I0672169

Diamonds and Deception

A Chili Beane Mystery, Volume 1

Dixie Leigh

Published by Dixie Leigh, 2025.

DIAMONDS AND DECEPTION

First edition. January 6, 2025.

Copyright © 2025 Dixie Leigh.

ISBN: 978-0987300324

Written by Dixie Leigh.

For George, with endless gratitude for your unwavering love, support, and belief in me.

You make everything possible.

Chapter 1

I could see the moment his eyes registered confusion. From then on, it was only a matter of counting down before he made a statement about what he'd read. Three ... two ... one ...

"Is this some sort of joke?" The man looked up from my loan application and raised an eyebrow, a manoeuvre I was certain he had perfected in front of a mirror. I fought the impulse to ask if the mustard-coloured suit he wore was his wife's idea of a joke and instead put on my perkiest and sincerest smile.

"No joke, that's my actual name." I pointed to the yellowed document peeking from under the mountain of papers. "See, it says so on my birth certificate."

He continued staring at me, clearly thinking my parents were crazy. Secretly, I agreed with him. But then I wasn't a bank manager whose last name was Cashman either. Looking around the wood-panelled office, I was thankful I didn't have to spend my day confined to a computer. The enclosed space would drive me nuts. Perhaps that's why I was a private investigator, so I could be on the road in the fresh air. Well, as fresh as the town air could get, anyway.

Mr. Cashman readjusted his glasses and cleared his throat. "Okay. Well, Miss ... um ... Beane, if you'll leave this with me, I'll get back to you as soon as I have further information."

Translated, he meant—after I find out if you're trying to pull a fast one.

I stood and shook his damp hand and resisted the urge to wipe mine down my pants leg. "No worries. Thank you for your time."

He opened the door, and I left, weaving my way through the throng of people waiting in line for an almost non-existent teller service. With only one cashier open, it looked like they were going to be there awhile. I stepped next door and grabbed a black coffee, the scent of roasted beans lifting my spirits. A light sprinkling of rain had me running for my car. The theme from Banana Splits filled the interior just as I'd buckled my seat belt. A sigh escaped as a picture of a gorgeous blonde filled the phone screen. My sister had interrupted what so far had been a not-too-bad-day. But to be fair, she probably had an insurance job for me to look at and right now, I needed the money. I answered on the fourth banana.

"Hey, Coco. What's up?"

"Just wanted to remind you that Dad's birthday bash is in three sleeps. Make sure you're on time. The caterers will have a fit if you're late again."

I closed my eyes and groaned, hoping she hadn't heard. How could I have forgotten? I glanced down at the Mickey Mouse watch gracing my wrist. If hurried I could make the shops in time and buy him something. The only problem was Thursday meant pension day. Every person in town would be out in full, blue-rinse force, so if I wanted to do any shopping, I'd better make it quick.

"I'll be there with bells on." I put my seat belt on and adjusted the rear-view mirror. "So, what did you get him?" I asked. I aimed for nonchalance, but Coco saw right through me.

She laughed one of those deep, full, throaty laughs that men loved and women instantly hated. "Don't worry, there's a present already wrapped with your name on it. You just need to pick it up from the jeweller before he closes at nine."

I pumped the air with my fist. It was a good thing she understood me so well. "You're a lifesaver."

"I know." She laughed again. "You owe me big time. Again."

She gave me the shop address and then hung up. For the millionth time, I was glad she was my sister. Okay, sometimes she could be a royal pain, but then just when the chips were down, she always came through.

I just wished I'd been born with her name instead of mine.

Coco Beane rolled off the tongue. It was cute and quirky, unlike mine, which didn't roll but clunked like the mysterious noise under my car.

Chili Beane. What parent in their right mind called their daughter Chili when their last name was Beane? My only consolation was my parents hadn't called me Fava, or worse still, Jelly.

Checking my watch again, I figured I had enough time to go home, shower, and feed Almond, my beautiful lilac-point Birman, before heading to the jewellers. I was actually looking forward to the party. It would be wonderful to catch up with friends and have a fun-filled night of family games. My sister always threw a great shin-dig.

With the key in the ignition, I drove home. This was the part of my day I loved the most. The sight of black cows against the green pastures never failed to instil a sense of calm. Windmills rising in empty fields stood like tall metal sentinels, their rusted arms turning in lazy circles. I loved everything about the country. Almost everything. A logging truck rolled by and my car reverberated like thunder. A sign industry had encroached on my world.

Five minutes later, I turned off the winding road and onto my driveway. Home sweet home. I'd fallen in love with the quaint mud-brick house when I first saw it. A rose garden lined one side of the house, while apricot poppies, multi-coloured asters and yellow nasturtiums wove their way through the rockery border—interspersed with the heady fragrance of lavender bushes. It seemed to say welcome. I'd been renting here for almost two years and now the owners were selling me this little one-acre patch of heaven. Hopefully, the bank agreed.

As the door opened, I stepped into the cool darkness and groped for the light switch. The light on my answering machine blinked, and I listened to the recorded voices while opening a can of cat food. There was a message from my boss, Pete, two from a company doing television surveys and one hang-up. Nothing else. Business was running a little slow lately.

I blamed the economic crisis; people were holding tight to their money.

Almond, rubbed against my legs, miaowing at me to hurry with her food. With her bowl set on the floor, I raced to the shower, snatching a can of soft drink en route. It was finished by the time my shower was hot. The water's touch provided a soothing sensation on my skin, easing the soreness in my muscles and weary feet after a lengthy day following a person suspected of insurance fraud. I brushed my damp hair and quickly put on jeans and a jumper, grabbed my keys and bag, and departed. It was a good thing the jeweller was in the next suburb or I'd never make it there on time.

Darkness fell, draping the world in a black and silver shroud as I drove to the shop. I'd tried phoning ahead, but no one had answered. I gave up on the third attempt. They were probably busy with late-night shoppers.

I drove down a main road toward an upper-class suburb where upper-class people lived their upper class lives. Don't get me wrong, I had nothing against them, really. Everything just seemed to come so easily for them, while poorer schmucks like me worked our tails off for them. I guess it all boiled down to jealousy on my part. I was getting sick of being a poor schmuck.

Grabbing my notebook, I flipped on the interior light, keeping one eye on the road while I tried to find the address. The store was in a strip of shops, unusual these days as most were in centres where extra security meant safety. But if Coco ordered the gift from this shop, then it must have been perfect. He was probably an ex-client. I crossed fingers he'd given her a good deal; otherwise my pay cheque was going to be disappearing.

I pulled my car to the kerb and got out. Street lights shone brightly on the row of storefronts. A dog barked in the distance. It was one of those steady, monotonous barks that probably drove the neighbours insane every night. That's why I had a cat. No barking, no whining, just a studied nonchalance. I approached the door and knocked. When no one showed, I pressed my face against the reinforced window. A light was on in a back room and I could see someone's shadow moving silently through the dark office. I thumped on the door, louder this time.

No such luck. I blew on my hands, shoved them in my pocket after stomping on the ground. A cold mist had rolled in, blanketing everything in its path. A part of me wanted to leave, go to my dad's party and say I'd forgotten the gift. The other saner part understood that would be inviting trouble with a capital B for Bonnie. Not that she was mean or anything. Quite the opposite. One of my mum's oldest friends, Bonnie, was exceptionally generous. Everyone loved her. But get on the wrong side and she could give you a look that made your guts wither and die.

I was in no mood to die tonight.

I pressed my car's remote control, and the ensuing double beep confirmed that I had activated the alarm. The last thing I wanted was to get back and find my car broken into. I didn't care what neighbourhood I was in, statistics showed damage to cars no matter where you lived. I followed the path around the side of the building, stepping over broken glass and empty cans, and walked toward the back.

The metal door was standing slightly ajar.

I opened it and stepped into the warmth the small room offered. Remnants of coffee making sat neatly on the counter. Two leather chairs were facing each other. Chocolate chip cookies sat in a glass jar, their golden edges and melted chips practically calling my name. A faint smear across the glass caught my eye, subtle but oddly out of place.

My stomach rumbled at the thought of food. The sooner I got out of here, the sooner I could eat. At the far end of the room was another doorway, the brocade curtain dividing the two rooms partially open; the room beyond brightly lit.

Ignoring the cookies, I walked toward the doorway and called out, "Hello? Anyone here?"

There was no answer. I parted the curtain, took a few more steps and glanced toward the jewellery cases on the right. I froze. My stomach heaved as a wave of nausea hit my throat, and I was glad I hadn't eaten. The body of a man lay face down on the floor. The metallic tang of blood mingled with the scent of freshly brewed coffee stung my nostrils. It reminded me of shows like Criminal Minds and CSI, only this was no actor playing a part. This was the real deal—a dead person, in the flesh.

I wish I could say I saw it coming, but I didn't. I just stood there, frozen like a dime-store mannequin, my usually sharp mind paralysed by the shock of what was in front of me.

I wish I could claim my survival instincts took over, but they didn't. The room seemed to shrink around me, the walls pressing tighter with every thundering beat of my heart.

Most of all, I wish I'd never set foot in that stupid jewellery store.

A soft footfall, barely audible, sounded behind me. My senses heightened, and I half-turned, my pulse pounding in my ears. An icy chill swept through my body. Someone was in here with me and the dead guy. Fear clenched my heart as the room contracted further, a tightening vice of dread.

Pain exploded in my head, a sudden and intense agony that sent shockwaves through my body. My vision faded as I fell. I landed on something large and unyielding; the impact sending another jolt of pain through my body. A fog of confusion clouded my mind as I struggled to make sense of my surroundings. A pair of worn brown boots appeared sideways in my vision.

The world around me greyed, edges blurring as if I was viewing reality through a smudged lens. The darkness that had been lurking at the edges of my consciousness closed in, offering me respite from the chaos and terror.

I found a strange solace as the world dissolved and I succumbed to the merciful embrace of oblivion.

Chapter 2

"**S**weetheart, are you awake?"

A soft hand stroked my forehead, gently pulling me from a world of dreams that held an eerie allure. The nightmare, thick with chilling images of bodies and diamonds sinking in rivers of blood, reluctantly released its hold as I surfaced to consciousness. I inhaled deeply, grateful to escape the nightmare and relieved to find myself in the waking world—far better than the one I'd just left behind.

I blinked twice, letting the light gradually sharpen my vision. The blinds were open, letting in a filtered stream of light that seemed to soften the sterile air around me. The unmistakable tang of disinfectant mixed with an unidentifiable scent, confirmed I was in a hospital. A dull ache in my head added to the evidence—an unwelcome souvenir from whatever had just happened.

At least I wasn't in the morgue.

Vague, disjointed flashes of memories flickered through my mind, their rhythm matching the thunderous bass of a heavy-metal band that seemed to have taken residence at the base of my skull. A dissonant melody kept playing on repeat—a Katy Perry song gone horribly awry. Just like the tune, my emotions were all over the place—hot and cold, in and out, up and down. And none of it had anything to do with love.

I turned my head, the motion slow and deliberate, and caught sight of familiar faces hovering near me—my family. Coco's face, framed by her hastily pulled-back hair, looked even paler than usual. Dad, standing beside her, had his signature copper curls—wild and untamed, just like mine. Their worried expressions were all too familiar, but they felt oddly distant, like they belonged to a dream.

"Sweetheart, are you all right?" Dad's voice, a comforting blend of concern and reassurance, filled the room. His words were soft, as if afraid to disturb the fragile peace in which I"d just woken up. "Just rest. We"re here. Everything"s okay."

I nodded cautiously, suppressing a groan that threatened to escape as I moved my head. The pain in my skull was enough to make me close my eyes again, craving a return to the comfort of sleep. But the familiar touch of someone's hand on my arm stilled me—a gesture of protection and love, like when I was little and sick. Deep warmth settled within me. It was a comforting experience to be cared for.

Footsteps echoed through the room—measured and sharp. The nurse's voice followed, professional and unbothered. "The doctor will be here soon. Perhaps you'd prefer to wait outside while he examines the patient?"

I cracked open one eye, trying to gauge the situation, and spotted Matron standing near the bathroom door. She had a presence that could tame even the rowdiest of men—or a misbehaving cat. Her hair was styled into an old-fashioned beehive, her posture rigid as she waited for a response. She was a no-nonsense woman, and right now, she was clearly waiting for Dad and Coco to make up their minds.

Dad cleared his throat and gave Coco a quick glance before squeezing my hand gently. "We'll just grab a coffee, honey. We won't be long."

I barely nodded in response, the wave of exhaustion crashing over me. The thought of what had happened sent a shudder through my body. This wasn't the first time someone had tried to hurt me. But next time? I might not be so lucky.

Matron ushered them out of the room, her steps fading into the hallway. I was about to drift back to sleep when another presence entered.

The clipboard rattled against the metal bed frame. Papers rustled. Warm fingers found my pulse.

I considered pretending to be asleep, but then the voice came—a smooth, velvet tone that instantly made my heart skip a beat.

"Hello, Chili. How are you?"

I froze, my heart leaping into a rapid, frantic rhythm. The words seemed to come from the depths of my past—memories I'd long tried to bury. A man's voice that I'd once known all too well.

Dr. Morgan Burns—ex-fiancé—hadn't changed a bit. In fact, if anything, he was even better looking. Tall, tanned, with golden blonde hair that seemed almost unreal. His blue eyes—still the same deep, piercing shade—could melt anyone, and once upon a time, they had melted me.

"When ... when did you get back?" The question spilled from my lips before I could stop it, the words laced with a mix of surprise, anxiety, and an unexpected rush of warmth.

"A week ago." He glanced down at his watch before reclaiming my wrist and continuing to check my pulse. "I missed you, Chili."

I swallowed, my face flushing as I met his gaze. His words seemed to hang in the air, weighty and laden with meaning. "I missed you too."

It was true. The memories of our time together—camping trips, hiking, and hot-air ballooning—flashed through my mind like old photos. He'd always been the adventurous one, constantly dragging me out of my comfort zone.

Just then, a nurse entered with my dinner tray, disrupting the moment. Usually, it was the food service staff that brought in the meals, not the nurses. She placed the tray on the over-bed table with a clunk, rolling it to the side.

I watched her for a second, a flicker of amusement mixing with my discomfort. Really? Was this how things were going to go?

She barely glanced at me before turning her attention fully to Morgan, fluffing out her curls in what looked like a practiced gesture. "Is there anything I can help you with, doctor?" she asked, the question dripping with enough overt sexuality to make my eyes roll.

Seriously?

Morgan caught my look and winked, his lips curling into a knowing smile as he responded without looking away from me. "That's okay, nurse. I've got everything under control."

"Okay. Well, if you need anything ..." Her voice trailed off, and she gave him one last lingering glance before sauntering out of the room.

As soon as she was gone, I let out a quiet sigh of relief. The woman had probably never faced rejection before. A small part of me almost felt sorry for her, almost.

Morgan held my wrist a little longer than necessary, his thumb brushing against my skin. "I really have missed you."

I pulled my hand away, suddenly aware of how intimate the contact was. "First, I'm not your girl," I said, pulling the blankets higher. "Second, you gave up that right when you left and took a job halfway around the world." I met his gaze, my voice steady despite the weight of the moment. "You didn't have to go."

He shook his head. "You're right. I didn't have to go. I wanted to. There's a big difference." He shrugged. "But you could have joined me."

"We've been over this before, Morgan," I snapped, frustration edging my tone. "I couldn't just up and leave. I have responsibilities here. People needed me."

He softened, his voice quieter. "I needed you, Chili."

I let out a long sigh, my heart aching at the words I had heard too many times. "Can we change the subject, please?"

He hesitated then nodded, picked up my chart, and read it. "You've got a slight concussion, so we're going to keep you here for a couple of hours. After that, you're free to go."

"So, no permanent damage?"

He met my gaze. "No. You're a very lucky girl."

Lucky? I should have been planning my wedding with this man, not sitting in a hospital bed, looking like I'd been dragged through hell. I wished for makeup, for the illusion of normalcy. But what I really wanted was to forget everything that had led me here.

"That was a nasty hit you took," he continued, his voice laced with concern. "Any idea how it happened?"

Before I could respond, a knock came at the door.

"Excuse me, doc. I get to ask the questions around here, not you."

I didn't need to look. That voice—rough, gravelly—was all too familiar.

Detective Senior-Sergeant Gideon St. James had entered the room, the man who both terrified and intrigued me. The man who had kissed me once and made me question everything about myself.

Morgan jumped to his feet, his posture stiffening, while Gideon strode into the room with all the confidence of a man knowing he had nothing to prove. Their eyes met, and I could almost see the tension crackling between them. It was like watching two wild animals sizing each other up before a fight—silent, loaded, waiting.

"I'm not sure my patient is up for an interview yet, detective," Morgan spoke first, breaking the silence.

Gideon's eyes flicked to me before narrowing. "Why? The nurse said she was being discharged." His gaze returned to Morgan. "Or have you changed your mind?"

Morgan puffed out his chest, but it didn't have the same effect as Gideon's quiet presence. The difference between them was stark—one was a doctor, the other a cop, and in that moment, the cop was clearly in charge.

I couldn't handle the standoff anymore. "Have you two finished?"

Morgan turned to face me. "You don't have to talk to him right now, Chili."

"Stay out of this, Burns. You stick to doctoring, and I'll handle the cop stuff," Gideon shot back, his tone sharp.

"She's got a concussion. It's probably better to wait until the morning."

"Don't get your knickers in a twist—"

"Enough!" I snapped, my patience worn thin. Both men paused and turned their attention to me. Did I really want Gideon here? After everything that happened between us? The memory of his lips on mine still lingered, warmth I couldn't shake.

"You're not my fiancé," I said to Morgan firmly. Gideon's smirk grew wider, his eyes glinting with mischief. I gave him a pointed look. "And you, enough with the bad cop routine. It's straight out of a 50s film."

They both had the grace to look sheepish. "Fine. Here's good," I muttered. "I just want to get this over with so I can go home and crawl into bed. Alone," I added, glancing at both of them. "It's fine, Morgan. I don't mind talking to him."

St. James smiled like a man who'd just won some sort of private victory. "Told you, doc. Me and Chili go way back." And then, as if on cue, he winked at me.

Morgan ignored him. "If you're sure. Press the buzzer if you need anything."

Gideon grabbed a visitors chair, spun it around, and straddled it with the cocky grin of someone who'd just claimed the high ground. As he settled, Morgan leaned over the bed, his hand covering mine for a moment. "I'll catch you later. We can talk somewhere ... private." He gave me a quick smile and was gone.

Gideon flicked open his notebook and glanced down at it. "I don't get what you ever saw in that guy."

"He's a good doctor," I protested. At his grimace, I nodded toward the scar on his face, "He did a decent job patching you up."

"Yeah, but as a man, he's a joke." His eyes met mine, locking onto me with an intensity that made my pulse race. "Are you into the weak, clueless, still-wet-behind-the-ears type?"

Heat surged up my neck, flushing my face. "He's not that bad."

Gideon snorted. "Not that good either." His gaze dropped to his notebook. "But you're right. The guy can't help being a tosser."

"That's not fair. Just because he's not like you doesn't make him a tosser."

"Oh, but it does."

"Gideon," I warned, my voice a low growl. "Enough."

He raised both hands in mock surrender. "Okay, okay. Let's get this over with so you can check out of this hospital nightmare."

Now we were getting somewhere.

"Why were you at the jeweller's last night?" Gideon asked his voice suddenly serious. All pretense was gone.

"Coco asked me to pick up a gift," I said with a shrug. "It's Dads birthday tomorrow night, and I forgot."

A crooked grin tugged at the corner of Gideon's mouth, lifting the scar on his cheek. "Ah, that explains it. You and dates, huh?" He teased well aware of my dreadful track record with remembering anything that wasn't immediately in front of me. "Anything strange about the store?"

"The back door stood unlocked. I opened it, called out, and walked in," I said. My stomach grumbled at the thought of the jar of cookies I had almost grabbed before the whole mess began.

Gideon's smile softened into something more genuine. "You haven't changed, Chili. Still an accident waiting to happen." He made it sound almost ... endearing.

He stood, scraping the chair across the floor. The sunlight caught a pin on his jacket and flashed brightly, momentarily blinding me. My heart dropped when I noticed the memorial pin for his wife and child—just a small, silver thing — but it hit me like a gut punch. A shadow seemed to fall and a chill ran through me.

He lifted the lid on my dinner tray and sniffed. "You gonna eat this?"

"No, go ahead," I replied, suddenly nauseous. My appetite had evaporated the moment he walked in.

Gideon took a spoonful of mashed potatoes, chewing slowly as he inspected my plate. "Not bad. Definitely better than the hospital food I remember," he said with a shrug, wiping his mouth with a napkin. "So, what happened?"

I recounted the events of the previous night as he jotted down notes between bites of my dinner. A single pea fell from his fork, bouncing across the floor and rolling toward the door. Hopefully, no one would slip on it later.

"So, who is this guy?" Gideon asked his voice serious again.

I shrugged. "No idea. Coco sent me. I assumed he was an old associate."

"Not unless your sister's got a thing for married men."

"Married?" I blinked, surprised.

"Yeah. William Van Horne married to Delia Van Horne. No kids."

I froze. "There's no way Coco would get involved with a married man. She must've known him from somewhere else."

I picked at a nail, trying to dismiss the uncomfortable sensation creeping up my spine. "So what do you think happened?"

"I'll have to wait for forensics to confirm, but it looks like a botched burglary. He'd been dead a while before you got there," Gideon said, pulling the lid off a carton of apple juice and drinking it down in one go. He sighed and looked at the now-empty food tray. I could read him like a book—now that the food was gone, he was ready to leave.

"Well, I'm off. I'll call you if anything changes."

"Sure."

He paused, a gleam of mischief in his eyes. "Oh, and Chili?"

"Yeah?"

"Watch out for sharks."

I narrowed my eyes. Somehow, I didn't think he was talking about the ocean variety.

Chapter 3

I was off work for the next twenty-four hours and Pete, my boss, had warned he'd take away coffee privileges if he saw me. I didn't mind, it would give me a chance to catch up on jobs around the house.

Dad had organised a security consultant to come over later this afternoon and chat with me about how to fortify my retreat against unwanted intruders. My recent hospital stay had convinced all of us we couldn't be too careful. The thought of the person responsible for killing Mr Van Horne and giving me the headache of the century coming back to take care of things was unsettling, to say the least. I'd triple-checked everything and locked all the windows before bed and even then I hadn't slept well.

While I waited for him, I checked out social media and uploaded a picture of Almond for 'Caturday', the cat lover's equivalent to the start of the weekend. A gentle breeze floated through my open windows, bringing with it the scent of lilacs. I showered, donned my gardening clothes, and set to work. Within a short time, the house was presentable, floors washed and dried and paperwork filed. I switched the oven on and placed cream, lemonade, and flour on the counter.

Cooking was not my forte, but even I could make scones from a simple three-ingredient recipe. I mixed everything in a bowl, then patted the dough out on a board and cut it into rounds. I had just placed the tray in the oven when I heard voices arguing outside. Drawing back the curtains, I looked out the window.

My elderly neighbour, Mr Dorsey, was berating a man I had never seen before. Next to him sat Dudley, his yellow Labrador. As much as I loved the bundle of fur, he was useless as a guard dog. He could track rabbits and bark at strangers, but to actually bail someone up or bite them? It wasn't happening. If you had the slightest whiff of food about you, he'd lick you to death.

Stepping outside, I made my presence known. If my soft-spoken neighbour had raised his voice, something was dreadfully wrong. I meandered over, ready to intervene, my boots crunching on red pea-gravel.

"Is everything okay, Mr Dorsey?"

He turned to me; face ruddy, fear and anger playing across his features. He jabbed his finger toward the man. "He wants to buy my property. I've said no, but he wants me to take these papers." His voice rose as he spoke until he ended in a bark.

"What papers?" I turned to the interloper. "Who exactly are you?"

He held out his hand. "Stan Tunbridge. You may have heard of me." At my quizzical look he continued, "Tunbridge Real Estate? Over in Comet Falls?" His shoulders slumped a little when I shook my head in the negative. "We have a client who's interested in purchasing Mr Dorsey's property for a very nice sum." He handed me the paperwork. "Perhaps you could show him how generous my client is once everything has settled down."

Without another word, he tilted his hat toward us, got in his car and, in a cloud of dust, drove down the road.

We both stood in silence for a few moments and then I ushered Mr Dorsey to my house. I didn't think he was in any state to be left alone. He mumbled something about people having no respect for their elders and I agreed, though I believed everyone was a target these days.

Social media was proof of that.

The aroma of slightly burnt scones greeted us, and I hurried to remove them from the oven. I settled both man and dog in the open-plan lounge room and set about making us morning tea.

"Why would anyone want to buy my house?" he asked. He'd run his hand through his hair and now resembled an absent-minded professor.

I picked up the paperwork Tunbridge gave him. "I'm not sure." The sum of money mentioned caught me by surprise. "That's a substantial amount they're offering, a lot more than the houses around here are worth."

He took a sip of the hot liquid; the cup quivering in his shaking hand. Tea sloshed in his saucer as he put it down. I'd only lived in the street for a couple of years, but he'd married, raised a family and buried his wife and only child while living here. I could understand why he was concerned.

"Are you positive you don't want to sell?" I asked.

He straightened. "Definitely not." He tapped his chest. "They'll be taking me out in a coffin before I give my property to anyone. It's my home."

"Did he say anything else?"

"Not really." He sighed. "Only that someone of my age might find it easier to manage things if I moved to a retirement home."

That seemed to be the answer to everything these days, out of sight-out of mind, until it came time to do a reading of the will. Then relatives came out of the woodwork.

"They can't force me to sell, can they?" His voice rose and Dudley raised his head and looked at his owner. Mr Dorsey reached down and patted him.

I chewed my lip. "I don't think so, but it's probably better if you talk to someone about it."

"The police?"

I smiled. "A lawyer might be better." I tapped my fingernail on the table top. "I think we might give Maisie a call. I'm sure she could help."

Mr Dorsey left, and I flicked a quick email through to Maisie McClintock, a legal-aid lawyer in town. She usually specialised in women's law, but I was pretty sure she'd make an exception this time, or at the very least find someone who could help.

A knock at the door announced A1 Security. After checking their identification, I allowed the father and son team to enter. The son was a younger version of his dad. Solidly built, both had a burgundy-red tint to their hair that women paid hairdressers a fortune to imitate. They deposited their cases on the floor and we did a lengthy tour of the property.

We discussed my needs and the various systems and setups and I listened to the suggestions, which included cutting bushes back from the house and installing timers for the lights. Eventually we settled on a twelve camera system with night vision plus a video doorbell and cyber security. There was also a back-up battery in case of a power outage. An app on my phone monitored everything.

A part of me was sad that it had come to this. Overnight, my relatively safe world had imploded. No longer could I relax, believing that I was untouchable. I had become a pawn in someone else's game.

I signed the invoice, and they got to work.

They worked well as a team, each deferring to the other's strengths. I got out my secateurs and trimmed the bushes while they mounted the cameras and installed the video doorbell. They even added locks to my windows as a bonus. When they'd finished and cleaned up, I was as safe in my home as I would be at Fort Knox. The only thing left was a timer for the lights and dad assured me he'd do that in the morning.

I slept with thoughts of land developers, elderly neighbours and cute, smiling dogs swirling through my dreams.

Chapter 4

Everything about the world the following morning seemed fresher, brighter as if my accident, and the knowledge I was no longer untouchable, had somehow caused everything to stand out in relief. Chocolate croissants and coffee from the local bakery sat on my table, waiting to be consumed. Dad and Coco were already eating, and I followed suit, taking a bite from one of the gooey confections. Melted chocolate filled my mouth and stuck to my teeth. I washed it down with a healthy swig of hot cream and caramel-laced java. Sheer bliss.

Blue wrens played tag in the garden visible through the window. Almond was curled on the back of a chair, soaking up the sun; tail flicking as she too watched the birds. She was too lazy to do more than just watch. That, plus the bell around her neck, meant she wouldn't catch anything. I loved these mornings when work didn't take precedence and leisurely breakfasts were the order of the day.

The only catch was dad obviously had something on his mind. My guess was that something was me. I drank the coffee, crumpled the paper cup and tossed it overhand into the bin. Score! Raising my clasped hands in victory, I thanked my imaginary fans. Coco grinned and leaned forward, her hand in high-five style. We touched hands and she winked, her way of conveying she understood what was ahead. Dad watched us over the rim of his cup. He didn't smile, which wasn't a good sign. We were a notorious family of jokers.

I leaned back and lowered my hands. "That was great, Dad, thanks. Just what the doctor ordered."

"My pleasure." He cleared his throat, a clear signal he was ready to speak. "Chili, we need to talk." He placed his cup on the table.

"Sure, what's up?"

"I want you to think seriously about giving up your job."

Now why didn't that shock me? Twenty-nine and a spinster seemed odd to everyone but me. He wanted me married, settled down and producing lots of grandbabies. I couldn't even keep a boyfriend, let alone get one to the altar. "Why?"

"You could have died."

"Yes, but I didn't."

"Your work is too dangerous. Next time you might not be so lucky."

"I understand, Dad. But this is my job; it's what I'm good at. Besides ..."

"What?" He tilted his head, curious at what I was going to say.

I shrugged. "It doesn't matter." I was better off letting him think it was work related. If he'd known I'd been picking up his birthday present, he'd be horrified.

He stood and walked to the window, his hand absently patting Almond. Her purring filled the room. Coco glanced at me, her face sympathetic. She understood how much I loved my job. She also realised Dad wanted me to quit.

"Chili ..." Dad turned and gripped the chair. He was struggling to keep control, and a boulder lodged in my throat. "I thought we'd lost you. When the police called ..." Dad's face flushed red, and his eyes held an unfamiliar gleam. "I can't go through that again." Two quick steps and he stood in front of me. His arms reached out, pulled me to my feet, and wrapped around me. "Promise you'll think about it?"

I nodded, my face pressed into his chest. His caring did something that most things couldn't. It made me cry. Tears dampened the front of his shirt, creating dark blobs on the brown cotton. My dad was hurting and that made me hurt. I hugged him hard. Coco joined us and we pulled her into our circle, one of The Four Beanes-kateers. Three, now that mum was gone. We stood like that for a while, lost in the 'what-if's.' He pushed me away gently and Coco passed the tissues. We all took one. She then disappeared into the bathroom, giving us a couple of minutes alone.

"So, have you heard anything more from Gideon?" he asked.

Wiping eyes that no doubt had me looking like a raccoon; I shook my head, grateful for the change of subject. "No. He wants me at the station later for an official interview. He just came by the hospital to check on me."

"That was thoughtful of him."

"Yeah."

"I gather seeing Morgan didn't impress him?"

"It didn't." I grinned, "Though the sentiment *was* mutual." A thought occurred to me. I turned to look at him. "Had you heard Morgan was back?"

He shook his head. "I had no idea until we saw him at the hospital. He must have kept his homecoming pretty quiet. His parents never mentioned it."

That was odd. Morgan's family and mine attended the same church and had since I was little. His parents would have told dad he was coming home. Why he would keep it a secret was beyond me.

"Morgan left his overseas job?" asked Coco, drying her hands on a towel. "When did that happen?"

"Not sure," I answered. "But from what I gather, he's back to stay."

She laughed. "I guess that means every single woman within miles will be at church this week." Her smile dropped. "I'm sorry, Chili, I didn't mean ..."

I waved her words away. "Don't be silly; Morgan and I are just friends." It was true. At the mention of his name, there were no butterflies, no feelings of giddiness, nothing. The feelings from a couple of nights ago were gone. "Besides, if he finds the right girl, I'm happy for him."

Relief crossed her face. She gathered up her bag, crossed the room, and hugged me. "I'm glad. He's not the one for you," she whispered. "Just in case you need it, there's a thermos of hot chocolate on the counter. Plus a bag of mini-marshmallows." Turning to dad she asked, "I'm heading downtown, do you need anything?"

He glanced at the watch I'd bought him for Christmas. "Can you drop me over at Glen's? I plan on catching some waves this afternoon." He pretended to ride a surf board—with a soulful grace I admired.

Coco and I exchanged glances, grinning. And he thought we were cheesy.

Ten minutes later, they were gone. I wandered to the mailbox and grabbed a bundle of letters. Across the road, Mr Dorsey was watering his lawn. He saw me and raised his hand in greeting. I loved this area. The neighbours were friendly without being nosey and there was plenty of space. Tall trees and distant mountains gave the illusion of being in the country.

Overhead, the sound of thunder rumbled. As I gazed upward, a raindrop struck my forehead. With the mail hidden beneath my shirt, I raced towards the house. Seconds after the sliding door closed behind me, hail pelted down, turning the paddocks into a green and white carpet. The temperature dropped, so I lit the logs in the fireplace. Ahead of me lay the perfect afternoon. The roller-coaster of the last twenty-four hours had put me in the mood for love songs to cry by. Coco had copied her favourites. It was in the CD player, ready to go.

I settled on the couch and hit play on the remote. There was nothing better, hot chocolate with extra marshmallows, a roaring fire and REO Speedwagon crooning 'how he'll keep on lovin' me'. I sighed. If only it were that simple.

Morgan's presence at the hospital had surprised me. Ending our relationship was the right decision, but sometimes I wondered if I had been too quick. He was like a comfy old jumper, always there when you need him. The problem was I wanted the entire package, not just comfortable.

Then there was Gideon.

If anyone could catch the murderer, it was Gideon. He was the type of cop you wanted on your side when the chips were down. He was also tough and smart, with an air of approachability. The scars on his face didn't bother me. It was the ones hidden underneath that were a concern.

The loud ring of the phone broke into my thoughts and I jumped, spilling hot liquid onto my pants. Muttering, I grabbed a cloth, swiping at the mess. Throwing it down, I picked up the offending machine.

"Yeah?"

"Chili?"

It was Morgan. I thought I'd have a few more days before being in contact. Apparently not.

"What's up?"

My feigned nonchalance didn't have the desired effect.

"There's a pot-luck picnic after church tomorrow. I promised I'd join my parents and wondered if you were going."

"Honestly? I hadn't really thought about it."

I'd be more than happy to drive you, and then perhaps we could talk?"

"I don't think that's a good idea." With Morgan, I was all talked out. We'd voiced everything we had to say a long time ago.

"We've already said all we needed to." I took a deep breath and steadied myself. "I think it's better if we keep everything professional."

He was silent for a while. "Okay, I understand. If you need anything, I'm here."

I hung up. My house suddenly seemed empty, and the temptation to call him back was strong.

I rang Coco instead. Sometimes a sister is the best kind of therapist.

Chapter 5

Private Investigation was nothing like you see on television. No red sports cars or rubbing shoulders with the rich and famous. It was all footslogging and interviews. Most investigators worked for insurance companies, recouping losses, checking out claims. Some agencies specialised in spousal surveillance.

The thought made me shudder. You either trusted your spouse or you didn't. These days it seemed most didn't. I preferred missing persons, reuniting loved ones, but even then, you needed to be careful. Not everyone told the truth about why they were looking for people. A concerned family member could easily turn out to be a jealous ex-lover.

I stuffed spare clothes and shoes in my backpack and glanced at my watch. My car was still at the hospital, so I'd have to bike it to work. There was just enough time to call the office and then head on my way to meet the walrus; my cheesy nickname for our local mayor.

The phone call with my boss, Pete Taylor, was brief. I'd spoken too soon. He had a surveillance job lined up that was worth good money. It involved a man who thought his fiancé was having an affair. Pete had taken names and done a background check on the client. Everything was kosher. Besides, he was right. Bills had to be paid. Pete's wife was due to have their third baby, and he needed the extra income.

So did I for that matter.

My car hadn't been returned so as I rode my racing bicycle down the cul-de-sac and onto the main road, I mulled over our conversation.

I couldn't believe I had heard nothing about my loan. How long did it take to approve these things? At least riding my bike was saving on fuel.

The sun had only been up for an hour and already sweat prickled my back and neck. The road wound through the bush and past paddocks. Potholes waited to catch unsuspecting drivers off guard while under Eucalypt trees kangaroos sat; a captive audience.

By the time I arrived at work, I was hot, tired, and in dire need of coffee. I prayed Pete had the pot on.

Our office sat in a small L-shaped complex, nestled between a beauty therapist and a dentist. Funny, but true. At least if either of us had an angry client, a dentist was at hand. We hadn't had to utilise his services so far, at least not in the line of work.

Pete sat at his desk when I walked in. The obligatory cup of green tea seated on the worn Formica table next to him. His wife had him on a health kick and to hear Pete tell it, the tea, not the lack of caffeine, was going to kill him.

"Hey, Chili." He grinned and nodded at my outfit. "Oh, Polyester. Nice. It suits you."

I looked down at my hot-pink cycling jersey, then back at him. "Get your facts right, Pete. It's Lycra. I don't do polyester."

He raised his hands in defence, his face lighting up. "Sorry, my mistake." His grin dissolved. "How's your head?"

"I'm doing fine. No tackling any rugby players for the next week, but I'll live."

Pete shook his head, his bald skull dotted with perspiration. He looked more like a middle-aged man every day—which wasn't a bad thing. It paid to be inconspicuous in this job. He preferred to rely on old-school technology rather than smart devices. He even had a Ham Radio set up in his basement. "The world's going to hell in a hand basket. I mean, what's it coming to? Anyone's a target."

"I know. It seems surreal." I sat in my chair and spun to face him. "On top of that, I've heard nothing about my loan, despite them guaranteeing an answer in twenty-four hours."

"Why?"

"I'm not sure. But, I'm gonna find out." I reached for the hands-free phone and dialled. A cheery voice thanked me for calling and asked me to choose an option. "Three." The words were out of my mouth before she'd finished advising the selection. That's what happens when you make a lot of calls; soon you understand the system better than they do. They transferred me, and I heard a familiar voice on the line.

"Cashman, speaking."

"Hi, Mr Cashman. This is Chili Beane ... we spoke the other day?"

He cleared his throat. "Oh yes, Miss Beane. What can I do for you?"

"I still haven't received an answer on my loan application. I was wondering if you'd made a decision?"

"Oh, yes. Um, Ms Beane. That's right. I remember."

Yeah right. Like he could forget my name, it wasn't exactly generic. Especially after the fuss he made over it. "I'm a little confused. The application was in order, my accountant supplied financials and I had good references. What's the holdup?"

He took a deep breath. "I'm sorry Miss Beane. I can understand you want an answer, but I'm unable to discuss the details with you."

My mouth hung open. "You can't discuss the details of my application with me?"

I shrugged in response to Pete's raised eyebrows. "What's up?" he mouthed.

Cashman continued. "I'm sorry, but it's company policy. All I can tell you is that your paperwork is in order. Someone will get back to you shortly."

"I don't understand— "

"I'm not at liberty to say anymore. Goodbye Miss Beane. We'll be in touch." He hung up.

I looked at Pete and pulled the hands free set from my head, letting it drop onto the desk. I raked both hands through my hair and glared at Pete like he was Cashman. He was right. The world was going to hell in a hand basket.

"What'd he say?"

"Only that he couldn't discuss it; but they'll be in touch."

Pete looked puzzled. "You're right, it makes little sense. If your application was no good, wouldn't they advise you straight away?"

That was the screwy part. Why indeed? I snatched up the phone and contacted the owners. I needed more time to come up with the money. Mary answered on the third ring. "Hi, Chil. How are you?"

"Good thanks, Mary. Are you enjoying caller I.D?"

She laughed. "Listening to you was the best thing I ever did. At least now I can screen my calls. No more pesky salespeople." She sobered. "I'm glad you called."

I got that hinky sensation as if ants had crawled up my spine and I was about to get bad news. "I'm glad someone's happy to hear from me."

"I got a letter in the mail this morning." Paper rustled in the background. "Have you ever heard about a company called 'Red Soil Developments'?" I sucked in a breath. That was the name on the top of Mr. Dorsey's proposal. What on earth was going on?

"I'm not sure. Why?"

"They want to purchase the property." She mentioned the figure and my stomach bottomed out. "Wow," was all I could utter. There was no way I could match that offer, it was more than double the sale price. Plus, taxes on the property had just skyrocketed.

"Isn't that the weirdest thing?"

"What's weirder is I can't find out if my loan's approved or denied."

"Oh. I'm sorry."

We chatted for a few minutes more. As we ended the call, I asked her to fax me through the offer. "Sure. And, Chili?"

"Yeah?"

"I'm really sorry."

So was I. It was one blow after another. The fax machine sounded, and Pete picked up the sheet of paper. He let out a low whistle. "Man. These people sure want her property. What makes it so special?"

"Maybe they want to subdivide?" I looked at him. "Mr Dorsey had a similar offer."

"The nice old guy across the street?"

I nodded. "The very one."

Pete handed me the offer, as well as a folder. "There's only one way to find out what's going on. Go see our illustrious mayor. And on your way, you can do a drive by and check out the client address. It's all there in the paperwork."

I was glad that our office had shower facilities. Twenty minutes later, I'd showered, changed and was ready to go. Pete flipped me his keys on my way out.

The council building loomed on the horizon, a monolith, cold and imposing. I climbed the stairs two at a time, entered through the automatic doors and turned right. Alfred Sealey, mayor, and in my mind, the secret walrus impersonator, sat at his desk, phone in hand. I stood at the door, my shoulder against the door frame.

Sealey's office eclipsed my kitchen and dining room combined. The decorator had masterfully mixed autumnal reds, brown and gold to create understated luxury. Maybe Sealey would give me her card. Though at the rate things were going, I was probably better off asking for rental advice.

Alfred looked up and raised his hand, beckoning me to enter. My shoes sank into the plush carpet, which probably cost more than my monthly wages. I hoped I wasn't tracking in dirt. I couldn't afford to pay for his carpet cleaning. A discreet check of my boots assured me all was soil-free.

He gestured for me to take a seat, but I declined. It was good to be standing after being seated all morning. His fingers idly rubbed the expanse of stomach protruding like a built-in table. He seemed in a good mood and I could picture him watching a movie, a beer can on his belly. With elections coming up, he probably thought he had it bagged like buttered popcorn.

That was the problem with small communities. Most people hated change, even if it meant keeping someone like Alfred Sealey as mayor.

After a few minutes of browsing the titles on his impressive bookshelf, he finished his phone conversation.

"Well, if it isn't little Chili all grown up." The way he said 'grown up' left me wanting a bath. He scanned his diary, running his finger down the pages. We both knew my name wasn't there. I got in quick.

"Tell me, what can you share about the land re-development project in my area?"

His eyes bulged as did his mouth, then a mask slid down to shield the look of shock. "Land development?" He leaned back, his chair groaning under his weight. Fat fingers stroked his greying moustache. "I have no information about that."

"You've heard nothing about someone offering huge money for houses?"

He shrugged his shoulders. "Haven't heard a thing."

I shoved the paper on the table in front of him. "Then have you any idea who owns 'Red Soil Developments'?"

He picked up the paper and perused it; his glasses perched on the end of his nose. "Hmmm ... I can't help you with that." He placed it on the table and leaned back in his chair. "But leave it with me and I'll have someone look into it." He steepled his fingers and peered at me. "I heard you were involved in that dreadful business the other night. I'm glad to see you're looking none the worse for your encounter."

His words didn't line up with his body language. I'd bet my last lollipop he was more disappointed than glad.

"Were you familiar with William Van Horne?"

"Of course. As mayor, I've met all the business owners in our wonderful community."

"Was he involved in anything shady?"

His eyes narrowed. "Are you suggesting that I am involved in his demise?"

I spread my hands in a placatory manner. "Not at all. But someone in your position is bound to hear the odd rumour or two."

"I can assure you I have heard nothing at all about dealings involving Mr Van Horne, shady or otherwise."

"And you've heard nothing about developers wanting to build a resort or housing development?"

"No, but as I mentioned already, I'll look into it for you."

He reached for the paper, but I was quicker. I folded it and tucked it into my bag.

"That's okay. I'll get your assistant to make a copy. That way, it doesn't accidentally get lost."

His smile didn't reach his eyes. "Fine. Now if you'll excuse me ...?" He stood and rounded the desk, opened the door. Gallantry was still alive and kicking.

I couldn't help a last dig. "We both understand rezoning would need to be voted on by the council."

"Yes, it would."

That took me by surprise. I expected him to confuse me. "And no one has approached you to sub-divide?"

"Not by the owners, no."

Ah, now we were getting somewhere. "So the owners haven't approached you, but the investors have?"

"No." The smug look on his face was annoying me. "If a developer wants to purchase land, that's up to them. I can tell you, however, that

Red Soil Developments have not approached the council to re-zone, anything. I think you're looking in the wrong place."

"Sounds to me like you're doing a cover up. But don't worry, I'll find out what it is." I waved goodbye and spun out of his office. It seemed I was looking in a lot of wrong places lately.

It was time to do some surveillance. The client's wife would head out soon on her daily trip to the gym. My job was to follow her, take photos if possible and report back. If I didn't move myself, we'd lose the client and Pete would never forgive me.

As I steered the car towards the upscale neighbourhood where the client lived, I switched on the radio. Soothing tones of classic hits from the seventies reverberated through my speakers. I sang along to Dancing Queen, glad no one could hear my tone-deaf warbling. I drove past the address at normal speed, pulled around the corner, and parked outside a corner store. The client's notes showed that his wife consistently took the same route. I was hoping this day would be no different.

I'd only been sitting for three minutes when her car zoomed past. I counted to five and pulled out, keeping a discreet distance. The woman was no slouch with driving. She kept just under the speed limit yet weaved in and out of traffic like a pro. It was a good thing she didn't deviate from her routine; otherwise, I may have lost her. It was also a good thing she was driving a hot pink sports car. The thing stood out like a neon light.

A few minutes later, she pulled into the parking lot and entered the complex. I pulled my hair into the requisite ponytail, swapped my jeans for tracksuit pants, and grabbed a towel from my bag. As I crossed the threshold, I waited for my eyes to adjust. A woman's voice screeched in the distance, advising whoever was listening to lift their legs higher. I hoped she wasn't my personal trainer. The voice would put me in an early grave.

The recreation centre was home to a swimming pool, gym, and coffee shop. I scanned my membership card and wound my way through spectators. Mothers were waiting for children's swimming lessons to finish, others waiting in line for coffee. I edged through a cluster of overweight women in too-tight, too-bright bike pants. My foot hit a half-eaten greasy chip, and I slipped, landing hard. One woman laughed. I didn't join her. A hand reached down. I grabbed it and hauled myself up. Pretending to get fit was going to kill me if I wasn't careful.

"Are you alright?"

"Yeah." I inspected my knee. It throbbed like the dickens. "Thanks for helping me."

"My pleasure. They should have that mess cleaned up."

"Yeah, they should." I looked up and almost fainted.

My rescuer was the very woman I was supposed to be tailing.

Pete was gonna kill me.

Chapter 6

"Are you sure you're okay? You look a little peaky."

I stood and dusted my pants off. My ego wasn't the only thing bruised. My knee throbbed and my ankle was tender, as if a tantrum throwing toddler had kicked it. "I'll be fine, thanks again." I took a step and winced. There'd be no pole dancing in my immediate future. The thought of me swirling around a pole was hilarious. Years ago I'd coolly leaned against one trying to impress my high school crush, missed the pole entirely and landed in a puddle of muddy water breaking my wrist.

"Here, let me help." She slipped her hand under my arm, placed her usual order for both of us, and helped me hobble to a table. This woman was good. Usually I waited in line for ages before even being noticed.

Soon we were drinking coffee, eating warm zucchini slice and laughing like old buddies. I liked her; she was nice.

"So, my name's Sommer Lewis. What's yours?"

I hesitated. I really didn't want my companion to laugh at me. "Chili Beane." I waited for the teasing that didn't happen. Everyone I met made some sort of comment, usually rhyming with harts or darts. My surprise must have registered with her. She leaned forward. "Guess what my maiden name was?"

I shrugged. "No idea."

"Camp." She grinned and sat back. "I couldn't wait to change it."

I blinked. "Wait ... your name was Sommer Camp?"

"Yep."

"Wow." Laughter bubbled up. I raised my salted caramel mugacino in a toast. "Here's to crazy parents everywhere. Thank you for not allowing us customised key chains." We clinked mugs and shared a smile. In that moment, I knew I'd gained a friend, or at least a co-conspirator, in the naming game.

"I don't think I've ever seen you here before." she said, taking a sip of her drink. The emerald solitaire on her wedding finger was the same colour as her eyes. She really was beautiful and not the slightest bit conceited.

"I've been a member for a while, but this is actually my first visit to the centre." I admitted.

"Oh you poor thing, that's awful. I hope it doesn't put you off coming back." She clapped, her eyes sparkling. "Why don't we come together? I'd love the company."

I shrugged. "Sounds great to me. We could all do with more friends, right?"

We sat by the water, observing the children splashing and laughing. I needed to get her to share more about her personal life with me. As I pondered my options, I considered reaching out to Pete and confessing that she had caught me red-handed. It would be such a shame if the suspicions about Sommer were accurate.

"Can I let you in on a secret?"

"Sure." I mimed locking my lips and throwing away the key. "What's up?"

She glanced around to ensure that nobody was listening. "I don't really come here to use the gym."

"So what do you do instead? Meet some hot guy?" I laughed. She didn't.

"That's exactly what I do."

Her confession shocked me. I was positive her fiancé was wrong. Was I losing my touch? Usually I was spot on about people.

Now it was my job to ensure no one heard us. "You're having an affair?"

She giggled. "No silly. I'm taking dancing lessons."

"You're what?"

Her eyes shone. "I'm having dancing lessons. My fiancé is a wonderful dancer, and well, I have two left feet. Our wedding is in a couple of months, and I wanted to surprise him."

I felt like a creep. A dirty, sleazy creep.

She placed her hand on mine. "It's nearly time for my lesson. Why don't you come and watch? I'm sure Felipe won't mind and it's only for an hour."

She grabbed my arm, and we walked to a door which said 'meeting room'. She knocked twice and we stepped inside. While a long table and chairs took up the front of the room, the back was clear. To say the man walking toward us was hot was an understatement.

I lowered my voice. "That's Felipe?"

"Sure is. He's a world champion ballroom dancer and was friends at school with my younger brother. That's his wife near the sound system". A petite woman waved to us. I waved back.

She introduced me to them and I sat and watched as they took to the floor. Felipe's wife handled the music while he coaxed and instructed Sommer until their dancing was flawless. The rhythm coursed through me, and my feet itched to join them. Her fiancé was a lucky man. I wondered if any guy would ever go to that much trouble for me. I hoped so.

They finished, and Sommer came back, wiping her face on a towel. "Well? Do you think Cade will like it?"

I reached forward and pulled her, my newest, and probably sweetest, friend, into a hug. She had restored my faith in humankind. "I think he's gonna love it." I whispered.

We promised to catch up the following week. After saying farewell to Felipe and his wife, I stopped by the cafe for a hot drink. As I took a few sips and headed towards my next destination, my phone rang. I quickly answered, balancing it between my chin and shoulder while making sure not to spill my drink or drop my bag. "Hello?"

"Chili?"

"Dad? What's wrong?" Slithers of fear pricked my skin.

"I'm glad I caught you. It's Coco ..."

"Dad, slow down. What about Coco?"

He took a deep, raspy breath. "Gideon just arrested her for murder."

Murder? My cup dropped to the floor and exploded. The remains of my hot chocolate fanned out across the tiles. Coco? Arrested? This had to be some sort of bizarre joke.

"What do you mean, they arrested her? Have you spoken to her?"

"I had a call a few minutes ago from the jail. The only thing I've been told is they arrested her about half an hour ago."

My thoughts whirled as I struggled to comprehend what he'd said. There was no way Coco murdered anyone. A staff member motioned for me to move out of the way so they could clean up the mess I'd made.

"Okay, I'll be there as soon as I can. Tell Coco not to say a word until her lawyer arrives."

We exchanged a few more words and Dad hung up. I pulled myself together and headed out the door. Regardless of what I thought before, as of this moment, Gideon was definitely off my Christmas card list.

Chapter 7

A million thoughts tumbled through my mind as I sped to the police station. How on earth could Gideon even imagine that Coco would commit murder? Surely there had to be some mistake. He understood her better than that. He'd shared countless meals with us, crashed on our couch to watch football or car racing or tennis. Both he and dad were sporting fanatics. The rest of us just played along.

Gideon knew us, knew Coco couldn't bring herself to kill an errant spider, let alone a human.

So what was he doing?

The tyres of my white Mazda skidded as I braked sharply into the parking lot. The police station and courthouse shared the same brick complex. A narrow walkway separated the two areas. Besides saving the public money on land, this setup also expedited the delivery of justice. Police could enter the building through the rear doors, avoiding families waiting in the lobby. No one liked to be confronted by angry loved ones. Well, an angry loved one was heading inside. Right now.

I skirted the main building and headed for the smaller one at the rear. Two Council workers in bright orange vests tended the surrounding gardens. Neat lines of fragrant rose bushes hedged cement paths. Near the front door, a sand-lined tray sat, waiting for half-smoked cigarettes to be thrown in. Six months ago I would have flicked my own hastily lit tailor-made in there. A brief tug of desire flitted through me. Every time stress hit, so did the siren's call of my favourite brand. So far, I'd been able to ward it off. But if Coco was facing murder charges—I forced my eyes away from the butts that would give me a hit or two and entered through sliding doors.

The desk sergeant looked up and gave me a lop-sided grin. Brian Johnson was a good friend of mine. "Hi, Chili." He nodded toward the hall. "Your dad's waiting for you. If you follow me, I'll take you through." He reached under the desk. A buzzer sounded and the door on my right opened. I walked through and it closed behind me with an ominous click. "Can I get you a coffee?"

"No thanks, Brian, I'll be fine," I lied.

He led me down a tiled corridor and to a window-lined room. Neither of us spoke. He couldn't answer my questions even if he wanted to, so what was the point? He knocked once, opened the door and shut it behind me.

The room was about as welcoming as a dungeon, though someone had tried.

A table took centre stage while green fabric-covered chairs surrounded it. A large fake palm sat in the corner. On the wall opposite the door hung a gilt-framed painting. At least, that's what I thought it was. It looked more like someone had got drunk and vomited blue, green and purple paint on it, then stood back and called it art. Some people s trash was another's treasure. It leaned at a slight angle, but not enough to make me want to straighten it.

A large two-seater chair fronted the window. My dad sat in the middle, hunched over, head in hands. He'd aged a lifetime since our phone call. I sat next to him and dried my sweaty hand on the chair before resting it on his shoulder. "How are you holding up?"

"Fine." He shook his head. "I can't believe any of this. She wouldn't hurt a fly."

"Yeah," I said, jerking my thumb toward the door. "But they don't." I rubbed his shoulder again. "What happened?"

Coco headed home to tidy up before the kids arrived from school. The police arrived and asked her to come down and answer some questions. That's it. No one's told me anything." He thumped his fist against the chair's back. "What's taking them so long?"

"I don't know." Dread reared its ugly head. "What about the kids?"

"Bonnie ... uh ... Mrs Murphy's going to look after them tonight. They think it's a special sleepover."

I sat back and rotated my neck, trying to ease some of the tension there. Coco's next-door neighbour was an angel. The twins would be safe with her. And they adored the older woman, though whether it was because of her amazing cooking or the extended bedtime curfews, I wasn't sure.

The door opened and Superintendent Gordon Barrett stepped into the room. Cheap cologne followed him like a hungry dog. As Gideon's boss, he made all the major decisions.

I'd never liked the man. I found him boorish on the few occasions I'd spoke with him. He appeared to find women a nuisance, a mundane necessity to life. It was a surprise to everyone that he'd married.

He didn't acknowledge us straight away.

Instead, Barrett walked over to the puke picture and tilted it an inch. He stepped back and studied it, rocking back on his heels. Satisfied, he turned and faced us.

"When can my sister leave?" I asked before anyone could open their mouth.

"She can't. Not yet." He pulled out a chair and sat, his legs crossed at the ankles. He brushed lint from his trousers. "We're holding her overnight on suspicion of murder."

"You can't be serious? What evidence do you have?"

"I understand you're upset, Mz Beane."

"Miss."

"Sorry?"

"It's Miss, not Mz." I wiggled my fingers at him. "Not married."

"Oh. Of course." He examined me over the top of his glasses. "I understand you're upset, but you of all people should understand I can't discuss the case with you or your father."

"Yes, but— "

He held up a manicured hand and continued. "Suffice to say, we're doing everything in our power to separate fact from fiction."

Dad leant forward, his face pale, teeth gritted. "Are you telling me you think my daughter's responsible for a man's murder?" He stood and leaned on the table, his voice rising in anger. "What are you? Some kind of idiot?"

Barrett sighed. "Mr. Beane, I can assure you— "

"You can assure me nothing. You're holding my daughter like some common thief while the actual murderer is still out there."

"I understand your concern, but getting upset doesn't help the matter."

"Listen, mate." Dad jabbed a thick finger at Barrett's face. "Stop pussyfooting around and fix this!"

"Mr Beane, you need to calm down." Barrett's steely gaze met first dad's then mine.

"Calm down?" Dad turned to me, his knuckles white against the wood grain. "Did you hear that, Chili? This moron wants me to calm down."

Barrett either didn't know my father very well or wasn't one himself. No self-respecting man would sit back and let his daughter get arrested and do nothing. Barrett was an idiot, if he thought otherwise.

The two men faced off over the table. There was plenty of bad blood between them. Barrett had dated my mother. When she met my dad, they fell head-over-heels in love and married a short time later. Barrett held a grudge ever since.

"This isn't getting us anywhere, Dad." I touched his shoulder, the muscles tense under my fingertips. "We need to get going, check on the kids."

The two men glared at each other for a few seconds more.

Dad sighed and straightened. "Fix it, Barrett." He rubbed his left shoulder, flexing the fingers. "This is wrong."

Barrett didn't speak, just eyed us both with distaste. The feeling was mutual.

I turned and reached for the door. A groan sounded from behind me. Swivelling, I managed to half catch dad as he crumpled to the floor, his face grey, his eyes bulging as if he were in shock. He clutched his chest. His eyelids fluttered once, twice, and then closed.

My heart froze then pounded through my chest painfully. He was having a heart attack.

I wheeled to face Barrett. "Get an ambulance!" I screamed. "Now!"

I tilted dad's head back, searching for a carotid pulse with my fingers.

Nothing.

Fear filled me, paralysing me with its strength. This couldn't be happening. Not here, not now. I shook my head. I couldn't do this. He was going to die.

My dad was going to die.

My hands clenched, nails driving into my palms. This was what first-aid training was for. I just had to follow the instructions drilled into me. I fought for calm, took a deep breath, angled my arm and brought it down on his chest with a precordial thump, then placed one hand atop the other and started CPR.

"Row, row, row your boat ... one, two, three, and four." I hated the childish song, but our trainer was right. It helped remember the timing of compressions.

Tears filled my eyes and stained his shirt. My arms burned, my eyes blurred. "Don't you do this to me? Don't you dare die." I squeezed my eyes shut. Memories of him and Mum flitted through my thoughts. I couldn't lose him, not like I'd lost her. "God, please don't let him die," I whispered. "I need him."

A flurry of activity filled the room as paramedics rushed in. Strong arms lifted me away from dad and led me out of the way. The paramedics inserted a breathing tube into Dad's windpipe. One paramedic continued compressions.

A weary ache crammed into my chest. Someone would have to drive me to the hospital; I didn't think my legs were going to hold me up for much longer. A pair of arms hugged me, while a voice whispered soothing words against my hair. Gideon had come. I was certain he would. I turned and buried my face in his jacket. His arms held me close, but he couldn't comfort me this time. "I hate you." I moaned. "If it wasn't for you, this wouldn't have happened."

He kissed the top of my head. His voice sounded as tired as I was. "I know."

Chapter 8

I finally made it to the hospital.

After clarifying that I had no desire to see Gideon, I'd been offered a ride in a police van.

He'd followed in his own car.

The man who arrested my sister stood in front of me. In his hands, he balanced a coffee and muffin-laden cardboard tray. The black suit and tie he wore not only looked good, it screamed cop. Patients and staff alike cast covert glances his way. I didn't care. Let them look and wonder what he was doing with me, the crazy, copper-haired chick. He sat and placed the tray on the cracked plastic seat between us. Smart guy. It's best to stay away from a woman experiencing PMS, especially when her life has blown up.

"Are you all right?"

I exhaled so hard my breath puffed out strands of hair. My hands knotted, and I had to fight an irresistible urge to punch him. "What do you think?" I hissed.

He shut his eyes, leaned back, and rested his head against the wall. Like I said, smart guy. Desperate to attack something, I grabbed a blueberry muffin and stuffed half of it in my mouth to keep from chewing on Gideon. People slumped in uncomfortable chairs, most in varying states of health; one guy had a bloodied towel wrapped around his arm. Others, like me, waited to speak to the medical staff. Two kids sat with their backs against a wall playing a video game. I envied them the ability to get lost in a fantasy world, instead of dealing with the cold reality of a hospital room. A dying father. An incarcerated sister.

I glared at Gideon, choking down the stale food. It lodged in my throat. One more thing to hold against him. He glanced at me and shook his head. "I'm not the bad guy here, Chili."

"Oh. Really?"

"Yes, really. I understand you blame me for what happened to your Dad." He sighed. "But honestly? His heart attack isn't my fault."

I couldn't answer. He was right. In all fairness, though, what did he expect? Heart-felt gratitude for arresting my sister? Fat chance.

Still, he met me here. Bought me food. At my age, bringing food counted for something. It entitled him to a little honesty.

"You're right. I'm angry about Coco." I nodded toward the emergency department. "I'm angry that Dad's in there." Our gazes met, and I allowed all the pain and turmoil to be visible on my face. "I'm angry that you betrayed me."

He flinched and leaned forward, his arms resting on his knees. "I didn't betray you, Chili."

"So now you're telling me you weren't involved in any of this?"

A woman with her arm in a sling sat opposite us. She stared open-mouthed at me. I stared back and raised a questioning eyebrow. She was no match for me—I could give a stare Medusa would be proud of. She looked away.

"If you'd just let me explain ... " He pushed his sunglasses back on his head and reached for my hand. His fingers were warm and calloused and did swirly things to my stomach. What was it with tough guys and their hands? I was like an addict craving a fix. I looked away from the perfect fit of my hand in his and shrugged. "Fine, go ahead."

"I'm not on the case. I got pulled."

My mouth fell open. I glanced at his face. The crooked half-smile told me he was being truthful. That put things on a new level.

"Why?" I clipped the edge from my voice.

He fixed his eyes on the dirt-smudged wall opposite. "Barrett knows I'm fond of you and your family." He lifted one shoulder. "He thinks I can't be impartial."

Impartial my foot. If Barrett thought Gideon was anything other than a total professional, he was way off base. "So you didn't arrest Coco?"

He nodded. "That I did do."

I jerked my hand away from his. He reached for it again, but I tucked it under my thigh.

"I thought I could help."

The knot in my stomach slowly unravelled. I was torn between relief that he was off the case and the realisation that he wasn't there for her. I swallowed hard. What a mess.

Footsteps clattered toward us. We both looked up. Just what I needed. Nurse Blondie and Doctor Morgan. Morgan?

I scrambled to my feet, knocking over the remains of our coffee. Brown liquid splattered Blondie's shoes. She glared at me while I pretended not to notice. Out of the corner of my eye, Gideon smirked.

"Hi, Chili." Morgan nodded coldly at Gideon. "St. James."

He turned to me, jutting his shoulder to block Gideon. "Your Dad's going to be fine. He's had surgery and we've placed a stent in his artery. We need to keep him in for a few days for observation." His eyes searched mine.

"Thank God." I grabbed Morgan and hugged him, my knees weak. Dad was going to be all right. Gratitude welled inside me until I thought my heart would explode. A cough sounded behind me. I pulled back, embarrassed, my hands dropping to my side. Two sets of eyes watched us and neither was happy. It looked like Blondie had set her cap on Morgan. Well, then.

"Are you his attending?" asked Gideon.

"No, Dr. Frank is. He graciously allowed me to tell you the good news."

I reached out and squeezed his hand. "Thanks, Morgan. When can I see him?"

"Now if you like." He looked at his watch. "Nurse Johnson can take you to him, but make it short, okay?"

"Of course." I turned to Gideon. "I'll be right back." It was his turn to hug me. Morgan stiffened at my side. Gideon let go and nodded. "I'll be waiting for you." I hurried off, wondering if anyone else heard the promise in his parting remark. It was great having them both there. If only they'd keep the testosterone under control. Our footsteps clattered on the floor as she led me through the double doors and into a curtained cubicle.

Monitors beeped, IV fluids dripped, while my heart revved like a Formula One car. My Dad lay among the various tubes, his skin paler than the sheet thrown over him. I stood, refusing to let my knees buckle. The last time I'd been here was the night Mum died. A drunk driver had hit her while she was out for a morning walk. He'd left her there, lying in the gutter like a piece of trash, and sped off. They found her and brought her here, but it was too late. A sense of déjà vu hovered in the air.

Blinking back tears, I walked nearer the bed, trying not to touch the tangle of machines keeping him alive. My hand reached out and touched his fingertips, his face. The rough bristles made me cringe. He was cold to the touch. Cold, but alive. That was all that mattered. I picked up a chair, sat and rested my face on the bed, his hand next to my cheek. Strength leached from my bones. This had to stop. I couldn't handle much more. My world had crumbled, and I wasn't sure how to fix it. I bowed my head. Tried to pray, but the words jumbled with remembered phrases from Mum's service. A hand touched my shoulder. I jumped and then tried to smile.

Jessica Rabbit was back. A slight smile touched her lips, but not her eyes, which remained as cold as my father's skin. "Time's up. You'll need to leave now," she murmured.

I nodded. Kissing Dad's hand, I whispered, "I'll be back soon, Dad. I love you."

Once again, I followed Jessica's swinging hips down a corridor. Stepping through the doors, I blinked. I must have been gone longer than I thought. Orange and pink fingers lit the room as the sun dipped its rays through the windows. Gideon was waiting right where he said he would. One gold star for him. He spotted me and headed over. Women turned to watch him, but he took no notice. I liked that about him. His bad-boy look was just an image that drew women like a magnetic charge, including me. Except the man who lay beneath the surface was decent and kind. One who would lie down and give his life for his brother.

"How is he?"

"Asleep. He's zonked out on medication."

We walked to the car and got in. Gideon drove back to my house. I sat in comfortable silence, lost in my thoughts. I stared out the window into the growing darkness. Houses flashed by, light peeking out from behind closed curtains. Families were getting ready for bed, tucking little ones in, watching television. Inside the cosy little boxes, were other people going through stuff like this?

The car breaking softly woke me. No way. I must have dozed off. Stretching, I wiped drool from the side of my mouth. Great. So much for being lady-like. As the door swung open, the interior light flashed on. Eerie shadows crawled away from the car. I shuddered. Now was not the time to let my imagination take control.

Gideon drummed his fingers on the steering wheel. He turned his head and looked at me, dark circles under his eyes standing out like bruises. I wasn't the only one who hadn't slept well. I forced myself to suppress any sympathy. His eyes caught mine and held. My stomach churned under his scrutiny. "I am sorry about your father, Chili. You need to believe that."

I did. And knowing that made everything worse.

He pushed a strand of hair away from my mouth, his fingers grazing my face. "You understand the system, Chili. Everything will be fine. Have a little faith."

That shook me. Faith in a flawed legal system? In him?

"Ha Ha. Hilarious." I grabbed my belongings. "I'd ask you in, but it's getting late."

He tilted his head. "And I arrested your sister."

"You bought it up, not me."

"Fine. I'm not arguing with you, Chili. Get some sleep and I'll call you tomorrow." He reached into his jacket. "Almost forgot, I picked up the mail for you." He handed me a small pile of envelopes, secured with a rubber band.

I walked to my door and fumbled with the lock. I peeked out the window for a last look at him. That rugged hand lifted in a wave. My hand lifted, though I ordered it to stay put. As he drove away, I watched the red taillights until they disappeared and a wave of loneliness hit.

As I deposited my keys on the counter, I removed my shoes and collapsed onto the lounge, exhausted and confused. Almond jumped on my lap and sharpened her claws on my leg. I wasn't sure what to do. I was so drained that I couldn't call Coco's neighbour to check on the twins. Another to-do item for tomorrow. Between visiting Dad and Coco, arranging for the twins to stay with Bonnie and checking in with clients, it was a good thing business was a little slow.

I grabbed the pile of letters and flipped through them. One caught my eye. The front of the letter prominently displayed the name of my lending institution. A beacon of hope. The bearer of good news. My bank loan was here. Soon I'd be the proud owner of one acre of heaven. Pictures of fluffy yellow chicks, home-grown vegetables and heavily laden fruit trees flicked through my mind like a well-loved video. Perhaps I'd even get a dog.

I scanned the pristine sheet of white paper, not registering what I read. I started again, slowly, each black word tattooing itself indelibly on my brain. I screwed up the paper and threw it against the wall. Tossing my head back, I curled my hands into fists and screamed in anger.

The bank denied my loan.

Chapter 9

I typed up my notes and emailed them to Pete, asking him to make sure my name didn't appear in his final report. Pete responded, assuring me I shouldn't worry because the company who hired us would create their own report and wouldn't mention us. No one likes someone else is taking over their case.

No other jobs had come in, so I could now concentrate on getting my sister absolved of a crime she didn't commit. I made a cup of hazelnut coffee, grabbed a handful of candy covered chocolate and fired up my computer. Almond watched me from her perch on the back of the armchair, her tail tucked around her. Rain drizzled against the window. I clicked the remote for the sound system and classical music played quietly in the background. It was my version of white noise.

My first search was for William Van Horne. The page loaded, and I soon looked through dozens of entries about him, his wife, and the many charities they'd sponsored. Connie was right about the South African connection; they'd both been born and raised there. They had three kids, all grown, a beach house and a penchant for Pomeranians. Mrs Van Horne was not only a highly regarded breeder but was popular on the dog show circuit. I couldn't find a link to anything remotely illegal.

I typed Morgan's name into the browser and popped a chocolate-covered peanut in my mouth. I chewed while debating the wisdom of researching an ex on the 'net. It was something I warned clients about doing, especially after partying or having a case of the blues. Since neither applied to me, I figured it couldn't hurt. I hit the enter key before I could change my mind. There didn't appear to be a lot out there. Most professional people kept their profiles pretty locked down. Apart from a few mentions with Border Doctors and a promotional photo of a group of them, Morgan included, helping children in Africa, I couldn't find anything.

A sigh escaped my lips. Why had he returned after only completing half of his three-year commitment? It wasn't because of me. There had to be another reason. Perhaps something was going on with his family, a secret we were unaware of. I rubbed my hands over my face and tried not to dwell on all the possibilities.

This was getting me nowhere. I was out of chocolate, out of clean clothes, and out of ideas. The clock chimed eight, and I realised I couldn't do anything else today. After a long, hot shower and some TV watching, I needed a good night's sleep. If I exhausted myself, I wouldn't be able to help anyone.

I was just searching the fridge for anything remotely edible when someone knocked on my door.

I picked up my phone and tapped the doorbell video app. Gideon. And bless him, he brought food.

"Hey," he said when I flicked the deadlock and opened the door. He held up a large bag. "Bonnie thought you might be hungry."

I stepped aside, and he entered. "You didn't have to go to so much trouble."

He smiled. "It's never any trouble. Besides, you don't live that far from town. And I was pretty sure you wouldn't have eaten." He put the bag on the counter and started searching cupboards for plates and cutlery. I tried to help, and he shooed me out of the kitchen. "Sit down. I can do this bit."

It was hard to relax and let someone else look after me. I was so used to looking after everyone else. I sat down, put my feet up, and watched him. From my vantage point in the open plan living area, I could view the kitchen, dining and lounge areas. It was kind of nice seeing him place food and drinks on a tray. Was this what Sommer's hubby did for her? A pang flowed through me as I wondered what else I was missing out on.

He soon appeared with steaming plates piled high with roast lamb, vegetables, and gravy. My stomach rumbled. Bless Bonnie, her cooking skills were legendary. I speared a roast potato, swirled it in the gravy, and sighed with contentment. It was delicious. The outside was crisp and caramelised to perfection, while the inside was soft and fluffy. We ate in companionable silence while the rain continued to drizzle outside. I finished my food and lit the fire. This was my favourite part of the colder months. The world could do whatever it liked outside my little haven.

He cleared up the plates, put the dishwasher on and came back with hot chocolate with lashings of cream and sprinkles, together with gooey chocolate brownie. Perfect. I indulged in a large bite of brownie and licked the leftover chocolate off my lip. A sigh escaped my lips as all the tension released from my shoulders.

"How are you feeling?"

I looked up at him and saw concern on his face. It was nearly my undoing. Why do we cry when someone shows us sympathy? Shouldn't we cry because we don't get it?

I choked down the lump rising in my throat. "Honestly?"

He nodded.

"Like I'm losing myself." I ticked off my fingers. "Between dad, Coco, the murder and the redevelopers wanting my house, I can't seem to catch a break." I sighed. "And I'm just so darn exhausted. On the plus side, I have a new friend." I relayed the whole thing with Sommer and he laughed at my clumsiness.

"Only you could take an unpleasant situation and turn it into something positive," he said. "What's your next step?"

I took a sip of my drink. "I need to see Mrs Van Horne and do some digging into Red Soil Developments. The Walrus was cagey when I spoke to him, so I definitely think he knows something."

"Cagey, in what way?"

I mentioned that any development plans must go through the council, but he argued that they never received them. "Actually, that's not true. He said, 'Red Soil Developments' had submitted none."

"Do you think someone else submitted plans, and he's not telling you?"

"You're probably right. I need to look into it some more, otherwise I'll end up homeless and on the streets."

He grinned. "I've got a spare room at my place." Almond miaowed. He reached over and rubbed behind her ears. "You're always welcome, too."

My heart melted. We'd been through a lot, Gideon and I. He was two years ahead of me in high school and the object of every girl's crush in the area, me included. It was he who drove me to the hospital when I broke my wrist and was the first to sign my cast. I was there for him when he got married and again-when in retaliation for him exposing a paedophile ring- his pregnant wife disappeared.

I hesitated, and then softly asked. 'Do you ever think about her? About Sarah and the baby?'

Gideon's expression darkened, his jaw tightening. "Every day, he said. "Some questions never stop haunting you." He continued his voice barely above a whisper, "We wanted it to be a surprise. We decided to wait until the birth to find out if it was a boy or a girl." He swallowed. "I'll never know. That's the hardest part—never knowing."

I reached out placing my hand on his arm. "I can't imagine how hard that is," I said. "But not knowing doesn't change the love you had, or still have, for them. That love is real, Gideon. It always will be."

He nodded, eyes clouded with unspoken pain.

It was time to change the subject.

I asked him how his day had been. "Not bad. I've been typing up reports, and the boss assigned me the missing person's case over in Hendley."

"Is that the teenager who didn't come home after cheerleading practice?"

He scratched his chin and nodded. "Good kid, good grades and hadn't done anything like this before. I've interviewed her family and friends and we've done a grid search. Tomorrow I'll speak to teachers and extend the search. Hopefully, something will turn up."

"What are your thoughts?"

"I don't think it's going to be good."

I sighed. I couldn't imagine having someone I loved go missing. The parents must be beside themselves. After what Gideon had been through with his own family, the case must've been hard for him to work on. If anyone understood my feelings, it was him. I'd sat with him when his wife and baby went missing, watching his world implode and knowing I could do nothing but be there. My thoughts drifted toward Coco and the Van Horne's.

"Chili?"

"Hmm?"

"You're not thinking of investigating the murder, are you?"

I blinked. How could he know that's exactly what I'd been thinking?

"No, why?"

"Because, as you're aware, if you interfere in a police investigation, then the powers that be would, and could, cancel your investigator's licence. Plus, you can face some serious jail time. And trust me; Barrett would throw the book at you, literally."

Heat filled my face, and I concentrated on swiping crumbs with my finger. I popped the last corner of the brownie in my mouth. "If you were me, wouldn't you want to find out who killed Van Horne?" The clock ticked off the seconds before he answered. "Yes, I would." He leaned forward and touched my knee. "So just think of this as a gentle reminder. You won't be helping anyone if you're behind bars or dead."

I didn't respond. There was no answer to that. He was perfectly right. The law prohibited Private Investigators in my area from trespassing, picking locks, or using illegal recording devices like hidden cameras. Any evidence used in court had to be got by legal means and apply to a case. Prosecutors couldn't use tainted evidence and it could even lead to dropping charges.

We sat in silence for a while, staring as the fire flickered and danced. My mouth stretched into a yawn, relieved that he had moved on from the topic. I lifted my head and met his gaze with my own. He smiled and just like that, everything was right between us.

He patted the seat next to him and I scooted across and rested my head on his chest. We watched a movie while the world outside grew silent. I must have dozed off as I woke when he carried me to bed and tucked me in. He kissed me gently and whispered good night. I heard the front door click shut and drifted back off, the warmth of his lips still on mine.

Chapter 10

One baby-faced angel was heaven. Two were enough to make me cry. Coco's twins were sitting on the front stairs when I pulled up. Their faces lit up when they recognised my car. They looked so cute sitting there, framed by potted ferns and hanging baskets. Hydrangeas grew in garden beds at the front of the house. Pink flowers grew along the right side, and blue on the left. It never failed to surprise me how Bonnie had separated the colours. My gardening thumb was the kiss of death to all plants.

Billy and Susie bounced on the step. Warmth floated through me. They were adorable and so loving. They made it easy to be the generous aunt, the one who spoiled them rotten, then handed them back to their mother.

"Aunt Chili! Look! Miss Bonnie gave us ice-cream!"

I grabbed two bags from the backseat and headed toward the kids. Sticky hands and lips greeted me. I held them both close and inhaled the scent of skin, fabric softener and chocolate ice-cream. Everything that was pure about children. It wouldn't be long before they grew up, and the world tainted them with peer groups and pressure.

"You guys are so lucky." I leaned back and looked at them. "Have you been good for Miss Bonnie?"

Two identical sets of moss-green eyes stared at me. A glance- and an unspoken message passed between them. "Yeah," Billy answered.

Susie looked at her foot. Her red sneaker drew patterns on the gravel driveway. I curled my fingers under her chin. "What's up Susie-blue?"

"I miss Mummy," she whispered. Her bottom lip trembled. Billy looked at his sister. His eyes filled with tears.

A lump formed in my chest. I pulled them both against me. Soft arms wrapped around my neck. Faces buried in my shoulders. "I miss Mummy, too." I let go of them and brushed hair from one face, kissed the other. "But, she'll be home soon and when she does, how about we have a surprise party?"

"Really?"

"Really."

Bright smiles beamed from trusting faces. I hoped I could live up to their expectations.

The screen door swung open, and Bonnie's generous frame filled the doorway. "How's your dad?" I glanced at the twins. They were too busy making party-plans to listen. "He's doing better. He should be home in a few days."

She grasped both my hands in hers and relieved eyes met mine. "He's a healthy man, your dad. He'll be fine." Her words filled me with hope and I hugged her. She was such a blessing to my family. She pulled back, wiped her eyes, and took a deep, shaky breath. "Coffee?"

I nodded. "That'd be great."

I gave her one bag and handed the other to Billy. "This is for you to share with your sister." Squeals of delight accompanied the discovery of the latest Disney movie.

"Can we watch it, Miss Bonnie?" Pleaaaaase?"

She smiled, dimples taking her face captive. "Of course you can watch it." She ruffled Billy's hair. "Wash your hands first. Your aunt and I are going to the kitchen. Call if you need anything."

They ran inside, the worries of a minute ago forgotten. I watched them go, envious. How I wished I was five again with nothing to worry about.

Bonnie led me through the house and into her kitchen. Like her, it was large and inviting. The smell of slow cooking Coq au Vin crept into my nostrils and embraced me like a long-lost lover. My mouth watered. My stomach growled. I couldn't imagine anyone resisting the combination of bacon, chicken, and mushrooms cooking in a savoury blend of onions and red wine. Bonnie was a masterful cook. Everything she prepared became a dish to be savoured, like a fine wine or chocolate. Rumours had it she'd even prepared meals for royalty. After sampling her food, I believed them.

She poured us both coffees. A delicate china plate sat covered on the table. Underneath the lace cover waited a decadent White Chocolate Mud cake. Bonnie cut a slice, placed it on a matching rose patterned plate and handed it to me. Good manners dictated I use the fork provided. I cut a sliver and ate, not bothering to suppress a sigh. I pointed my fork at her. "This is heavenly. You really should open a bakery."

Her eyes twinkled. "If I did, who would look after your family?"

"True." I took another bite. "Forget the bakery. We need you more." I wondered if Bonnie made wedding cakes. Not that I needed one soon, but it was handy to know. She waited until I'd finished the treat before leaning forward.

"Are you okay?"

"Fine." I took another slice. "Tired, more than anything."

"Well, that doesn't surprise me." She spooned whipped cream on my cake. My waist-line was going out the window. Good thing a wedding dress wasn't on my horizon. At least that deep down urge for something sweet was being assuaged. "You've got too much on your plate." She glanced at mine. "No pun intended."

"I just feel so useless."

"I understand. But you're a good woman, Chili. Don't let anyone tell you differently."

My ego expanded to meet my waistline. I'd been called a lot of things, but good wasn't one of them.

Bonnie's cheeks flushed. "I'm sorry. I didn't mean to embarrass you."

"There's nothing to forgive." I reached out and patted her hand. "You're part of the family. Even Dad says that."

"Really?" The cream covered spoon poised in mid-air. "Your Dad says that?"

I added more sugar to my coffee. "Of course he does. He's always going on about you. It's always Bonnie this and Bonnie that."

She gasped. Clumsy fingers dropped the spoon into the bowl. Her face reddened even more while her eyes widened. Cream flicked up and landed on my chin. I wiped it off, and honed in on the trembling hand, the flushed face. What had I said? I was missing something. Somethi— Oh. *Oh*.

Bonnie was in love with my dad. Man, I could be so blind. Why hadn't I seen it before? I stirred my coffee while she cleaned up the mess, my thoughts moving in time with the spoon. It all made sense now. The cooking, helping with the kids ... her way of being close to him. It didn't hurt, though. That surprised me. Shouldn't there be anger or indignation on behalf of my deceased mother? Mum always liked Bonnie; the two had been friends since childhood. Somehow, I thought she'd approve. "What does Dad think of you?"

"He likes me, I think. We haven't really talked about it. He didn't want to upset either of you."

"Why would that upset us?"

She fingered the lace edge of the tablecloth. "Because of your mum. We were both such good friends, and when Frank died ... well, I thought that was it. Who'd want an overweight, almost sixty-year-old woman?"

"Trust me. Anyone who can cook like you do is bound to have a tonne of admirers."

"But they don't want me for me."

I could see her point. Some guys only wanted a maid or bed warmer or, as you got older ... a nurse. Finding someone who was interested in the total package was harder. "Well, my dad isn't like that." I squeezed her hand. "I'm happy for you both."

A smile lit up her face. "Thank you."

Not being able to share her feelings about dad must have been hard, especially with him being in the hospital. "I'm heading back to the hospital later. Why don't you join me?"

Tears filled her eyes. "I'd like that very much." We sat lost in thought for a few moments.

"How is Mrs Van Horne doing?" she asked.

The change of subject threw me. "Who?"

"Mrs Van Horne, the jeweller's wife." At my questioning look, she continued. "The one you found dead?"

"Oh, her!" I shook my head to clear the confusion. "I forgot he was married. Had you met them before?"

"Only socially. His wife took my cake decorating class. Her wedding cake was beautiful."

"So you do bake wedding cakes?"

"Yes. Why?"

I waved my hand in the air. "No reason. A friend was asking, that's all." I helped myself to more coffee. At this rate, I was going to spend the rest of the afternoon in the bathroom. "So, what were they like? The Van Horne's."

"Wealthy. Not old money, mind. They were more 'Nouveau-rich.'" Bonnie got up, her chair scraping on the floor. "They emigrated from South Africa about thirty years ago. From what I hear, they escaped from Mugabe's tyrannical reign with only the clothes on their backs and each other."

"Wow. That must be some story."

"It is. You should pay Delia a visit. After all, it was you who found her husband."

"Yeah, I just might do that." I caught her smile. "Pay my respects and all." I glanced at my watch. "Right now, I'd better go see Coco before they revoke my visiting privileges. So far, no one's been able to tell me exactly why she's in custody."

"Really? I would've thought something would have been said by now." A crease appeared between her brows. "I hope she's alright."

I nodded. "Me, too. I learned from previous cases they can hold her for 48 hours without giving her a reason, just on the suspicion of a crime. So I'm not really sure if it's just that suspicion, or if they have something they believe connects her to the crime."

I helped clean up, hugged the munchkins and left with dread circling my chest.

Chapter 11

The dread hadn't lifted as I drove downtown to the jail. I fiddled with the radio knob jumping from station to station, then with a frustrated jab turned it off, letting silence fill the air. Everything seemed to rub me wrong. The air-con was too breezy against my skin, the sun too hot against the window. I wound it down and stuck my elbow on the door ledge. My throat was sour with the taste of bitter coffee and I'd run out of antacids. I pulled up behind the police station, turned my engine off, and sat there.

What was I doing? Running around trying to solve a homicide had more than my reputation at stake. My sister was going to be facing some serious jail time. I couldn't imagine how her kids were going to cope without her if I failed.

Minutes ticked by as I sat waiting for something, anything, to show me what to do. When nothing happened, I grabbed my things, locked the car, and made my way inside.

Officer Johnson wasn't in charge this time, so there was no idle chit-chat or promises of a drink. A dark-haired woman with a chip on her rather broad shoulders led me down the corridor and to a small, windowless room. I took two steps into the room and the door behind me clanged shut. The room was part of a newer extension only built a couple of years ago. Grey paint covered the walls, and a metal table with two matching chairs sat in the middle of the room. A faint musty odour hung in the air.

Waiting for me was Coco.

Not waiting for permission, I walked forward and hugged her. A chill came off her body, and I pulled her even closer. It was only when the officer told me to let go I did. We sat on either side of a table and the officer moved to a corner of the room, giving us a small amount of privacy. I swiped my hand across the dust-covered table and looked at my dirty fingers. I wiped them on my pants. Only then did I really observe at my sister.

Awful couldn't describe how she looked. Her face had lost its tan and in its stead was a ghostly pallor. Dark purple smudges sat under her eyes. She hunched her shoulders, and her clothes hung loosely on her frame. Had it really only been twenty-four hours?

Coco brushed a limp strand of hair away from her face. "Hey, Chil," she said, her smile moving the corners of her mouth but going no further.

I swallowed and touched her hand. "Hey."

We sat that way for a few minutes, letting our eyes search each other for clues about how we were really handling things. Neither of us was doing well.

"How are the kids?"

"Doing great. Bonnie's been feeding them loads of goodies, and I took over a movie and ice-cream. They're probably all sugared out and sleeping it off."

She gave a tired smile. "I'm glad. Any news on dad?"

"Morgan says he's doing well and we'll hear more in the next couple of days. Once released, he's going to stay at your place so Bonnie can monitor him." I chewed the corner of my lip. "Speaking of dad; did you know about him and Bonnie?"

She sat back, confusion etched on her face. "What do you mean?"

"It appears they've been secretly dating."

Her mouth dropped open. "What? Why didn't they say anything?"

I shrugged. "They probably thought we wouldn't approve because Bonnie was mum's friend."

"I guess it's not really a tremendous surprise." She worried the skin around her fingernail. "As long as they're happy, that's the main thing."

"That's what I said." I pulled a packet out of my pocket. "This is for you."

The officer came over and inspected the packet. Anger prickled my skin, and I swallowed a nasty retort. It wasn't as if the package was big enough to house a file. She nodded once and gave it back to Coco.

She opened it and grinned. "I love Rock Cakes!"

"I thought it might cheer you up."

The pastry was huge. A conglomeration of dough, glace cherries and sultanas, they were a mainstay of our lunchboxes growing up. The addition of glace cherries was mine. I threw in a handful when making them with mum and after that we always included them.

She took a bite and a genuine smile lit her face. "This is *so* good!"

We chatted about inconsequential things while she finished her treat. The cold metal of the chair had seeped through my jeans and judging by the way Coco wiggled on hers, she too was suffering from a frozen butt. I took my pen and notebook out of my jacket pocket and put them on the table. It was time to get down to business.

"So tell me more about William Van Horne."

"We met years ago at a financial conference. We exchanged business cards, and I redecorated his house when he and his wife were overseas. They liked it, so always sent work my way. In return, I'd buy gifts for clients from his store."

"What gifts?"

"Pens, jewellery, pocket watches; that sort of stuff."

I jotted that down in my notebook. "Why do the police think you killed him?"

She shrugged. "Well, according to Gideon, he was hit over the head with my jar of biscuits."

I recalled seeing a jar on the counter, a dark and sticky smear standing out against the delicate vine pattern etched on the thick bottom.

"The biscuits were from you?"

"I ordered a speciality jar online as a thank you gift. They were gluten-free and with dairy-free chocolate in them. They think that's what killed him. The jar not the biscuits."

"I remember seeing it. The jar looked expensive."

"It was but with the deal he did with me on presents, it was worth the extra."

"Didn't they have a gold seal around the edge?"

She shrugged. "I think so. I dropped them off just before phoning you." That was interesting. The jar I saw still had the seal intact, even though there were biscuits sitting next to two cups of coffee.

"Did you have anything to drink while you were there? Wine? Coffee?"

She shook her head. "He offered, but I wanted to get home in time for the kids."

"Okay, so other than the biscuits, which you ordered online and hand delivered, there's really nothing else tying you to the murder?"

"No, nothing that I'm aware of." She sighed. "I understand they have to look at every avenue, but I didn't do it."

I took her hand and squeezed it. "Once they've done the autopsy and reviewed everything, they'll release you."

"I hope so, Chilli, I really hope so." A strand of hair flopped across her eyes and she tucked it behind her ear. "It's like I'm in a recurring nightmare with monsters chasing me and I just can't wake up."

The thought of my close encounter with the killer had me nodding in agreement. Even with the extra security precautions at home, I still felt naked and vulnerable. I kept checking the rear seat of the car for someone hiding there, kept my keys between my fingers like a modern day 'Wolverine', kept wondering if I should get a guard dog.

"It'll get better, I promise. Soon you'll be out of here and back home where you belong."

She nodded. "Thanks for coming down."

"We're family, right? You'd do the same for me."

The guard tapped her finger on her watch. It was time for me to leave.

I gathered my things and turned back to Coco. "One more question. Do you have any idea who might have held a grudge against him or his wife?"

A wrinkle formed between her eyes that hadn't been there before. "I'm not sure. I mean, he had mentioned an argument at a dog show. Some lady accused them of cheating." She shrugged. "If I think of anything else, I'll let you know."

We hugged, and I left. As I stepped through the front door, strands of brilliant sunlight pulled everything out of focus. I donned my sunnies and waited for my eyes to adjust. A group of people appeared to be standing near my car, taking photos and chatting with excitement. I walked toward them, a pit opening in my stomach. People taking selfies en masse either meant someone famous was nearby or an accident had occurred. I was hoping for the former.

When I reached the pavement, I pushed through the crowd and stood looking at what had once been my beautiful white car.

Someone had slashed one tyre, threw a bucket of rhubarb-red paint onto the roof, which now dripped down the windscreen and bonnet, left the bucket upended on the aerial, and hastily misspelled the words "Back Of" in a scrawl on the doors.

I was wrong; it appeared I was famous after all.

Chapter 12

S omeone damaged my car, Dad was in the hospital, Coco was in jail and they had denied my loan. My life was a crime scene playing out before my eyes. And now I was being interrogated, or at least that's how Barrett's questioning appeared.

"It's beyond me why someone would want to damage my car." I was back inside the police station cradling a cup of tepid coffee while my life crumbled around me. Annoyance flared, and I took a deep breath. "Did any of the surveillance cameras catch who did it?"

"No. It appears someone spray painted over the lens." He got up from his chair and perched on the edge of his desk. It was a classic technique meant to place him above me. Two could play at that game. I leaned back in my chair, stretched my legs out, and crossed my ankles. He asked, "Why do think they'd want to do that?"

"Well, I guess that would depend on how long they've been out for." I waited, but he didn't respond. My money was they hadn't been functioning for a while and he didn't want to admit it. I couldn't blame him—public confidence in the police was at an all-time low. "I don't think someone would go to all that trouble just to damage *my* car. It was probably an end-of-year high-school prank that someone has forgotten about by now." School finished three weeks ago.

I changed the subject, hoping to catch him off guard. "Do you really think Coco had anything to do with Van Horne's murder?"

He raised his hands as if to hold off my question. "Now I'm pretty sure Detective St. James has already informed you we can't discuss an ongoing case. We especially cannot discuss that with a relative of a suspect in custody." A smirk touched his lips. "Even if that relative happens to be a private investigator."

I shook my head and tried to play up to his ego. "Oh, I know that. I was really only wanting your personal thoughts from your own experience." I looked down as I played with the handle of my bag and made my voice small. "Do you think they're somehow connected?" I asked. "Could someone have damaged my car because of Coco?"

"Oh, don't you go getting worried about it. I'm sure what happened to your car, as bad as it is, was just the prank of some bored kids." He stood and hitched his pants, his stature growing with his self-importance. "We'll get to the bottom of Mr Van Horne's murder." He winked. "I can promise you that."

There was nothing more I could say. Barrett wouldn't let anything spill, and it was time for me to head out.

"You're right. I'm sure you'll work out who the actual killer is ... eventually." His smile dropped and the air chilled. If I wasn't careful, I'd end up in a cell next to Coco.

Barrett stared at me for a few seconds more and nodded toward the door, dismissing me. "You can go, but just remember ..."

I stood and grabbed my bag. "Yeah, yeah. Don't leave town."

He sighed. "I was going to say, 'try to keep out of trouble.'"

I opened the door to the station and stepped outside. The air under the portico was cold and my breath became frosty. As I stepped out into the sun I wished I'd brought gloves.

Rusty, our local mechanic, had parked his tow-truck in the middle of the road and was just off-loading an old pickup truck; an F100. I waited while he parked it and then began loading my car onto his truck. I'd called him earlier before going inside the station to make a formal complaint. He promised he'd have a loan car waiting for me by the time I was finished.

He saw me, grinned, and waved me over.

"Hi Rusty."

"Hey Chili." He nodded toward my car. "Who's got their knickers in a knot with ya this time?"

I winced. He made it sound like I deliberately tried to upset people. Though being fair, I seemed to have more than my fair share of trouble.

He patted my arm. "Just joking with ya. Whoever's done this needs a good smack up the side of the head."

"Thanks, Rusty. I think you'll need to get in line for that one. How long do you think it'll take to fix it?"

The trailer winch ground to a halt and he hooked the control box in its bracket. He removed his baseball cap and smoothed his hair before replacing the cap. "It's probably going to be a couple of weeks, unfortunately. I'll have to check with the manufacturer on the paint colour, get the supplies in and then have Gaz do his thing."

"How is Gaz these days?" Rusty's brother had just gone through a messy divorce which had divided the town. His wife had racked up thousands on their joint credit card and walked out, leaving him floundering in bills while she partied in Bali.

"Yeah, not bad." He leaned forward and spoke in a low voice. "Gaz had a win on the horses so could pay most of the debt back."

"Really? Wow."

"Yeah, but say nothing. If Sheila gets wind of it, she'll want some and she's already taken almost everything he had."

I mimed locking my lips and throwing away the key. "I won't say a word to anyone."

He fished a set of keys out of his pocket and handed them to me. "Only reason I said something was 'cause you've never been a gossip. Here's the key to the pickup. You can borrow it until your car's ready."

I was surprised they allowed me to borrow the pickup. The truck held sentimental value, as it had belonged to their late father, and both brothers were very particular about who drove it. Their generosity and trust touched me in.

"Thanks Rusty, I really appreciate it."

"No worries." He cleared his throat. "I was sorry to hear about your dad and Coco. Sometimes life really sucks. You guys have always been there for us, so loaning you a car is the least we could do."

I swallowed past the lump in my throat and hugged him hard. "Thank you." We pulled apart. Rusty winked and walked over to his truck. He paused and called over his shoulder, "Left you a present on the seat!" A few minutes later, he pulled away, my car in tow.

I hopped into the cab of Rusty's pickup and sat, my gaze locked on the peaceful scene outside. Rain had fallen, and the air filled with the scent of petrichor, that sweet, heady fragrance of bacteria in the earth mingling with water and ozone. It smelled better than it sounded. People ran for cover, hastily opening their umbrellas. Purple-blue flowers gracefully floated from the heavily laden boughs of a jacaranda.

A ticker tape memory of dancing in puddles flooded my senses and brought with it a touch of sorrow. Life was simple when you were a child with a loving family and the world was full of wonder.

I sniffed. My emotions were all over the place, and a dull ache pulsed behind my left eye. For a moment, I considered going home and sliding into bed, but from previous experience, sleep would elude me. I placed my bag on the floor. The car was too old to have blue-tooth, so I left my phone in the glove box within easy reach. On the passenger seat was a small cardboard box with the logo of my favourite bakery on it, which also happened to be the only bakery in town.

My throat closed and tears blurred my vision as I took an enormous maple-bacon cinnamon roll from the package. Food was my love-language, and it touched me that Rusty remembered. I bit into the gooey morsel and savoured the sweet-salty flavour.

I retrieved my pen, folder, and a bottle of water from my bag and balanced the roll on my knee, wiping a stray bit of icing from my mouth. I'd already made notes in a chronological format, starting with the murder of William Van Horne, and my hospitalisation, and ending with Coco's arrest. It was my own simplified version of a homicide detective's murder book. The section regarding the victim contained all the personal information I'd found during my internet search. Crime scene notes contained just that; as well as a description of the jar of cookies Coco had given as a present.

I didn't have access to the Medical Examiner's report but added cause of death, as suspected head trauma. My last section was simply titled, suspects. This was where I drew a blank. It felt like a betrayal to include Coco's name, so I split the page into three sections and wrote 'dog breeder', 'jewellery store', and 'personal'. I added the details Coco had relayed regarding an argument at a dog show in the relevant column.

I took a large bite of my roll and was chewing slowly when someone knocked on the window next to my head. Panic flowed through me and I fumbled for the door lock. Bacon pieces sprayed the interior as I started choking. The folder slid off my lap and I grabbed for the bottle of water. The door opened, and a hand pounded on my back. Snot and tears flowed down my face as the coughs finally subsided. I wiped my face with a hankie, blew my nose, and drank some fluid.

"Oh my gosh, are you okay?"

I slid out of the car, and bending over, nodded. Two pairs of boots were in my vision. A memory teased me, but it floated away before I could grasp it.

Straightening, I blew my nose again, wiped my hands on the back of my jeans and allowed myself to be hugged.

"I'm so sorry, Chili, I didn't mean to scare you. I just saw you sitting there and wanted to introduce you to my fiancé." Sommer pulled back and our eyes met. Hers were full of concern.

I attempted to speak, cleared my throat and waved off her apology.

"It's okay," I answered, my voice hoarse. "I was off in dreamland." Doubt flickered across her face. I rubbed her arm. "Seriously, I'm fine." I cleared my throat and turned to the man beside her. "You must be Cade. Sommer's told me all about you."

He laughed and stuck his hand out. "Only good things, I hope."

"They were so good I don't think any man could match you," I said. His laugh was infectious, and I smiled. He was just as nice as Sommer had said. "So, what are you guys up to?"

Sommer linked her arm through Cade's. "We were just heading to that cute little cafe you told me about for a bite to eat. Wanna join us?"

I tried begging off, but they both genuinely seemed to want me to be the third wheel, so I agreed. Soon we were sitting inside Rosie's Café. We chatted while Rosie took our orders and disappeared into the kitchen, where her husband performed the magic that the cafe was renowned for.

"So, Chili, what do you do for a living?" Cade sat closest to the bay window, pots of herbs intermingled with violets lined the windowsill. A basket filled with cascading geraniums hung from the ceiling, while a row of homemade jams and preserves adorned the counter. This was my go-to place whenever I wanted to meet someone for coffee. Or a snack.

I wasn't sure how to answer him; after all, it was he who organised for Sommer to be followed. My dad always said truth telling went hand-in-hand with truth living; words he'd gleaned from James E. Faust, an American clergyman.

"Actually, I'm a private investigator." Cade's eyes widened slightly as he took in my words.

"Really?" Sommer bounced in her seat. "That must be so exciting."

I moved my arm as Rosie placed drinks in front of us. Steam rose from my coffee to flavour the air with a touch of hazelnut. I shrugged, keeping my face bland and disinterested. "Not really. I work for a small business in town, so it's mainly missing pets or insurance work." I dipped my spoon into the foam on my coffee. "Pretty boring, really."

Cade's shoulders relaxed. The company he'd hired was a large firm, so he had no reason to think I was involved. "But it pays the bills and I'm lucky I have a great boss."

I turned the conversation away from myself. "So what have you guys been up to?"

Sommer grinned at me. "Remember how we met at the gym?" I nodded. "Well, I couldn't keep my dancing lessons a secret any longer, so I showed Cade what I can do." She nudged him with her shoulder. "He's joining me to brush up on some steps and then we're going to go ballroom dancing! Isn't that amazing?"

We toasted their love of dancing and each other. My heart swelled watching them. This is what I wanted, a love shared with a special person. Gideon's face flickered into my thoughts, and I smiled at the possibility.

Our share meals arrived, soft, pillowy baked gnocchi sprinkled with toasted almonds, rustic Tuscan pizza complete with charred edges and, my favourite, shrimp and lobster ravioli in a lobster bisque sauce. If I was lucky, there'd be leftovers to take home. Our plates filled with food and our tastebuds tantalised, we chatted.

Between finding out about where they worked—Cade in finance while Sommer was an artist—and the latest gossip, both celebrity and local—the time slipped away. The sky was awash with a symphony of colours and my thoughts centred on the peacefulness of when their conversation pulled me out of my reverie.

"... I don't know how they'll manage it, what with the price of diamonds dropping so dramatically," said Sommer.

"Do you think it will have that much of an effect on business?"

"Shannon says it's that bad that they might have to lay off staff."

I interrupted. "Sorry, what's happening to diamonds?"

Cade explained. "Diamond prices, well, most jewellery actually, peaked during COVID-19. Now the prices have plunged so investors lost a significant amount of money."

"Plus, many people are turning to lab-grown diamonds," added Sommer.

I was confused. "Why would anyone prefer a lab-grown diamond over a natural one?"

She shrugged. "They're indistinguishable from a mined one, which means you can get a larger diamond for a smaller price." She held up her right hand and waggled her fingers. The square cut solitaire sparkled against her pale skin. She continued, "and remember what they say, "Diamonds are a girl's best friend.""

I nodded, because regardless of whether it was mined or natural, it was still an impressive rock. "So how much have they dropped in price?"

"About 25%, but it's predicted the drop could go as low as 40%," said Cade. "There are also labour costs not only with the production but also in the making of the actual jewellery."

"And what if that happens?"

He smiled. "Good question. I guess a lot is going to have to change for confidence to return to the market. As long as there's an imbalance between supply and demand, things won't improve. Effectively, we're in a diamond industry recession."

He took a sip of his coffee. "The primary target market of fine jewellery and diamonds, in particular, are younger generations and they're demanding social responsibility from the industry. Especially with 'blood diamonds' and the fact that lab-grown diamonds are mass produced, and cheaper, doesn't help."

I'd never heard about lab-produced diamonds before and said so. "Most people haven't," he agreed. "And remember, diamonds aren't just for engagement rings, they have a lot of practical purposes." He ticked off his fingers. "Dentist drills, cancer treatments, bio-imaging, beauty treatments and there are even clinical trials in its effectiveness for orthopaedic medical devices because of its low friction and durability. Ultimately, diamonds will even replace silicon."

I wondered if William Van Horne used mined or manufactured diamonds in his work and made a mental note to jot this information down in my murder book.

We discussed the sanctions imposed on different countries, and companies, over dessert; lemon soufflé and crème anglaise. With full stomachs and promises to catch up, we said our goodbyes, picked up our doggie bags, thanked Rosie and her husband, and left.

Chapter 13

Frustration edged my thoughts as I drove home, my grip on the steering wheel a little tighter than usual. My memory, once razor-sharp and reliable, now seemed to have diminished in the attack's wake. Along with the sleeplessness and the constant dull headache, these symptoms served as unwelcome reminders of the violence that had shaken my life a few days ago.

Morgan had warned me I might have trouble, but I hadn't wanted to admit it. Strength was something I prided myself on. Anything less seemed like a failure on my part. I wasn't sure where that came from. It certainly hadn't come from my family, who were always supportive and loving. Perhaps it was just a societal issue where the perception was single women didn't need anyone to lean on and could do absolutely everything for themselves.

Society was wrong. We all needed someone.

Recording even the simplest of tasks on my phone had become a necessary routine. Things I could usually remember were slipping away like a mist. Gideon would say that was a good thing. The notes, not the memory lapse. Notes were reliable, but memories weren't. Perhaps that was a lesson I needed to learn.

I flicked the radio on and caught the beginning of the hourly news bulletin. I turned up the volume to listen as the commentator reported the discovery of a body downstream near Hadley's bend. The police were keeping other details under wraps for now. A sinking sensation filled my stomach. The only person I'd heard was missing was the girl Gideon and his team had been tirelessly searching for; Harper Foley. An ache grew inside as I thought of her family and friends and the burnishing hope that had now perished.

Pulling over to the side of the road, I retrieved my phone from the glove box and quickly typed out a text message to Gideon. He wouldn't answer until he'd finished work, but at least he would have a reminder that I cared.

The phone rang just as I was putting it back. I was surprised to see Gideon's name appear on the screen. With a mix of curiosity and concern, I answered the call, trying to keep my voice light despite the heaviness in my chest.

"Hey you," I said.

"Hi, Chili. Thanks for the message. It was sweet of you." Gideon's voice came through, carrying a subtle weariness that immediately tugged at my heart. I swallowed the lump that had formed in my throat before responding.

"Are you still at the scene?"

"Yeah, the guys are just doing their thing. We should be finished in a couple of hours." The thought of what he might deal with sent a shiver down my spine.

"Are you holding up alright?"

He hesitated for a moment before responding, his voice carrying a hint of exhaustion. "Yeah. It's just been a rough night."

"I'm sorry."

"Me, too."

We shared a brief silence, the weight of the situation hanging between us. Eventually, he asked about my evening, and I recounted the dinner I'd had with Cade and Sommer, even though he was only half-listening. His mind was likely preoccupied with trying to piece together the puzzle of what had happened to the missing girl. My voice was white noise to the reality of what was going on at the crime scene. I was just finishing when I heard animated voices in the background.

As Gideon's voice crackled through the phone, a mix of concern and urgency clear in his words, I couldn't help but hold my breath, waiting for him to continue.

"Look, something's come up and I have to go. I'll call you as soon as I can, okay?"

"I understand," I replied, my voice laced with concern. "Please be safe, Gideon. Call me when you can."

He hung up before I could say anything more. I hoped whatever happened was good news under the circumstances.

By the time I reached my driveway, the evening had grown darker. My heart raced as I noticed a car parked in front of my house. Fear tightened its grip around my chest, and I hesitated for a moment, unsure whether to proceed or retreat. After locking the car doors and staring at the parked vehicle in my rear-view mirror, my fingers resting on the keys in the ignition as sprinkles of fear trickled down my spine. The interior light flickered on, the faint amber glow revealing Morgan's familiar figure. Relief washed over me, and I released the breath I hadn't realised I was holding.

Perhaps dad was right, I should move closer to town, closer to safety, closer to friends and family. I was becoming fearful of every shadow and seeing death in every corner.

My legs had stopped wobbling like jelly as I climbed out of the truck and waited for Morgan. The shaking was just stopping when he stepped in front of me.

"Hi, Chilli," he said, a grin tilting the corner of his mouth up. "I realise it's late, but I really needed to see you."

His belief that he could just drop in whenever he wanted, combined with a rotten couple of days, fuelled a surge of irritation through me.

"Yeah, well, next time try calling before you just rock up out of nowhere," I retorted, my voiced edged with a mixture of annoyance and exhaustion." I pointed my finger at him. "We are no longer engaged and you don't have a right to just show up whenever you want."

My voice wavered as the weight of my recent experiences, combined with the sudden appearance of Morgan battered my resilience.

"You scared the daylights out of me, Morgan," I admitted, my voice breaking. "I thought you were here to finish me."

He took a step back as if I'd hit him, his face registering shock. "I am so sorry, Chili, I didn't think."

"That's obvious. Can't—whatever it is—wait till the morning?"

He side stepped a few paces toward his car. "Of course it can. I'll ... um ... I'll give you a ring tomorrow and see if you want to catch up." He threw the last couple of words over his shoulder as he hastened away.

A curtain twitched at Mr. Dorsey's house. It briefly comforted me, realising he was looking after me.

I exchanged a wave with Mr. Dorsey, his thumbs-up gesture reassuring me that someone was nearby, ready to lend a hand if needed.

Guilt for earlier behaviour edged its way into my thoughts. Perhaps I was being too harsh. Guys like Morgan failed to understand that the worst thing they could imagine happening to them while being alone somewhere at night was having their wallet stolen. That was the least of a woman's concerns.

I bit my lip and called out. "Morgan, wait." He turned and slowly came back, his shoulders hunched and hands deep in his pockets. "I'm sorry, I shouldn't have snapped at you." I gestured toward the house. "Why don't you come in and we can have coffee on the verandah?"

Wariness tinged his face. "Are you sure?"

"Positive."

He followed me in and helped me make coffee. Almond flicked her tail and turned her back on him. I smiled. She had never really warmed to Morgan in the way she had with Gideon. I heated the leftovers from Rosie's, grabbed a fork and plate each, and we headed out the back. This was one of my favourite spots and one I rarely shared with others; however, I wasn't comfortable chatting with Morgan in the intimacy of my home.

Trust, once broken, is hard to restore.

The Jarrah verandah where we sat was spacious and purpose-built to the owner's specifications. The soft glow of evening light filtered through the leaves. I'd placed comfortable lounge chairs, partially hidden by ferns, in quiet areas to sit and watch the birds while a long rattan table and chairs took up centre stage, for those rare times I entertained. A hammock swung, at the other end, from hooks, for when I wanted to read in the warmth or take a nap. Plants, rugs, and an assortment of ceramic figurines completed the tableau. It was where I greeted the day when I couldn't sleep, or when I had a rare lazy morning to myself.

We sat at the table across from each other. A comfortable silence lingered between us for a moment, the unspoken understanding that we both carried our own burdens and uncertainties.

I studied him over the rim of my coffee cup. He was still the same Morgan I'd fallen in love with a lifetime ago. He'd cut his hair differently and a faint scar rested above his left eyebrow, but essentially nothing else had changed.

"It's been a strange couple of days, hasn't it?" I said.

"Yeah, it has. I never meant to add to your worries by showing up unannounced."

"I appreciate that, Morgan. But sometimes even well-intentioned actions can have unintended consequences."

He nodded in understanding, and a moment of shared vulnerability passed between us. Despite our differences and the history that had led us to this point, there was a connection that hadn't completely faded.

As we sipped our coffee and shared a meal, the rhythmic creaking of the hammock and the gentle swaying of the ferns seemed to mirror the ebb and flow of our conversation.

"What was it like, over in Africa?"

He sat back. "Hard. There are so many people in need of help. It was tough in ways I hadn't expected."

I listened as he spoke about the death and destruction he'd witnessed.

"Most people imagine Africa as this exotic paradise," he continued, "but there's a harsh reality that goes unnoticed. I stayed in an area where blood diamonds were a rampant issue. The stories I heard, the lives affected—was heartbreaking."

His words hung between us. "It must have been incredibly difficult."

"It was," he admitted. Morgan's voice carried a mixture of hesitation and longing as he finally broached the subject which brought him to my door.

"Chili," he began, his words carefully chosen, "I've had a lot of time to think while away. And I realised how stupid I was to let you go."

I met his gaze, my heart softening at his vulnerability. Morgan had always been a good man, and I couldn't brush aside our shared history, however my feelings for Gideon had developed in ways that I hadn't anticipated.

A quiet sigh escaped me. "Morgan, you've always been an important part of my life, but eighteen months is a long time and things have changed...for both of us."

He nodded, understanding in his eyes. "I know I messed up, Chili, especially with everything that's happened. I got caught up in my world and didn't pay attention to you."

"It's not just about that," I continued gently. "We've grown in different directions." I waved my hand toward the expanse of the sky. "You ventured out into the world to be a doctor. I stayed here."

"Do you think there's a chance for us to try again, to rebuild what we had?"

I took a deep breath; the words forming in my mind as I tried to convey my feelings without causing unnecessary pain. "No, there isn't. We both need to move on. What about that new nurse at the hospital?"

"You mean, Jessica?"

I held back a snort as I thought how apt my nickname for her had been. "Yes, Jessica. She seems like a nice person and she's certainly interested in you."

"Do you think so?"

I reached out and placed my hand on his, a gesture of comfort and understanding. "Morgan, we can't force feelings that aren't there. I'd love for us to remain friends, to continue being a part of each other's lives."

He nodded, his fingers intertwining with mine. "I want that too, Chili. I value our friendship more than anything."

A sense of relief washed over me. I had never been good at holding grudges.

As we fell into a comfortable silence, my mind raced. There was something I had forgotten to ask him, something important about his return that I needed to know. But the conversation had taken its own course, and I had missed the opportunity.

After a moment, Morgan stood up, his eyes meeting mine. "I should go, Chili. It's been good catching up."

A pang of regret hit me, and I forced a smile. "Yeah, it was nice seeing you again, too." He hesitated, his gaze lingering on me. "Take care of yourself, Chili."

"You too, Morgan."

With that, he turned and walked away, disappearing into the night. I watched him go, the weight of my forgotten question heavy on my mind. In the verandahs stillness, I leaned back in my chair and closed my eyes, trying to remember what I had meant to ask him, and hoping that maybe, just maybe, our paths would cross again soon.

Chapter 14

My dad was coming home.

Excitement had my knee bobbing in time to the radio with a joy I couldn't contain. We had always been a close family and mum's death had brought us even closer. The thought of losing him as well as her was more than I could endure. I pulled into the hospital car park, locked the pickup, and hurried through the main entrance and into the foyer. The message I had this morning was that he would meet me down here.

People like me filled chairs, either waiting to pick someone up or having a rest from the ward. Some were reading - others playing on their phones - while one little boy had two long strands of mucus hanging out both nostrils, reminding me of the sage green tapered-candles I'd received for Christmas the year before. His mother seemed oblivious to the fact her child needed a handkerchief, or three. She was more occupied with flicking through a dog show magazine than monitoring her progeny.

A noticeboard full of articles caught my eye. Next to it, nestled between a large ficus and a square metal rubbish bin, stood a vending machine.

I walked over and placed the correct coinage in the machine. My finger hovered over the buttons and I was torn between two choices; a chocolate and cherry bar, or pistachio nougat covered in gooey caramel. From out of the corner of my eye, I watched as a little pink tongue darted out from the boy's mouth and swiped at the mucus. No longer torn, I pressed the button and retrieved my pistachio-less bar.

Different coloured flyers filled the noticeboard, ranging from water births to progressive belly dancing. I was just pondering what I would look like in harem pants and a veil when a voice sounded behind me.

Dad was sitting in a wheelchair, his bag on his lap, a grin on his face. I reached down and hugged him hard, tears escaping their confines. I stood and grabbed his bag. A nurse smiled as she asked if we were ready to go. I followed as she waved away my query about taking over and wheeled him through the foyer "Tis me job to make sure your pa gets into the car safely, mind," she said. "Once that 'appens he's all yours."

As they left, I discarded a tissue packet on the chair next to the boy. He looked up and grinned at me, eyes the same colour as the mucus he was sniffing. He was such a cute kid. I could never look at a pistachio ever again.

The nurse wheeled dad to the pickup and I opened the door and helped him into the cab, stashing his bag on the floor at his feet.

"Ye right now, love?" the nurse asked.

"I am now, Mary," he responded. "Thank you for all your help. I appreciate you looking after me the way you did."

She patted his arm. "My pleasure. Now ye got everything?"

He nodded.

"Righto then, take care. Give my love to Bonnie when you see her." Closing the door, she waved and started heading back inside. My instructions were to drive dad straight to Bonnie's and not dawdle, so I'd already picked up some things from his house. It would only be a week and he'd be fine to go home as soon as his doctor said he could look after himself.

We drove down the main street and pulled up at a set of lights. I glanced over at him and a shock ran through me. His dark ginger hair and freckles, so much like mine, stood out against his pale skin. The sunlight caught the deep purplish bags sat under his eyes and he had a look of fragility which wasn't there before. I reached over and squeezed his hand. He smiled. "Thanks for picking me up, love."

A car next to us revved and took off as the lights changed. "Well, I couldn't have you walking the streets in that getup."

He looked down at his tie-dyed t-shirt, brown leather vest and matching jeans. "Nothing wrong with this 'getup', love. If it was good enough for John Sebastian ..." I chimed in, "... it's good enough for me." We both laughed. My dad had been at conceived at Woodstock while the founder of 'The Lovin' Spoonful' had been rocking it, acoustic style, on stage. Nanna and Pop were both diehard hippies and they'd passed that love of everything psychedelic on to my dad. He'd even learned to play an autoharp just like his hero.

"Have you heard from Coco?" he said, breaking into my thoughts.

"Not since I saw her yesterday." I shifted gears and flicked on the right-hand indicator. "My guess is that as soon as the lab reports come back, they'll release her."

He sighed. "Surely even Barrett knows she's innocent. He's known our family for years."

"Yeah, well, I don't want you getting yourself worked up again, dad. The doctor said you're not supposed to have any more stress."

"Can't be helped, love. Neither of my girls would hurt a fly and Barrett's a moron."

"Now that is something we can agree on." I reached over and squeezed his hand. "As long as Coco is safe, that's all that matters. And while jail isn't much fun, at the moment everyone's working on getting her out sooner rather than later."

He waited a few minutes, and then cleared his throat. "It's none of my business, but have you heard from Morgan?"

I glanced over at him. "He came by last night."

"Really? What did he want?"

"To see if we'd get back together."

Shock registered in his voice. "You don't say. What did you tell him?"

"That there's no chance of that happening." I shrugged. "I was nice about it, even suggested he ask the nurse at the hospital on a date."

"How'd he take it?"

"Okay, I guess. I think a part of him expected it."

We drove on and enjoyed each other's company. We were a few minutes away from Bonnie's when I broached the subject of their romance. "I forgot to mention there's a present in the glove box for you."

He opened the compartment and took out a bag of lollies. "Licorice allsorts. My favourite." He opened the bag and passed me one with black strips blanketed between pink fondant. "I haven't had these in ages."

I peeled the top layer off the sweet and sucked on it. "They're not from me. They're from your Bonnie."

He pretended indignation. "What do you mean 'My Bonnie'?"

I grinned. "No need to play coy. I had morning tea with her yesterday. Why didn't you tell me you two had a thing going?"

"A, we don't have a 'thing' going and B, it's none of your business."

"It's okay, dad. Coco and I are fine with it," I whispered. "You're both terrific people."

He chewed for a few seconds. "I guess I was just worried you'd both be upset because of your mum."

"Neither of us is upset. We miss her too, but you both deserve some happiness." I exited the main road and turned up Bonnie's street. "We're glad you found it with each other. Besides, she's a terrific cook."

"You know what they say, love. The easiest way to a man's heart is..."

"Through his stomach?"

He chuckled. "Nope. Through his chest."

I groaned. "Your jokes are getting worse, dad."

"Yeah, but they still make you laugh."

We pulled up outside the house and grabbed his things. The front door flew open and Bonnie, together with Billy and Susie, Coco's kids, came running out. I watched as they surrounded dad. The twins gave him a rundown on their latest escapades while Bonnie hugged him. It was a beautiful sight. The only thing missing was Coco.

I followed them up the stairs, my steps as slow as my thoughts. I sat on the top step, leaned against the rail and closed my eyes - the sunlight infusing my body with warmth. Near my shoulder, bees droned in the subtle fragrance of the hydrangeas. Behind me, laughter echoed through the house. While the world continued to turn around me, I was cocooned in my own precious moment. I took a deep breath and pushed myself up from the step and dusted the back of my jeans. As I stood, the distant thrum of a perfectly tuned V-8 caught my attention. My heart sped up, and a smile curved my lips.

I'd recognise the rumbling sound of Gideon's restored XY Falcon, anywhere.

As the big orange beast came to a halt, the doors swung open, revealing two people. A sudden shock gripped me, and I moved down the path toward them, the world seeming to slow around me.

As the bees continued their dance and laughter echoed in the air, Coco and I embraced.

My sister was home.

Chapter 15

The din inside the house was incredible. We were all laughing and talking over each other in our delight that Coco was home. Moving toward the table with Billy and Susie wrapped around her legs, Coco smiled. Some of the earlier strain from yesterday had disappeared from her face. She sat down with a child on either side, leaned back and sighed. "You have no idea how good it is to be home."

"I can't imagine what you've been through," Bonnie replied. "Fancy anyone thinking you could do something ... " she glanced at the twins and tailed off, " ... like that."

"Where did you go, Mummy?" asked Susie. "We missed you."

She kissed the child's head and pulled her close. "Just on a little holiday, honey. Mummy's home now and that's all that matters."

A pang of guilt flitted through me. I kept wondering if I'd done enough to help. *If* I was doing enough to help.

"How did you know to pick her up?" Dad asked Gideon.

"I was doing some paperwork when Coco walked out, so I thought the least I could do was give her a lift."

Billy pinched his nose with two fingers. "Mummy, you don't smell so good."

Coco laughed, raised her arm and took a whiff. "Well, I guess I better go take a shower then, hadn't I?" She nudged Billy. "Good idea?"

He nodded emphatically. "Def'nitly."

While she and the children were gone, Gideon made coffee and Bonnie prepared brunch. I removed the vase of roselillies from the table and placed them on the sideboard. Their understated elegance drew me and I rubbed a velvety red petal between my fingers, the slight coolness a contrast in the warm house. The subtle fragrance reminded me a little of vanilla, together with a spicy undertone. Little wonder perfumers sought after it.

Dad started setting the table with cutlery. "Are you okay, love?"

I sighed. "Honestly? I'm so happy Coco's home, but I keep thinking that I'm letting everyone down. I'm not sure why."

"You've always been like that, even when you were little, always needed to be the one to fix everything." He placed a knife on top of a napkin. "A lot like Nanna Mae. Never happy unless everyone around her was too."

He straightened and looked at me. "The thing is; it's impossible. There's both good and evil in the world and it touches everyone. As long as we do our best and don't go out of our way to hurt anyone, well, that's all the Good Lord asks of us."

"But is it enough?"

"Is what enough?" Gideon asked, pushing open the kitchen's swinging door. The smell of bacon frying followed him. He placed a stack of assorted dishes on the table, as well as a set of serving spoons.

Dad nodded his head toward me. "Chili thinks she's responsible for everything that's happened, that somehow she could prevent anyone from ever getting hurt. I've told her she can't fix everything. "

He chuckled. "Listen to your dad, Chili. He knows what he's talking about."

The way Gideon brushed off my concerns nettled me. "I know, I know. I just want to do more. Like this whole thing is a jigsaw puzzle and if I only had the right piece, I could solve it."

Gideon raised an eyebrow. "I seem to remember a conversation where you agreed to leave it to the authorities, remember?"

Heat suffused my face. "Perhaps."

He gazed at me for a few seconds, and then held out his hand. "Come on, let's go take a walk."

We left and crossed the road to the park, at the edge of the estuary. A children's play area was in one corner, complete with a wooden castle and swings. I sat on one and twirled from side to side while Gideon sat on the other—his large frame looking comical on the small seat.

"So, what's really going on?"

I drew a swirl in the sand with the toe of my shoe. "Honestly? Here I am, a licensed private investigator, and I can't figure out who'd want to frame Coco."

"Why do you think she was framed?"

I tsked. "Because she was arrested!"

"She was arrested on suspicion of murder, not murder itself. And she was released, so what does that tell you?"

"That she's innocent?"

"That they believe she's innocent," he stated. "If forensics had come up with anything to link her to the murder, she'd be facing an arraignment, not getting ready to have a meal with her family."

He was right, but I still couldn't let it go.

"So why was she arrested in the first place?"

"You mean why did I arrest her?"

I nodded.

Gideon's jaw tightened, the scar on his lip becoming more pronounced. "I can't discuss an ongoing investigation, Chili."

I snorted. "Oh, please, since when have rules ever stopped us? Remember the Great Cafeteria Caper of '05?"

A ghost of a smile flicked across his face before disappearing. "This isn't high school anymore, nor is it another one of your wild schemes. This is serious."

He sighed and brushed sand off his leg. For a moment, I glimpsed the boy from school, hidden beneath the hardened detective exterior.

"Coco was the last person to see him alive. And witnesses informed us they'd seen both of them arguing just before she drove off. The altercation was pretty nasty." He paused. "Coco hit him."

I shook my head. My sister hadn't hit anyone in her life. She was kind and considerate and pretty much perfect. I said as much.

"We have the entire incident on security footage and she admitted it."

I couldn't contain my shock. "Why?" I glanced at him. "Why would she hit him?"

"You'll have to ask her that yourself."

My spirits sank. Not only had I not saved Coco, but she'd actually hit another person. It's possible she wasn't the person I thought she was. If Coco had concealed that from me, her sister, I wondered what else she was hiding.

The aroma of hot chips floated on the breeze and I watched a family fend off a flock of seagulls. One cheeky sod stole a chip out of a child's hand and hopped away with his prize.

I was still eager to learn about the cause of Van Horne's death and the identity of the person who hit me. Gideon seemed to read my thoughts.

"You need to leave this alone, Chili. Next time you might not be so lucky."

"I just keep thinking I could have done more."

He took my hand in his. "Chili, I say this with all love and kindness. Not everything is about you. "

Startled, I stared at him. His thumb rubbed over the palm of my hand with soothing strokes, even as his words stung. "Did you listen to me, a friend and a detective, when I advised you to keep out of everything? Did you try to ease Bonnie's burden with the twins and your dad?" He sighed. "You're not a cop, Chili; you're a private detective and a great one at that. You're dedicated to your job, but it can make you selfish and one-eyed."

I snatched my hand away and got to my feet, taking a few steps. I turned, the rising wind whipping my hair across my face.

"Selfish? One-eyed? That's rich coming from you, Mr. I-Work-Alone-Because-No-One-Understands-Me."

Gideon's eyes flashed. "That's not fair, Chili."

"Neither is calling me selfish when I'm just trying to help my sister!" I snapped, my voice rising. "You don't understand what it's like, Gideon. You don't have family left to worry about."

The moment the words left my mouth, I regretted them. Gideon's face slackened, that old pain flickering in his eyes.

"Gideon, I'm sorry, I didn't mean—"

He held up a hand, cutting me off. "And that is where the problem lies. You only think about how things affect you, what you can say to others." He spread his arms wide. "Take a good look around you, Chili. We've all got things going on; life doesn't just revolve around you."

My face flushed with shame and anger. Part of me wanted to lash out again, to defend myself, but a small voice in the back of my mind whispered that perhaps Gideon had a point.

"Fine," I said, crossing my arms. "Enlighten me, Detective. What am I missing?"

Gideon leaned forward, his eyes softening. "Your sister's scared, Chili. She's not just worried about herself, but about how this will affect your father, the twins. And Bonnie? She's been running herself ragged trying to keep everything together while you've been chasing leads. On a case you're not supposed to be working on."

I opened my mouth to protest, but he continued, "And me? I'm trying to do my job, to find the truth, while also keeping you from compromising the investigation. Do you think I enjoy this? You at arm's length when all I want to do is ..." He trailed off, running a hand through his hair.

My breath caught in my throat. "When all you want to do is what, Gideon?"

His eyes met mine, and for a moment, I was vulnerable, uncertain. "When all I want to do is protect you," he mumbled. "To keep you safe from all of this."

The air between us crackled with tension. I wanted to reach out, to bridge the gap that had grown between us, but I held back.

"It's not protection I need," I said, my voice low. "It's the truth that's important. About Coco, about the Van Horne's, about all of it."

"The truth isn't always simple, Chili. You, of all people, should understand that."

A small ember of irritation caught on the edges of my skin, red-hot and prickling with annoyance. "What's that supposed to mean?"

Gideon sighed, his frustration only just contained. "It means you're too close to this, Chili. Your emotions are clouding your judgment. You're trying to force pieces together that don't fit, and it's going to get someone hurt."

My chest grew hot, my pulse quickening. "So what, you think I'm just a liability now?"

"No," Gideon said, his voice softer but no less firm. "I think you're too involved. You can't see clearly."

"Too involved?" I repeated, the words tasting bitter on my tongue. "Because I got hurt? Because Coco is my sister? Because the Van Hornes are—what? Connected to something I am unaware of?"

He shook his head, exasperated. "It's more than that. You've always been reckless with people you care about. It's dangerous."

I froze, unable to believe what he had just said. I attempted to speak up, but he interrupted me and kept talking. "And as for me? I'm trying to do my job, appease Barrett's demands, and prevent you from interfering with the investigation."

He sighed. "Look, I should have chosen my words more carefully; you're always hell bent on trying to fix the world's problems regardless of how it affects those around you. The past is the past, Chili. Sometimes we just have to deal with it and move on." He shrugged, hands parted in a plea for understanding. "Or at least that's how I see it."

"I don't have to 'fix the world's problems,' as you put it." Even as the words left my mouth, I felt their emptiness, the lie barely veiled. "I can't believe I'm hearing this. Especially from you."

His expression hardened, a shutter falling over his face like a barrier between us. His lips pressed into a firm line, his arms crossed over his chest. "And what exactly is that supposed to mean—'especially from me'?"

I held his gaze. "It means you've always had this need to protect everyone. It's who you are. But sometimes, that need to shield people from everything becomes too much. It smothers. You hold on so tightly, Gideon, you can't let go."

His jaw tightened, the flicker of something—anger, guilt, maybe both—crossing his eyes before he spoke. "You think I don't know that?"

"I think you do," I said. "But knowing it doesn't mean you've dealt with it. You carry the weight of the world because of what happened to Sarah, always trying to fix things for everyone, but you can't protect people from everything. Sometimes, you have to let them muddle through life even if it's hard, even if they muck up."

"I'm sorry I'm such a disappointment," he said, his voice laced with bitterness, each word cutting through the air like a blade. The bitterness wasn't just in his voice—it was in the way his shoulders sagged, the way his hands clenched into fists at his sides, trembling slightly. It was a bitterness born from hurt, frustration, and something deeper, something raw that I couldn't reach no matter how hard I tried.

"I never meant to smother anyone," he added after a beat, the anger fading to something quieter, more vulnerable. His jaw tightened as if he were trying to choke back the emotions threatening to spill out. "I tried ... I really tried."

I opened my mouth to speak, to tell him he wasn't a disappointment—that he mattered, but the words wouldn't come. The silence between us grew thick, filled with everything I wanted to say and everything I couldn't. Without waiting for a response, he turned and walked away, his shoulders tense as followed the winding path back to the road.

I stood frozen, wishing I could pluck the words from the air, erase them before they landed. But it was too late. He reached his car, the slam of the door cutting through the stillness like a finality I couldn't undo.

The engine roared to life, the distinctive rumbles of the motor echoing down the empty beach as he drove away. I watched until the tail lights disappeared into the distance as a fractured ache supplanted my earlier anger.

My words had been a cheap shot aimed at a man I was falling in love with. A man who had lost his wife and unborn child and, rather than let it define him, faced each day with a strength I couldn't comprehend.

The wind continued to lash sand against my legs as I trudged toward the house—the gnawing ache in my chest deepening with each step. I pulled the collar of my coat up and thrust my hands deep into my pockets. Gideon was right; my actions had been driven by my own insecurities and fears. Instead of facing that, I'd chosen to be cruel to a man who was trying to protect me.

I couldn't face anyone after the chaos I had caused, so I did the only thing I could—I got in my car and drove away, just like Gideon had.

Chapter 16

The interior of the car had warmed by the time I got to the main road. Outside, the wind had died down, leaving small branches strewn across the road. I turned left, heading for Caulfield Springs, thirty minutes away. From the glove box emerged the unmistakable opening riff of 'Summer in the City'. I ignored my dad's ringtone. The last thing I wanted to do was open up about my argument with Gideon and why I'd left. Coco's reason for being arrested only added another complexity to the drama. It was as if the universe had conspired to heap chaos in my life. For the time being, I needed distance, both physical and emotional, from the storm brewing around me at home.

It didn't help that I was responsible for some of it; maybe all of it. I turned up the radio and found solace in the rhythmic beat of the music and the open road stretching out before me. Row upon row of pasture was being replaced by cookie-cutter families in their cookie-cutter homes.

The sun had mellowed its intensity, casting a warm golden glow as I pulled into the Exhibition grounds. Parking in the designated area, I took a moment to collect myself. My goal was to connect with the woman who had clashed with Mr. Van Horne and find out what had happened.

Stepping out of the car, I rolled my shoulders and walked through the entrance, trying to shake off the lingering tension from this morning's argument. The ticket vendor, a friendly-looking woman seated behind a counter, was talking with a couple who appeared perplexed their dog hadn't placed in its class. Nearby, an official hovered, ready to step in if needed. I realised the world of dog shows could be just as intense and charged as the turmoil I had left behind at home.

Conversation over, the woman smiled and asked if I was an exhibitor or spectator. When I replied to the latter, she gave me a pamphlet which outlined dog breeds and their respective showing times. I headed toward the spectators stand and took a deep breath. This was my chance to make a connection, and inch closer to uncovering the truth about Mr. Van Horne's death.

The shaded stands filled with various people. Dog owners buzzed with excitement. I sat down near the end of one row, next to a woman who reminded me of a TV show personality. Her blue-rinsed hair, styled in a shoulder-length bob, provided a striking contrast against the backdrop of her mauve pantsuit. On someone else, the combination may have appeared gaudy. On her it was chic.

"Are you showing, dear?" she asked.

"Pardon?" I replied, momentarily lost.

She inclined her head toward the bustling arena. "Dogs, dear. Are you showing today?"

"No. I'm just here to watch."

"If you need anything, just ask." She leaned forward, her voice carrying a conspiratorial tone. "I'm an official." As she drew closer, a subtle, exotic aroma enveloped the space between us. She reached across and shook my hand. "Isabella Fairhaven."

The name rang a bell, sparking a memory from just days before. I had read an interview with her in a woman's magazine while waiting at the doctor's office last week. The interview had painted a vivid picture of her life and achievements both in and out of the dog ring. Her commitment to the welfare of animals had left a lasting impression on me.

I took a chance to confide in her. If anyone was privy to the secrets of the canine show world, it would be her. "Can I let you in on a little secret?"

Her eyes twinkled. "Of course."

"I'm here researching an incident which occurred a few weeks ago."

"An incident?" A slight line appeared between her brows. "Are you a journalist?"

"Let's just say I'm trying to get to the truth." I leaned toward her, allowing a shadow of concern to cross my features. "We don't want the club tarnished by a silly misunderstanding."

An unspoken agreement passed between us. She tapped the side of her nose. "I understand," she assured me, cementing our newfound alliance. "Now, which incident are we talking about; the one where Mrs Horowitz used eyeliner on her Shetland sheepdog or someone slipping a sleeping tablet to Mrs Cairns' poodle?"

My mouth gaped. I hadn't realised so many secrets and intrigues hid beneath the gloss surface of the canine realm. It had always seemed, on TV at least, to be a serene and idyllic world where well-groomed canines, and their owners, paraded before judges in pursuit of trophies and titles.

Isabella noticed my astonishment and offered a knowing smile. "You see, dear, the dog show world is like any competitive arena. Behind the scenes, passions run high and not everyone plays by the rules."

"I see. The incident I was referring to was about Mr Van Horne."

"Ah, yes. That was a very sad affair indeed."

I wasn't sure if she was talking about the incident here or his untimely death. "How so?"

"Most of the rumours surrounding dog shows are just that, rumours," she remarked. She leaned back in her chair, the ambient sounds of the current event echoing around us. "With William, however, that wasn't the case. Humphrey had indeed had his coat clipped."

"Humphrey?"

"Yes, William's pride and joy. Humphrey Bogarter, his Pomeranian."

I couldn't suppress a snort of amusement. "Humphrey Bogarter?" I repeated. An image of a Pomeranian donning a bow tie and asking Sam to 'play it again' sprang to mind.

She continued, ignoring my outburst. "William was quite the character in the dog show world. "It was almost impossible to find anyone who didn't adore him," she said.

"Not everyone." I pointed out. His dog had been shorn, and he murdered.

"It was such a shock to everyone here," she confided. "There have been earnest calls to rename the grounds in his honour."

"He was that well-liked?"

She nodded. "He was."

I sat back and joined the spectators watching the dog arena. Soft mown grass cushioned the paws of canine contenders as they paraded with their handlers. Excitement rippled through the stand as one woman in a crisp, flowing dress stood out. She was running alongside her Afghan hound, moving in perfect harmony with her four-legged partner.

The judge held a clipboard in one hand and a pen in the other, jotting down notes. The judge carefully scrutinised and recorded each detail, from the dog's gait to its posture.

I nodded toward the woman. "Do you think she'll win?"

"I hope so." Isabelle smiled. "That's my daughter." The warmth in her voice spoke volumes; she was a very proud mother. As we continued to observe the proceedings, I ventured further into my chosen subject.

"Is cutting a dog's hair that serious an offence?"

Isabelle shook her head, her expression shifting to one of mild amusement. "Yes, of course. Someone took to his coat with a pair of scissors and gave him a trim." She glanced at my head. "Imagine if someone had done that to your hair."

The thought of a well-coifed Pomeranian undergoing an unsolicited haircut was enough to elicit a wry smile from both of us.

"And that destroyed his chances of winning a trophy?"

"Indeed," she explained. "Every detail is under scrutiny in all competitive sports," she explained, "and even the smallest change to a dog's appearance can affect the judge's perception. Unfortunately, it wasn't a minor change; some had shorn his hair completely off. By the time they'd finished, he looked more like a disgruntled miniature lion who lost a wager with a lawnmower."

I laughed at the picture her words painted. "Oh, that's terrible," I said between chuckles. "Wouldn't someone have seen who did it?"

"You would think so," she said. "But if anyone saw who it was, no one admitted it." She leaned toward me, casting a glance over her shoulder. Her eyes sparkled with a hint of conspiracy. "It was as if a secret society of rogue groomers conspired to turn poor Humphrey into a walking punch line."

As I wiped away the tears of laughter streaming down my face, I imagined a covert team of doggy hairdressers, clad in black and armed with clippers, carrying out their clandestine mission under the cover of the night. I wondered if the leader was called the 'Clipper Commander.'

I nudged her arm. "So, who do you think was responsible?"

She pursed her lips. "I think it was an accident."

"Really?" I responded, taken aback by her unexpected perspective. After her earlier hints at the darker underbelly of the dog show community, this surprised me.

"Yes, really." She tilted her head. "At least, I don't believe someone who intended harm did it."

People around us broke into applause as the judge awarded Isabelle's daughter with a trophy, stopping me from asking any more questions. It appeared she was following in her mother's footsteps as someone to be reckoned with in the dog world.

A movement at the doorway I'd come through caught my attention. A woman entered with a small boy in tow. I recognised them from this morning at the hospital. I hoped the little candle-boy's nose had cleared up; I didn't want to catch anything.

Isabelle nudged my arm and nodded toward the pair. "In my belief," she murmured, "there's your culprit."

"The woman just entering?" I clarified.

Isabelle shook her head. "No," she said. "The boy."

The disclosure sent a chill racing down my spine. The ordinary mother and child became pivotal figures in the unfolding drama of the clipped Pomeranian. It was a twist I hadn't seen coming, and I wondered what secrets lay hidden behind the innocent façade of the young boy and his mother.

Chapter 17

They moved through the stands at a sedate pace; the woman clutching the boy's hand while he clutched the paw of a rather thread-bear teddy. They stopped three rows below us. Unhurried, the mother placed her bad gown on one side, her son on the other, and balancing a coffee cup in one hand, took notes on the events in the ring. Long chocolate hair shimmered in the sunlight, reminding me of a model from a shampoo commercial. I wondered if the colour came from a bottle and was a little envious that her hair was elegant where mine corkscrewed like a Botticelli painting gone wrong.

I leaned closer to Isabella. "What makes you think the little boy shaved Humphrey?"

"Helene, my daughter, interrupted him in his attempt to trim her dog, Farrah's, hair. When she asked him why he did that, he replied, 'to make her look pretty.'"

That didn't sound a motive for murder to me, at least not the way it stood. I couldn't see a mother murdering a jeweller over a haircut, unless he threatened harm on the little boy.

"What did Helene do?"

My phone chirped, and I glanced down at the message. It was Coco asking if I was going to be back in time for dinner. I decided not to respond. I needed space to process what Gideon had said.

"He is truly gifted."

"Who?"

She nodded toward the boy. "Alexander. He's quite the pianist. Have you ever watched the movie Rain Man?"

I shook my head.

"Alexander is also an autistic-savant, except his gift lies with music, not numbers."

"Really?" I knew nothing about autism and whether his piano playing was unusual.

"Yes. His mother, Marjorie, works long hours to in order to support them. She's hoping he will win a scholarship to Julliard."

I looked at the woman sitting next to him. "She sounds like a very dedicated mother," I said. "Is she also into showing dogs?"

Isabella scoffed. "That's not her mother. That, my dear, is the nanny. One Patrice Harris. She's supposed to watch him while Marjorie is at work." She leaned toward me. "The unfortunate incident happened under her watch. Let s just say she's not very good at her job and leave it at that."

I sat there and watched the rest of the dog show competitors and let the noise drift over me. The crowd clapped when Helene and her dog walked to the centre of the ring for awards. Alexander's nanny joined in while the boy sat listened to music, presumably, through headphones.

The more I heard, the more it appeared that the murder had nothing to do with this area of William Van Horne's life. I exchanged contact info with Isabella, thanked her for her time, and left.

Chapter 18

I updated my murder book, fleshing out my thoughts and ideas. I lived by the mantra that feelings weren't facts but also that women had an innate hinky-meter for things that weren't right. Mine was working over-drive.

My phone chimed again, and this time I checked the messages. Coco said we needed to catch up that night, grab a bite to eat, and talk. Our standing reservation was at a club near to home, one we'd both frequented. The food was great, and the drinks were cold. The other was from dad asking me if I was okay. I quelled the impulse to call and apologise. I refused to feel guilty about my behaviour. After all, I wasn't the one who kept lying and hiding secrets.

If I was going to meet Coco, I needed to change. I typed a quick message to both of them, selected an audio file on my phone, and headed home. Soon I was following along with Welsh language lessons. I'd become intrigued with everything the country offered after doing a DNA test and learning I had ancestors from there. One day I'd head over on a holiday. Until then, I had work to do.

Thirty minutes later, I was home.

It was country and western night at the hotel and my favourite local band was playing. My spirits rose at the thought of a night out. I fed Almond, checked my messages, and showered. I pulled on jeans, boots and shirt and spritzed myself with my favourite perfume. I was on top of the world.

I had plenty of time before my catch-up with Coco, so I thought it was time to visit the widow-Mrs Van Horne. Her hotel was a few blocks away from the club in the swankier part of town. I rang ahead to advise her I was coming, and she agreed to meet me in the lobby. I gave Almond a kiss and headed out.

Traffic was light, and it took me no time to get there. I parked and checked my watch. Mickey's gloved hands said I had about ninety minutes before catching up with Coco. It was more than enough time.

I walked into the lobby and informed the concierge of my arrival. A leather chair in the corner beckoned me. It afforded me a view of the entire area and entrance. From my seat, I had a view of the person who entered a few minutes later. The woman was tall with coiffed hair and clothing, which wasn't bought from an online catalogue or the sale rack at K-mart. I hazarded a guess I was looking at the widowed Delia Van Horne; wife of the dead jeweller.

I got up and walked toward her. Up close, the woman was stunning. She had pulled her honey blonde hair back into a chignon with one long tendril resting against the side of her face. On some women, it would have looked coy, but it added to a presence only money could buy. I introduced myself, and she nodded.

"I'm pleased to meet you," she said and introduced herself. "Bonnie explained it was you who found my husband."

It was my turn to nod. "Yes, it was. I'm sorry for your loss." I gestured toward the hotel bar. "Why don't we go through so we can talk somewhere a bit more private?"

I followed and motioned for her to take a seat. She took the sofa while I sat in one of the comfortable-looking chairs facing her. Crossing her legs at the ankle, Delia sat side on. They may have been nouveau rich but her deportment shouted finishing school. Her gaze travelled around the room, taking in the soft furnishings and neutral palette designed to make guests, of any gender, comfortable.

I waited for the woman opposite to finish her perusal.

"I'm hoping you can help me, Mrs Van Horne."

"Delia, please." She smoothed her skirt over her knees. "To be honest, I'm not sure why I'm here. It's just … I guess I wanted to meet the person who found my husband. That probably makes little sense …"

To me it made perfect sense. She was looking for that last connection to her husband before his death. I wasn't it.

"Have the police spoken to you at all?" I asked.

"Yes, however, they had little information, other than he died of anaphylaxis and the case is ongoing." She looked at me. "Bonnie mentioned you were looking into his death and that your sister had been arrested. Is that true?"

A dark hole opened in my chest. I hadn't officially received an invitation to investigate anything, and until then, I couldn't do much. The police turned away private investigators and didn't want them investigating where they weren't welcome. I counted to five before I answered. "Yes, she has. But you have to believe me; my sister would never hurt a fly, let alone kill someone."

"Bonnie said the same."

She took a slimline gold cigarette case out of her bag, clicked it open and offered me one. "Do you mind?" I didn't, but my craving was getting out of hand. Soon I'd be sniffing complete strangers for a hit.

I told her as much.

She smiled and put the case back in her bag. I wasn't sure why, but it was like I'd just passed some sort of test.

"I met her once. Your sister, that is."

"I didn't realise." It wasn't true. If Coco used her husband to buy expensive gifts for clientele, they were bound to meet up at some stage.

She told me they'd met at a garden soiree and discovered a mutual love of vintage furniture combined with soft, romantic furnishings. Later, when Delia discovered Coco was an interior designer, she commissioned her to redesign their penthouse apartment. It was all done via email, as Delia was overseas with her husband.

I wasn't sure where this conversation was going, but I enjoyed listening to her espousing my sister's ability to turn an ordinary house into a cherished home.

When she'd finished, she cleared her throat. Not in a five-pack-a-day way like most of my clients, but more of a delicate 'ahem'. Now we were getting somewhere.

"I want to offer you a job."

"A job to do what, exactly?" I asked.

"I want you to find out who killed my husband."

Surprise must have registered on my face. She waved her hand. "The police have let your sister go, so now whoever's in charge will decide it was a random junkie who believed murder was the only way to get their fix. The police won't make any arrests and they will close the case."

This wasn't what I thought she was going to say. My mind seized and discarded a million reasons I shouldn't take the case. I must have taken too long, as she continued. "I loved my husband, Miss Beane. We were planning on retiring and moving to Italy. Now he's gone and I have nothing." She choked on the last word and my resolve wavered.

"What if I can't find out who it was?"

"Bonnie has faith in you and so do I. Will you help me?"

A part of me wanted to say no, that this was a matter better left to the police, but the image of my sister in jail while my dad collapsed weakened my resolve. Would Barrett give this case the attention it deserved, knowing my family was involved? I wasn't sure, but as long as I was careful, this would give me the edge I needed to find the murderer.

Besides I could always give any information I'd gather to Gideon.

I told her about my pay rate and conditions. She didn't bat an eyelid even though I'd doubled the price I'd usually charge.

She had food delivered; just-baked croissants and fresh fruit salad with steaming cups of coffee. We spent the next hour delving into their family life, both here and in South Africa. We spoke about friends and acquaintances, plus everything in their past and plans for the future. Delia had bought photos and an address book with her. By the time we finished, I had an extensive case file to start with.

She left me with a shoebox of old photos and I sat pondering her words, my fingers tapping out a rhythm with the pen I was holding. While her perfume surrounded me with the fragrance of a rose garden after a spring rain, my heart was heavy with a trepidation I couldn't shake.

Chapter 19

The club was already rocking by the time I got there. I waved to the band and threaded my way to our usual table. Coco was already there with two glasses of Moscato and a packet of sea salt and cracked pepper chips, my favourite.

I bent to hug her, and she responded by pulling me into an embrace and kissing my cheek. Her lips warm against the coolness of my skin.

I slid into the seat opposite and deposited my bag and scarf next to the wall, where no one could grab it. Once bitten, twice shy. Though I was pretty sure the guy who'd tried to make off with my bag a couple of months ago wouldn't try it again.

Coco spoke over the music. "I hope you don't mind, but I ordered spring rolls, chips and a steak burger to share." No wonder I could never stay mad at her for long.

I snorted. Let's face it; I couldn't stay mad at anyone where food was involved.

"Sounds perfect." I picked up my glass and took a sip. The wine's sweetness lingered on my palate, enticing me to take another sip as I gazed around the room. People packed the room. Some lined up at the bar waiting to be served, while others crowded the dance floor. It seemed like every table was full.

Our food arrived on a share platter with a trio of house specialty sauces. I chose a spring roll, dipped it in a spicy mango sauce, sat back and took a bite. My eyes closed in sheer bliss. Even after munching my way through one or two croissants with Delia, I was starving.

We ate for a while in a comfortable cocoon of silence, even while music reverberated around us. With a satisfied sigh, Coco pushed her plate to one side and looked at me. She dabbed her mouth with a napkin. "I'm sorry, Chil. I wasn't honest with you about what happened to William."

I sat back and folded my arms. "Go on."

She took a deep breath. "I was arrested, not because of the cookies, but because I hit him."

"You hit him?"

She bit her lip and nodded.

"Where?"

"Outside his shop. Old Mrs Murchison called the police."

I'd been waiting for her to spill the beans, so to speak, yet the admission still came as a surprise. This Coco was not the one I recognised.

"What happened?"

"I've been buying my gifts for clients through him for quite a while. I'd gone to pick up my last order, and he said I'd already taken delivery of it the day before. But I hadn't. Things escalated. I walked out of the shop and he followed and called me a liar." Her voice quavered, and she stabbed the table with her finger. "Right there in front of a crowd of onlookers."

"So you hit him?"

She nodded again. "I was so embarrassed—and angry. I've never stolen anything in my life and to be accused of stealing from him ..."

I picked up a chip and swirled it in sauce. "Does dad know?"

"Yes. He had to come and bail me out."

"So why didn't you ask me to help?"

Coco's eyes welled up with tears. "I was ashamed, Chil, and didn't want you to see me like that—arrested, humiliated. I've always tried to be the perfect big sister ... the one who has it all together. "

"Nobody said you had to be perfect."

She gave me a watery smile. "I understand that. But I just panicked. I thought if I could sort it out quickly and quietly, no one would ever be the wiser."

"But it didn't work out that way," I mumbled. "When William Van Horne died, it changed everything."

"And now the whole town probably thinks I'm some kind of criminal."

I leaned back, considering. "Perhaps not. This is a small town and people gossip, but they also feel connected to you. They've seen you grow up, run your business and contribute to the community. One mistake won't erase all of that."

Coco dabbed at her eyes with the napkin. "I hope you're right. I've just been so stupid and worked so hard to build my reputation, and now ..."

"Now you're human," I finished for her. "Like the rest of us."

She let out a shaky laugh. "I suppose so."

We sat in silence for a moment. I stared out the window, trying to process everything she'd told me.

"So what happens now?" I asked.

Coco sighed. "I honestly have no idea. William dropped the charges and the police are aware I had nothing to do with the murder."

"That's good news, right?" I asked, with a flicker of hope for my sister.

Coco shrugged, her shoulders sagging. "I guess so. But the damage is already done. People saw me get arrested. I've already had a few cancellations ..."

I reached across the table and squeezed her hand. "We'll figure it out, okay? Your business is going to be fine. You've built something amazing, Coco. Your clients love you. One misunderstanding won't change that."

She met my gaze, a hint of her old spark returning. "You really think so?"

"I do," I said firmly. "And anyone who thinks otherwise can deal with me."

A genuine laugh tumbled out of her. "My fierce little sister, always ready to fight my battles."

I stood and picked up my bag. "This little sister has to go to the bathroom. Want me to grab another drink on my way back?"

"Why not?" She winked. "I don't have to go to work in the morning."

I groaned and wound my way toward the bar. Halfway across, I turned back to ask Coco something. She sat slumped in her chair, shoulders rounded and utterly dejected, her face drawn and her eyes fixed on the table. For the first time I realised just how much the arrest had taken out of her.

She'd been putting on an act for my benefit.

I hesitated to leave her like that, but I also knew how mortified she'd be if she knew I'd been watching.

Threading my way to the bar a flash of vivid colour caught my eye. I turned and craned my head to see above the dancers. I spotted a familiar form on the edge of the dance floor, the posture distinct even in the dim lighting.

Gideon. He was leaning against a mosaic wall talking to someone.

I took a deep breath and steadied myself. It was time I apologised for acting like a child. As I walked toward him, the crowd parted for a second. My heart sank as I watched him tuck a piece of hair behind Maisie McClintock's ear.

I froze; the pulsing music fading to a dull throb in my ears. All I could focus on was Gideon's hand lingering near Maisie's face. She giggled and leaned in closer to Gideon, her hand resting on his chest. A wave of nausea washed over me.

I should have known better. Of course he'd moved on. Why wouldn't he? I'd pushed him away, acted like a petulant child. And now here he was, with Maisie, of all people.

I turned on my heel, no longer interested in that drink in the bar. I needed air. I needed to get out of this suffocating club with its too-loud music and too-many people. Not caring who I bumped into or what drinks I might have spilled, I pushed my way through the crowd.

As I neared the exit, a hand grabbed my arm, pulling me back.

I spun around, ready to snap at whoever had stopped me only to find myself face-to-face with Coco.

"Where are you going?" she yelled over the music, her brow creased in concern.

I opened my mouth to reply, but the words caught in my throat. How could I explain what I'd just seen? How could I admit what I'd done? That I'd probably destroyed my chance at happiness before it had even started?

Coco steered me outside. The darkness hit me like a wave; the streetlights casting a hazy glow over the deserted footpath. The crisp air was a welcome relief from the stuffy club. A door opened behind us and the faint aroma of cigarettes and alcohol wafted through the night.

We walked in silence, vehicles honked in the distance and the occasional burst of laughter from other late-night revellers echoing off the buildings. We got in her car, Coco thrusting our bags in the back seat. "What happened?" she demanded.

I took a deep breath and let it out. "I saw Gideon."

"And?"

"He was with Maisie," I said, the words bitter on my tongue. "They looked ... close."

"Maisie McClintock—the lawyer? Are you sure?"

I nodded, trying to blink back the tears that threatened to fall.

Her face darkened. "That jerk," she muttered. "I'm so sorry."

"It's my fault. I was going to apologise to him and try to work things out."

She rubbed my arm. "Come on, let's get you home. We can stop for ice cream on the way."

We drove off, the neon lights of the club fading in the distance. I leaned my head against the cool glass of the passenger window, watching the town blur past us.

"You want to talk about it?" Coco asked.

I shook my head, not trusting my voice. The lump in my throat threatened to turn into full-blown sobs if I tried to speak.

True to her word, Coco pulled into the car park of our favourite ice cream shop. "Two double scoops of rocky road coming right up," she said, squeezing my hand before getting out of the car.

As I waited, I pulled out my phone, my thumb hovering over Gideon's name in my contacts. Part of me wanted to text him, to demand an explanation, to pour out all the hurt and anger I held inside. But what right did I have? I was the one who pushed him away.

I was still staring at his name when Coco returned, balancing two enormous ice creams.

"Here," she said, handing me one. "Eat your feelings. They have scientifically proven that it helps.

I managed a weak laugh and took a bite. The rich chocolate and marshmallow swirls melted on my tongue, momentarily distracting me from the ache in my chest.

"So," Coco said, licking her own cone, "what's the plan?"

"Plan?"

"Yeah, the plan." she repeated. "For getting over Gideon and moving on with your life."

I sighed, taking another bite of ice cream. "I'm not sure if I have a plan. I mean, it's not like we were exclusive or anything. We haven't even really gone on a proper date."

"In that case, you owe it to yourself, and him, to find out what's really going on." She wiped her hands on a paper towel. "We've known Gideon since high school and he's always been a straight shooter." She shrugged. "I say give him a chance to explain and then make your decision based on facts, not feelings."

I leaned my head against the seat and groaned. I knew my mantra would come back to bite me on the butt, however she was right. The truth might tear my heart apart, but I needed to hear it.

But before that I needed the comfort of my bed and a weighted blanket.

I turned to Coco and gave her a slight smile. "Home, James, and don't spare the horses."

Chapter 20

The next morning, I woke to Almond purring and kneading my chest, her whiskers tickling my nose. I groaned and gently pushed her aside, rolling over to check the time on my phone. 8:37 AM glared back at me, along with a missed call from an unlisted number.

Memories of last night came flooding back—Coco's confession, seeing Gideon with Maisie, the ice cream therapy session with my sister. I buried my face in my pillow, tempted to just stay in bed all day and wallow. But Almond had other ideas, the insistent miaows for her breakfast becoming louder.

"Alright, alright," I muttered, dragging myself out of bed and threw a turquoise robe over my pyjamas. "I'm coming."

After feeding Almond and making myself a strong cup of coffee, I settled on the couch with my laptop, the weather outside in keeping with my mood. The grey skies and rain pattering at the window made for a day designed to close the world and all its madness out.

How could I have been so wrong about the direction Gideon and I were heading? It was bad enough that we fought ... but Maisie? Where did she fit into all of this?

I opened my laptop, determined to distract myself with work, but my fingers hovered uselessly over the keyboard. The words wouldn't come. Instead, my mind kept replaying the scene from last night—Gideon's hand near Maisie's face, their heads bent close together, laughing at some private joke.

Almond jumped onto the couch, purring as she curled up next to me. I absently stroked her fur, grateful for the companionship. My phone buzzed on the coffee table, and I hesitated before picking it up. A text from Coco: *How are you holding up, hon? Want to grab lunch later?*

I sighed, torn between wanting to hide away and knowing that isolating myself wouldn't help. Before I could reply, another message appeared: *Don't even think about saying no. I'm not letting you mope all day. I'll be there at 1. Wear something cute – we're going to that new bistro downtown.*

I couldn't help but smile. Coco knew me too well. I sent back a quick 'OK' and set the phone down, feeling a small spark of motivation. Maybe getting out of the house would do me some good.

I spent the next couple of hours half-heartedly attempting to work, but my mind kept drifting. By the time Coco arrived, I had showered and put on a semblance of a presentable outfit—dark jeans and a soft rose-gold sweater that brought out the green of my eyes.

"There's my favourite sister," Coco said as I opened the door. She enveloped me in a tight hug, the scent of her familiar perfume comforting. "Ready to face the world?"

"As ready as I'll ever be," I replied, trying to muster a smile. "And by the way, I'm your only sister."

She winked. "That's why you're my favourite." Coco linked her arm through mine as we headed out, chattering about the bistro's supposedly amazing 'Croque Madame'. I let her words wash over me, grateful for the distraction.

The rain had let up, but the sky remained stubbornly overcast as we made our way downtown. The bistro was cozy and warmly lit, with vintage posters adorning exposed brick walls. We settled into a corner booth, and I relaxed slightly as we perused the menu.

"So," Coco said once we'd ordered her no-nonsense stare as sharp as ever. "Spill. What's going on in that head of yours?"

I sighed, tracing patterns on the condensation of my water glass.

"I just ... I can't stop thinking about it. About them. I keep replaying everything in my mind, wondering if I missed some signs. Was Gideon interested in Maisie all along? Did I completely misread our relationship?"

Coco reached across and squeezed my hand. "Honey, you can't torture yourself like this. You don't know what's really going on between them."

"But I saw them together," I protested. "They looked ... close."

"One moment doesn't tell the complete story," Coco said gently. "Remember when everyone thought you and Jake were dating because of that photo at the Christmas party?"

I grimaced at the memory. "That was different. Jake and I were just friends."

"Exactly. And maybe Gideon and Maisie are just friends, too. You won't know unless you talk to him."

I sighed, stirring my coffee. "I know you're right, but I can't bring myself to reach out. What if he confirms my worst fears? What if he tells me he's moved on with Maisie?"

Leaning back, Coco studied me. "Isn't that better than tormenting yourself with 'what ifs'?"

Before I could respond, our food arrived. The Croque Madame looked amazing and was certainly a step above an ordinary toasted sandwich, but my appetite had vanished. I picked at my food while Coco dug in enthusiastically.

"Look," she said between bites, "I'm not saying you have to call him right this second. Take some time to process. But don't let fear keep you from getting closure."

I nodded, forcing myself to take a bite. The rich, creamy sauce and perfectly runny egg yolk melted on my tongue, momentarily distracting me from my troubles. I had to admit; the food was delicious.

"You're right," I said finally. "I can't keep avoiding this. But I need a few days to gather my thoughts. Maybe I'll text him next week, see if he wants to meet up and talk."

Coco beamed. "That's my girl. And in the meantime, we're going to keep you busy. No more moping in your apartment."

A part of me wondered if keeping busy was more for my benefit or hers. It was time to find out. 'Are you okay, Coco? You don't seem quite like yourself.'

She sighed. "Is it that obvious?"

"It is to me."

She put her napkin on the table and took a sip of water. "To be honest I'm exhausted. Everyone keeps tip-toeing around me like I'm going to break."

"They're just worried about you."

"I get that, but I have to put on a happy act like everything's fine." She rubbed her cheeks. "My face aches from smiling so much."

I reached out and patted her hand. "Enjoy it while it lasts. Being a mum is hard and what you went through harder still. Pretty soon everything will be back to normal and you'll wonder why you didn't take advantage of the extra attention."

She tilted her head to one side. "Since when did you become so clever?"

"Since forever. You've only just noticed."

As if on cue, my phone buzzed. I glanced down to see a message from Bonnie asking if we wanted to come over later and taste-test some new recipes.

I showed Coco the text, and she nodded with approval. "Perfect. Family time is exactly what we both need right now."

As we finished our meal, I felt a small weight lift from my shoulders. I wasn't ready to face Gideon yet, but I now I had a plan. And more importantly, I had people who cared about me.

"Thanks, Coco," I said as we left the bistro. "I don't know what I'd do without you."

She grinned, linking her arm through mine again. "Probably wallow in bed all day eating ice cream. Speaking of which, want to hit that new gelato place before I drop you off at your ride?"

I laughed, surprised by how good it felt. "I forgot all about picking up the ute!"

As we strolled down the street, the clouds finally broke, allowing weak sunlight to filter through. It wasn't exactly a perfect day, but it felt like a metaphor for my current state of mind—a glimmer of hope peeking through the gloom.

The gelato shop was bustling with people seeking a sweet escape from the dreary weather. Coco and I squeezed our way to the counter, admiring the colourful array of flavours.

"I'll have the pistachio," Coco decided. "What about you?"

I scanned the options, my eyes landing on a rich, dark chocolate. "I'll take the chocolate hazelnut."

As we savoured our gelato on a nearby bench, I smiled. The creamy sweetness was delectable; a simple pleasure that momentarily pushed my worries aside.

"So," Coco said, licking her spoon, "what are you going to say to Gideon when you talk to him?"

I paused, considering. "I guess I'll just be honest. Tell him I saw him and Maisie and ask what's going on between them. And ..." I took a deep breath, "I'll tell him how I feel about him. Really feel. No more dancing around it."

Coco nudged my shoulder with her arm. "That's brave. And necessary. Whatever happens, at least you'll know you put it all out there."

We finished our gelato in companionable silence, watching people hurry by on the sidewalk. As we stood to leave, Coco pulled me into another hug.

"Remember, I am here if you need anything. Day or night."

"I know," I said, squeezing her back.

Afterward, Coco insisted on driving me back to Rusty's ute still parked near the bar where the night had taken its unexpected turn. We chatted lightly during the drive, avoiding any heavy topics, but as we neared my car, I felt the weight of reality creeping back in. She pulled up beside the kerb, idling for a moment as we said our goodbyes.

"Remember what you said," Coco reminded me, her eyes searching mine. "Be honest. With him and with yourself."

"I will," I promised, unbuckling my seatbelt. "And thanks for everything, really."

"Anytime," she said, flashing a supportive smile. "See you tonight." I stepped out, waving as she drove away, her car disappearing into the drizzle.

I climbed into the ute, pausing for a moment to collect my thoughts. My phone buzzed in my bag. Another call from a blocked caller ID number. I stared at the screen, my heart thudding. Two calls in less than 24 hours—it couldn't just be a coincidence.

I hesitated, debating whether to answer, but before I could decide, the ringing stopped, replaced by a notification: one new voicemail. With trembling fingers, I tapped to listen.

A muffled voice crackled through the speaker, distorted as if the person were speaking through a faulty connection or intentionally disguising their voice.

"Didn't I tell you to back off? Keep poking around, and next time, it won't just be your car that gets messed up."

The line went dead, and I sat there, frozen, the words echoing in my mind. I replayed the message, hoping to catch something I missed, but it was the same garbled warning. I looked around, suddenly hyper-aware of every car, every passer-by.

What had I stumbled into?

Chapter 21

I didn't feel like going home after the call, so I headed to the office instead. Pete was away for a few days, so I'd have the space all to myself. The late morning traffic was light, but every car that zipped by felt like a threat. Every flash of headlights in my rear-view mirror made my heart jump. Someone had threatened me before, but something about that voice—a low, gravelly whisper that sounded almost like a poor imitation of a movie gangster—had left me shaky. Maybe it was the fact that whoever it was knew exactly what they were doing, making it clear they weren't just messing around.

By the time I parked outside the office, my arms ached with tension. I locked the car twice, as if that would somehow stop my nerves from buzzing. Whoever called knew exactly how to get under my skin. And blocked caller ID numbers? They were about as traceable as a shadow on a moonless night. I could always ask the police for a malicious call trace on my phone, but with the way things were between Gideon and me, that wasn't going to happen.

I fumbled with the keys to the front door, dropping them twice before finally getting the lock to click open. Inside, the familiar scent of old wood and faint coffee grounds greeted me, a comfort I hadn't realized I needed until I was there. Files I hadn't touched in days, a half-eaten bag of pretzels I kept telling myself I'd throw out, and the cheap desk lamp flickering slightly as if even it couldn't decide if it was in the mood to work today, cluttered my desk.

I tossed my bag on the chair and sank into my seat, my fingers tapping absently on the desk. I should have been focusing on the case, on the tangled mess that William Van Horne's murder had become, but all I could think about was the call. 'Stop sticking your nose where it isn't needed,' they'd said. I couldn't help but wonder how much deeper this all went and how far I'd already pushed my luck.

I opened my laptop, scrolling through emails without really reading them. My mind kept drifting back to that voice. Someone was getting nervous about how close I was getting. And if there was one thing I'd learned, it was that nervous people made mistakes.

Tempted to call Gideon I reached for my phone. He'd know how to calm me down, maybe even help me piece together who might have made the call. But then I thought of Maisie and that night at the bar—the way Gideon had looked at her, and how stupid I'd felt standing there, a third wheel in a situation I hadn't been prepared for. I dropped the phone back on the desk with a thud. No, I wasn't ready for that conversation, not yet.

Instead, I pulled up the file on the land developers, my eyes scanning the familiar names and faces. I was onto something, I could feel it, but the pieces weren't fitting together yet. It was like trying to finish a jigsaw puzzle when someone had hidden half the pieces. And now, with Morgan's sudden return and Gideon's behaviour the night before, everything felt more tangled than ever.

I leaned back in my chair, staring at the ceiling. "Get a grip, Chili," I muttered to myself. "You've dealt with worse." But I wasn't sure if that was correct anymore. I couldn't shake the feeling that I was way out of my depth this time, and the deeper I went, the more dangerous it was getting.

I was still trying to shake off the unease when the door creaked open. Morgan stood in the doorway, looking like he'd been dragged backwards through an awful week—rumpled clothes, dark circles under his eyes, and that guilty slump in his shoulders. His sudden reappearance after 18 months away was enough to make anyone suspicious, but today he looked more lost than dangerous.

"Morgan." I tried to keep my tone neutral, but even I could hear the edge. "What are you doing here?"

"Sorry, I just ... I didn't know where else to go," he said, closing the door behind him. He stood near the threshold, unsure if he could go any further.

"You look like someone's after you." I asked, half-joking, half-serious. When he was younger, Morgan had a knack for stumbling into messes, but the look on his face told me this was no small fry problem.

He sighed, sinking into the chair opposite my desk. "You could say that. I, uh ... I need to talk to you about something." His eyes shifted around the room. "I think I'm in trouble." He sighed. "Actually, I know I am."

My stomach tightened. "What happened?"

"I'm not sure where to start."

"The beginning's as good a place as any."

"You're right. When I was in Africa," he began, rubbing his temples like he could massage the guilt away, "I got involved with some people. They convinced me to bring back diamonds, said it was to help fund clinics—real sob story stuff. And I believed them."

"You what?"

A flicker of defiance crossed his face. "I thought I was doing something good."

I crossed my arms, my mind working overtime. This was typical Morgan—thinking he was saving the world, only to get played. "So you brought diamonds back and then what ... you handed them over to someone?"

"Yeah. But the people who met me weren't the same ones who d set it up. They were rough, shady. I didn't ask questions—I was in too deep."

"So, where did you meet them?"

"At a jewellery store."

My jaw dropped. "Please tell me it wasn't William Van Horne's store?"

He nodded.

I couldn't believe what I'd heard. My voice raised an octave. "You gave smuggled diamonds to William Van Horne, the same jeweller who was murdered?"

"Technically, no. I dropped the diamonds off, but it wasn't Van Horne who took them. It was some other guy."

"What other guy?"

"Medium sized, brown hair, moustache. Mousey looking. The guy with him called him Stan."

My mind raced, puzzle pieces slotting into place. A medium-sized mousey-looking man with a moustache, called Stan. And the last detail— "Did Stan have a lisp?"

His eyes widened, as if the memory had just sharpened in his mind. "Now that you mention it, yeah, he did."

The room felt smaller, the air thicker. A million thoughts collided in my head, each one more damning than the last. Stan. The man with the lisp. He'd been hovering around the edges like a shadow I couldn't quite catch. I remembered his nervous energy, the way he skulked around Mr Dorsey trying to persuade him to sell his house.

This wasn't just some guy picking up a package; it was deliberate. Someone else had delivered the diamonds directly—someone who definitely wanted Van Horne dead. Stan wasn't just a go-between; he was a key player, manipulating events from behind the scenes, orchestrating the handoff like a conductor leading a symphony of chaos.

"I think Van Horne was being blackmailed by developers who needed a front for their dirty money, I said."

Morgan blinked, my words sinking in. "Blackmailed?" His voice dropped to a whisper. "I had no idea."

I stared at him, trying to read between the lines. Morgan wasn't a saint, but he wasn't this stupid. Or maybe he was just that desperate to believe in a cause, any cause, to justify why he'd abandoned everything else. "I bet they're laundering money through Van Horne's shop. The diamonds are part of it. He got caught up with some developers who are in deeper than just property schemes. Then they killed him to keep him quiet."

Morgan's face blanched. "I didn't know, Chili, honestly. I was just a courier—I didn't know what I was walking into."

"Now you do," I said, a little sharper than I intended. "This entire operation isn't just about Van Horne's little shop. It's about power, money, and the lengths people will go to protect their interests. And they're willing to kill to keep it quiet."

Morgan leaned forward, elbows on his knees, head hung low. "I'm sorry, Chili. I never meant to bring this to your doorstep."

"It's not just my doorstep anymore, Morgan. Van Horne's dead. And someone's trying real hard to make sure I back off." I could still hear the echo of that call in my ears, the threat lingering like smoke. I wasn't going to, but it definitely made me pause.

We sat there; the silence growing thicker. I could see the fear on Morgan's face.

"So what do we do now?" he asked, breaking the silence.

I stared at the files on my desk, a mess of leads that all pointed in different directions. But there was a pattern here, one I was seeing more clearly. "We find out who's really behind this. And we shut it down."

Morgan nodded, but his eyes were far away, lost in some thought I couldn't quite reach. "I'll help however I can. I just ... I can't let this go on."

"Good," I said, though I wasn't sure if I was reassuring him or myself. "You can start by telling me everything you know."

We talked for an hour my notepad filling with all the information he knew. At times I wanted to shake him, to snap him to his senses. How could a doctor who was so clever, be so stupid?

When he left, I stayed behind, staring at the closed door. There was still something I couldn't quite put my finger on. A connection between Van Horne, Morgan, and the developers that went beyond simple greed or fear. Whatever it was, I had a feeling it was the key to everything. And if I was going to find it, I needed to be sharper, faster, and one step ahead of whoever was already watching my every move.

Chapter 22

With Morgan gone, I went through the shoebox Delia had left with me. The room was a haven of quiet, the only sound being the faint hum of the city outside. I sipped my now-cold coffee and stared at the mix of black-and-white and faded colour photos. Each image felt like part of a mystery no one had fully put together, least of all me.

I flipped through the photos, each one revealing a fragment of Van Horne's past. There were pictures of him as a young man, Delia in her youth, and shots of glamorous social events and business meetings. One or two featured our mayor—the walrus—grinning widely for the camera. There was nothing in these images to suggest anything beyond a business relationship, but it was something I'd have to confirm later.

Photos bound by an elastic band caught my attention: desert landscapes, village scenes, and wildlife typical of Africa. My pulse quickened when I found a photo of a much younger Van Horne standing with a man who looked vaguely familiar. It was a candid shot, snapped outside a modest building that could have been located anywhere. The two men were smiling, each seeming to enjoy the other's company. I started as I realised why the second man looked familiar- it was Morgan's dad. The connection between these men—one now dead, the other very much alive—had to mean something.

I set the photo aside and picked up another. This one was even older. I recognized the man from my childhood—Morgan's grandfather—he had that same stern, unwavering look he always wore in pictures, dressed in a crisp suit that seemed out of place against the dusty, sun-baked landscape behind them. But it wasn't his familiar figure that caught my attention; it was the woman beside him.

She stood close, her posture protective, with one hand resting over her swollen belly, the other held in the crook of his arm. While her expression was softer and warmer than his, there was something undeniably strong about her. She differed from the grandmother I remembered, and she wasn't like anyone described in the family stories circulating around town.

And that she was standing next to Henry, visibly pregnant, spoke volumes.

I turned the photo over, hoping for a clue, but the back was blank—no date, no names, just a faint smudge of dirt that hinted at years spent hidden away.

Perhaps it was time to speak to Morgan's dad and find out what the connection between the two families was.

First, I needed to gather a little more context. Bonnie's invitation to rally the family together for dinner was the perfect pretext to gather more information.

The sun was low and golden as I pulled up to the familiar curb outside Bonnie's place. Her front screen door was closed, but the lights inside were warm and inviting. I walked in, greeted by the mingled smells of fresh herbs, baking bread, and something deliciously spicy simmering on the stove.

Bonnie was bustling around the kitchen, looking every bit the food enthusiast she was, with her apron dusted in flour and a pot of something bubbling on the stove. My dad sat at the dining table, sampling a dish of what looked like a savoury tart. Coco was leaning against the counter, trying her best to look unimpressed but failing as she popped a small spoonful of whatever concoction Bonnie had whipped up into her mouth.

"Hey, sis," Coco said, her mouth half-full. "You're just in time. Bonnie's got us taste-testing her new recipes. I'm not sure if she's trying to feed us or poison us, though."

"Hilarious," Bonnie said, waving her spoon. "I promise it's all edible. Mostly."

I grinned, grateful for the bit of normalcy amidst the chaos of the investigation. But this wasn't just a casual family gathering for me—I had questions, and I intended to get some answers.

"Hey, everyone," I greeted, taking a seat next to my dad. "Smells amazing, Bon. What are we trying today?"

"Everything!" Bonnie declared, setting down a platter of freshly baked rolls. She tapped the spoon on the edge of a plate. "But these, in particular. Wild mushroom and caramelized onion tartlets. Dig in."

We all helped ourselves, the kitchen filling with the familiar sounds of clinking cutlery and appreciative murmurs. I nibbled at a tartlet, my mind still half on the photos I'd found. My dad was busy telling Bonnie about his latest project at the surf shop, and Coco was making a show of critiquing each bite, like she was a judge on some fancy cooking show. The twins sat at their own table, munching happily on homemade chicken nuggets and tomato sauce. I waited for a lull in the chatter before steering the conversation.

"Dad, do you remember Morgan's grandfather?" I asked casually, picking at my food.

My dad looked up, surprised. "Yeah, I remember Henry. Good man. Tough as nails. Why do you ask?"

I shrugged. "I came across some old photos Delia gave me. Henry was in one of them, standing next to a pregnant woman. I didn't recognize her, though."

Bonnie paused, mid-pour, her eyes flickering with recognition. "That must've been Anna," she said thoughtfully. "She was ... well, it's a bit of a family secret, I suppose. Henry was involved with a woman before he met Morgan's grandmother, but no one really talked about it much."

The room fell into a curious silence as everyone digested this new information. My pulse quickened, but I kept my tone neutral. "What happened to her?"

Bonnie set the pitcher down. Her expression softened with old memories. "I don't know all the details, but from what I heard, Anna disappeared not long after someone took that photo. Rumours were Henry's parents paid her off, and she went back to her family, but it was always hush-hush. I remember your grandmother mentioning it once—she said it was as if Anna just vanished overnight."

Coco, now interested, chimed in. "Sounds like a soap opera. How come no one's ever mentioned this before?"

"Because nobody discussed it," my dad said, his voice tinged with a mix of nostalgia and caution. "Henry was always a private man, and whatever happened with Anna was painful for him. People in town respected that."

I nodded, trying to piece together what this new revelation might mean. If Anna had vanished without a trace, had she remarried? Could there be an entire branch of Morgan's family that he never knew about—one that connected him, even indirectly, to Van Horne?

"How did they meet?"

"Anna was originally from South Africa. They met here in town when she gave a talk about her work over there. Henry signed up and travelled to Africa with Anna's humanitarian team. Mind you, this was long before it became fashionable," dad responded. "She was a nurse and Henry, as you know, she was a logistics coordinator. His job was to ensure resources reached the right places."

Bonnie passed the butter to Coco. "I remember one thing," she said, almost to herself. "Henry went off the rails for a while after that. There was some talk about him bringing trouble back home, but I don't know if any of that ever came to anything."

A chill ran down my spine. The diamonds. Morgan's involvement. The cryptic family connections. It all felt too intertwined to be coincidence.

"What kind of trouble?" I asked, my heart thudding in my chest.

Bonnie shook her head. "Oh, Chili, it was so long ago, I can't recall the details. I think he got involved in something shady, but Henry never spoke of it. It was like some part of his past he'd rather forget."

Coco leaned in, resting her chin on her hand. "I wonder what happened to the baby? It must have been horrible for Anna to be in that predicament back then."

I murmured my agreement.

"I don't know," Bonnie replied. "No one's ever heard from her."

Another line I'd have to find out more about.

"Did Morgan's dad ever go to Africa?"

"I seem to remember he worked as a geologist for a mining company when he was younger," dad answered. "He'd been married a couple of years and had to leave Morgan's mum behind here as wasn't safe."

If Van Horne knew about Morgan's connections, that could explain why he got pulled into the money laundering scheme. And if Morgan's own father had been involved without realizing the true nature of the family ties, it would add another layer of complexity to the whole mess.

"Has this got something to do with the murder?"

"I'm not sure yet," I admitted, "but something tells me this isn't just a coincidence. There's a deeper connection between Morgan's family and Van Horne, something neither of them might have fully known."

"Be careful, Chili," my dad warned, leaning back in his chair with his arms folded. "Digging up the past can get messy, especially when it was buried for a reason."

I nodded, understanding the reason for his caution. But I also knew I couldn't stop now. The closer I got to the truth, the more dangerous it felt, but there was no turning back. Whatever lay at the heart of this tangled web, I was determined to untangle it—one secret at a time.

Chapter 23

After we finished eating, it was time for me to head off. Dad rested a gentle hand on Bonnie's shoulder before walking me out, his touch light but full of that quiet, unspoken affection he had for her. I watched as she leaned into it, eyes closing for just a second, as if soaking up the reassurance. He gave her shoulder a little squeeze, something so simple yet full of meaning, and then turned to me. We stepped out onto the porch together, the screen door creaking behind us. The night air was cool against my skin, a soft hum of cicadas filling the silence.

Dad leaned against the newel post, his eyes fixed somewhere out in the dark, like he was searching for something beyond the gloom. For a moment, neither of us spoke, just listened to the soft rustle of the wind in the trees and the distant sounds of the night. Finally, he broke the silence, his voice low and thoughtful. "You know, when you were little, you'd tell me anything," he said, a hint of a smile tugging at his lips. "Didn't matter what it was—bad dreams, lost toys, or which boy was flavour of the week. You never held back."

I shifted on my feet, feeling a mix of guilt and something else, something heavier. I looked at him, the way his face was half in shadow, the lines deeper than I remembered. He wasn't pushing or prying; it was just a quiet reminder that the door was still open, even if I didn't walk through it as often anymore.

"You can still tell me anything, Chili," he continued, his gaze still fixed on the night, like he was giving me space to find the words I never quite knew how to say. The question was almost my undoing. A soft ache rose in my throat and I swallowed before turning to him.

"I had a fight with Gideon," I blurted, my voice barely louder than a whisper. Dad glanced at me, his expression softening, but he didn't interrupt. "It was stupid, really. We were on the beach, and I guess ... I just lost it and said some pretty horrible things. Then when Coco and I went to the club he was with Maisie, and I—," I paused, swallowing hard, the hurt still fresh in my throat. "I didn't expect it to bother me, but it did. And then, I just ... I don't know." I shrugged. "I thought we had something special."

Dad didn't move, just kept his gaze out into the night, listening. I could tell he was weighing his words, figuring out the right thing to say without making me feel worse. "You know, Gideon's a good guy," he said finally, his tone even. "Always has been a straight-up kind of man. I've seen the way he looks out for you, and I don't think he's the type to play games."

I nodded, the sting of tears threatening to spill down my cheeks. "I know, Dad. I do. It's just—seeing him with her; it felt like I was being pushed aside." I looked at him, his face tinged with worry. I took a deep breath. "I've been digging into things, Dad. About Morgan and Van Horne. I found something, something big, and I know I need to take it to Gideon. But now, after what happened, I just ..."

"You're scared he won't listen," Dad finished for me, hitting the nail right on the head. I nodded again, the admission making my chest feel tight. "Chili, you've always had a good head on your shoulders, but you've also always been stubborn as a mule when you think someone's wronged you. I get it. But the thing about people like Gideon is they don't just walk away because you had a bad day or got into a fight. You've got something to say, he'll listen. You just gotta give him a chance."

I chewed on his words, letting them settle. It was so much easier said than done, but deep down, I knew he was right. Gideon wasn't the type to hold grudges, and despite how raw everything felt, I owed it to him—and to myself—to get this all out in the open.

"You know what else?" Dad added, finally turning to look at me. "It sounds like there's a lot going on right now, more than just you and Gideon. If you've got something important, something about Morgan, or the murder, you can't sit on it. You need to get it to the right people, and you need to do it before it's too late."

I knew what he was saying, even if he wasn't spelling it out. I couldn't just keep playing detective on my own. I needed to speak to Gideon, and I needed to do it soon.

"I will," I said, my voice firmer now. "I'll talk to him. I just ... I need to sort this out, Dad. It's all tangled up, and I feel like I'm drowning in it."

Dad nodded, his eyes softening. "You'll figure it out, Chili. You always do. Just don't forget—you've got people in your corner. You're not alone in this, even if it feels like it sometimes."

I leaned into him, and he put his arms around me. We stood there a moment longer, the quiet settling between us like an old friend. When I finally pulled away, I felt a little steadier, a little surer of what I needed to do next.

I drove home with the windows down, the cool air rushing in and clearing my head. By the time I pulled into the driveway, I'd decided I wouldn't wait any longer. Tomorrow, I'd go see Morgan's dad and tell him everything I'd found. Then I'd see Gideon. Whatever came next, it was time to stop running from it.

I stood there for a moment, staring at the house, my heart thumping in my chest. I wasn't sure how it would all play out—with Gideon, with Morgan, or with the tangled mess I'd uncovered—but for the first time in a while, I felt like I was finally ready to face it.

Chapter 24

I kicked off my shoes, half-heartedly aiming for the shoe rack, and missed. My cat, Almond, gave me a judgmental look from her perch on the armchair, tail flicking in lazy disapproval. Yeah, I knew I looked like a mess.

My eyes caught the blinking red light on my answering machine. I wasn't expecting anyone to call. Most people knew to text or email me unless they were technologically illiterate or a telemarketer. I hit the play button as I dropped onto the couch, sinking into the familiar worn cushions.

"Chili, it's Delia. I need to speak to you. There's something you should know. Please call me back as soon as you can."

Delia's voice, calm yet laced with an undercurrent of urgency, hung in the air. I checked the clock on the microwave: 9:38 PM. Not too late. I sat there for a second, my finger hovering over the phone, weighing whether I was emotionally prepared to take on whatever new bombshell Delia had to drop. It wasn't too late. Maybe Delia was up, staring at the same old photo albums, asking herself the same questions I was.

Wasting no time, I picked up the phone and dialled. It rang twice before Delia's soft voice came through the line.

"Chili," she said the relief evident, "thank you for calling back."

"No problem, Delia. What's going on?"

There was a pause on the other end of the line. I could hear the faint sound of something clinking, like ice cubes in a glass. She was probably sitting in her fancy house, sipping something expensive, trying to make sense of her husband's mess.

"I ... I didn't tell you everything before," she started, her voice shaky, as if she were choosing her words carefully. "There's more to William's business than I let on."

I leaned forward, suddenly more alert. "More than just the jewellery shop?"

"Yes. For years, William had a silent partner, someone who wasn't part of the day-to-day operations. I never met them, but William trusted this person more than anyone else."

"A silent partner?" I frowned. "Did he ever tell you who it was?"

"No, he didn't. He kept it quiet. But I know this partner had something to do with those land developers you mentioned."

A knot twisted in my gut. The land developers again. This whole thing was like a spider's web. "Do you think this partner is involved in the blackmail?""

"Yes," Delia said her voice firmer now, like she was certain. "I'm sure of it. William was a proud man, but for the last few months, fear had gripped him. More scared than I'd ever seen him. I think this partner—whoever they are—is the key to everything."

Delia's words sank in, deepening the mystery. A secret partner? This explained why William had been so tight-lipped in his later years. His blackmail must have come from more than just his involvement with the developers.

I chewed on my bottom lip. "Do you think there's any proof? Something we could use to identify this partner?"

"There might be," she said, hesitating. "William kept things hidden. I wasn't one to snoop, but I overheard him talking about important documents he kept at the shop. He always said, "If anything ever happens, you'll find what you need there.""

Of course, Van Horne kept secrets locked away in his shop. It was too perfect, too cliché, but it made sense.

"I need to get into that shop," I said, more to myself than to Delia.

"I'll make sure no one stops you," Delia said quickly. "You have my full permission to search through anything you need. Please, Chili, I need to know what' going on. I'm not sure I ever fully knew the man I was married to."

Her voice cracked on that last line, and something inside me softened. As much as Delia was part of this mess, she was also a victim in her own right; married to a man with more secrets than anyone deserved to carry.

"Thanks, Delia," I said gently. "I'll head over tomorrow and see what I can find."

We hung up, and I sat alone in the quiet of my apartment and stared at the ceiling for a moment, running through everything we had discussed.

William Van Horne had a secret partner. Someone tied to the land developers. Someone powerful enough to blackmail him, to make him afraid. And if this person was still out there, then I wasn't just chasing shadows. I was getting closer to the truth.

I tossed my phone onto the table, the sharp clatter breaking the stillness in the room. Everything felt off-kilter, like I was living in a half-dream. My house, usually my haven, seemed quiet, too empty. And I felt a presence. I rubbed my temples, trying to shake off the uneasiness settling over me.

But there it was again—that crawling sense of being watched, or followed, or ... something. I felt spooked, no doubt about it. That distorted voice from the phone call earlier that day still lingered in my ears, low and deliberate, like it had wrapped itself around my nerves and wouldn't let go.

I walked into the kitchen and poured myself a glass of water, my hand shaking just enough to spill a few drops on the counter. Almond watched me from her perch, her amber eyes unblinking. If only I had her kind of confidence.

"You're paranoid, Chili," I muttered to myself, staring down at the puddle. "Shake it off."

But as I reached to grab a tea towel, something out of the corner of my eye caught my attention. The sliding door to the back verandah—was barely open. Not enough to notice at first glance, but just enough to make my skin prickle. I stopped mid-motion, tea towel dangling in my hand, staring at the inch-wide gap.

Hadn't I locked that door earlier? I always locked it. It was automatic, a habit. And yet ... there it was, slightly ajar, the curtains fluttering in the soft night breeze.

My pulse quickened. I put the glass down slowly, trying to breathe through the growing tightness in my chest. I didn't want to jump to conclusions, but my mind was already racing ahead. A sliding door left unlocked. A warning call that was more than just words. Was it a coincidence, or was someone here?

I moved closer to the door, inch by inch, listening for anything that might break the silence. Nothing. No sound from the hallway, no shuffling footsteps. Just the soft hum of refrigerator. But the hairs on the back of my neck were standing up, every instinct screaming that something wasn't right.

Maybe I had forgotten to lock it. Maybe the wind had nudged it open. Maybe. But I knew better than to trust coincidences, especially after that phone call. My brain was going a mile a minute, analysing every scenario, every angle.

Had someone been inside my home? Or were they just letting me know they could be? The thought made my stomach flip.

I reached out and slid the door shut, locking it with a decisive click. Then I stepped back, eyeing it like it might open on its own. I turned and looked around the room, trying to shake the feeling that I wasn't alone.

Maybe I was just on edge, letting my imagination run wild after the call. Or maybe someone was playing with me, making sure I knew they had access, could get in anytime they wanted. It was a subtle threat, more unnerving than a straight-up attack.

I circled the apartment, double-checking the windows, the door, even the vents, like I'd suddenly fallen into a spy movie. But I found everything securely locked, exactly as it should be. Almond gave me a slow blink, as if to say, "You're losing it, lady."

Maybe she was right. But maybe she wasn't.

I pulled up the footage from the security cameras, my stomach twisting tighter with every second. The feed showed exactly what I was afraid of—someone had been here. In the grainy black-and-white video, a hooded figure moved through the hallway with ease, like they'd done it a hundred times. I replayed the video a few times, searching for any identifying marks, logos, or facial features which could give me a clue who it was. They were clever. No forced entry, no hesitation, no clues. They had a key. I leaned back, my heart thudding in my chest. No wonder the alarms hadn't gone off. They had access to my home through their own key. Whoever it was didn't need to break in—they belonged here. Or at least, they thought they did.

I grabbed my phone off the couch and considered calling Gideon. I could already picture him showing up, half-dressed and tired, looking at me like I was crazy. And maybe I was. Once he'd seen the video, though, he'd take me seriously, and things would spiral into something bigger, something I wasn't ready to face yet.

No. I couldn't drag him into this—not yet. Not when I wasn't even sure what 'this' was.

Instead, I sank back into the couch, my heart still racing, the glass of water abandoned on the counter. I tried to focus on the case, to push the nagging fear to the back of my mind.

But that door ... the way someone left it unlocked, just enough to make me question myself ... it was a message. Subtle. Clever. Designed to get under my skin, to make me doubt everything around me.

Well, congratulations, I thought. It's working.

I took a deep breath and closed my eyes, trying to calm the storm of thoughts racing through my head. I needed to focus, to think clearly. Whoever was behind this was smart. They wanted me to feel vulnerable, to hesitate.

I couldn't let them win.

Chapter 25

I spent a sleepless night with my phone and baseball bat in immediate reach. Almond didn't seem to have the same problem. She'd curled up on the pillow next to me tail tucked firmly around her, and resisted the urge to keep me company.

I envied her. No thoughts of mysterious phone calls, or unlocked doors, or faceless threats to disturb her slumber.

I couldn't get the sound of that voice out of my head. The message, low and growling, replayed over and over in my brain: Stop sticking your nose in where it doesn't belong.

It was almost dawn when I gave up on sleeping entirely. There was no peace to be found between these sheets. Instead, I threw on yesterday's jeans, tied my hair back, and grabbed the car keys. I needed answers more than I needed sleep. And Van Horne's shop was calling to me like a beacon of unfinished business.

The streets were empty, the city still caught in that strange pre-dawn quiet when even the traffic seemed to hush. The jewellery shop loomed ahead, its sign dark, windows reflecting the faintest glimmers of streetlights. There was something almost eerie about it at this hour, like the building itself knew more than it let on. Secrets hidden in plain sight.

I reversed down the laneway next to the shop, just in case. Not that I expected anyone to be watching at this hour—but paranoia had its perks. Sliding out of the truck, I hurried, not letting my gaze linger on any one spot for too long. The air was biting, which made me regret not bringing a jacket. Hopefully, I wouldn't be long.

I punched in the code Delia had given me, tapping it into the lockbox mounted on the wall just outside the back door. It sprang open to reveal the key lying just inside. I picked it up, the metal cold in my hand, and inserted it into the lock.

The door creaked as I pushed it open, and I winced at the sound. So much for being stealthy. The place smelled faintly of old wood and dust, with that metallic tang of forgotten jewellery lingering in the air. The counters gleamed under the faint light I flicked on, casting long shadows across the floor. I stepped deeper into the shop, my sneakers making the faintest squeak on the linoleum as I went.

"Alright, Van Horne," I muttered to myself, casting the beam of my flashlight around, "what were you hiding?"

The office in the back was cramped, Coco's jar of biscuits no longer sat on the counter and, along one wall, filing cabinets that looked as ancient as the store itself. I started there, fingers running over the handles of the drawers, hoping for some obvious clue. But no. Just the regular business files, invoices, receipts—nothing that screamed money laundering or blackmail. Nothing I didn't already know.

I searched through the drawers and workspace on the counter, moving paperwork and even checking under the keyboard pad for the computer. Nothing.

I sat in the worn chair and swivelled slowly from side to side, examining the room, trying to see if anything was out of place. I had just given up when I saw it behind the water cooler, an anomaly in the corner where the walls met.

The seam in the wall looked out of place, barely noticeable but just enough to raise suspicion. I manhandled the cooler to one side and peered at the area, running a hand along it. The plaster felt uneven. With a slight push, the panel shifted, revealing a hidden compartment.

Inside the hollowed-out space, nestled securely, was a small, key-locked safe.

I smiled, recalling my first job working for a locksmith back in high school. Mr. Harrow, my boss, was a grouchy genius who taught me everything from cutting keys to picking locks. "You never know when this'll come in handy," he'd said, handing me my first set of lock picks. He wasn't wrong.

I pulled the slim tools from my bag, grateful I'd kept them all these years. Mr. Harrow's voice echoed in my mind: *Patience and precision. The lock tells you everything you need to know if you're willing to listen.*

Kneeling before the safe, I inserted the tension wrench first, applying just enough pressure to hold the mechanism steady, and then slid in the pick; its slender tip seeking out the pins inside.

My fingers moved with practiced easy, probing gently, feeling for the faintest resistance. The first pin gave a satisfying click. Then the second. Each one fell into place, the lock's internal mechanics yielding to my steady rhythm. Sweat pricked at my temple, the smallest misstep could reset the entire process.

Finally the last pin clicked and the lock turned with a soft *snap*. A wave of relief swept over me as the safe's door creaked open, revealing its hidden contents.

Inside, there were stacks of papers, yellowed and frayed at the edges, but carefully organised. My heart thudded as I pulled them out, spreading them across the floor like puzzle pieces. Fake diamond certifications. That, I expected. Van Horne had been pushing these for years, making a killing off of unsuspecting clients. But that wasn't all.

Financial records. Bank transfers that led nowhere—no, wait. They led everywhere. Offshore accounts, shady transactions, amounts that didn't add up. It wasn't just about the diamonds.

I'd been right. Hed been laundering money for someone. The developers. They were in deeper than I'd realised.

My stomach twisted as I uncovered the last piece of the puzzle: a blackmail note. The handwriting was precise, almost elegant, but the message was chilling. Do as you re told, or this won't end well for you. No signature, of course. But I knew who was behind it. The developers had Van Horne under their thumb, using his business as a front for their dirty money.

And now he was dead.

I photographed everything and then shoved the papers back into the safe. This was big. Bigger than I'd thought. Bigger than just a missing diamond or a corrupt jeweler. This was a full-blown operation. Blackmail, fraud, murder. And I was right in the middle of it.

I had just cracked the door open and was about to leave when something tugged at my senses. A shift in the air. A strange, almost pungent scent. I froze, sniffing the air. Cigarette smoke. Faint but unmistakable; the smell of burnt tobacco mingled with the hint of something sweet and slightly acrid. My pulse quickened. I pulled the door closed, and I moved cautiously toward the front of the shop, peeking through the window.

Across the road, half-hidden in the shadows, was a car I hadn't noticed before. It was parked too far from any house to belong to a neighbour. And there, by the driver's side window, was the tell-tale orange glow of a cigarette. Someone was sitting there. Watching.

I stepped back from the window, my heart hammering in my chest. My mind raced through possibilities, but none of them were good. Was it the developers? Someone trying to spook me, make sure I knew they were watching? Or was I just being paranoid?

No. The smoke. The car. The cigarette. This wasn't just paranoia. I stayed low, creeping back into the office.

My hands trembled slightly as I reopened the safe and shoved the contents into a duffle bag I found under the desk, my nerves fraying at the edges. I couldn't risk leaving anything behind in case anyone else found it. Whoever was outside hadn't made a move yet, but the message was clear enough—they wanted me to know they were there.

Just as I was about to push the safe door closed, I noticed a small hole in the floor of it right in the far corner. Putting the bag down, I knelt, put my finger in it and lifted. The panel came away to reveal a secret compartment filled with bags containing jewellery, passports, and photos. I scooped up everything I could find, closed the safe, slid the wall back, and moved the water cooler to its original position. Satisfied that everything was back to normal, I glanced at the door, considering my options. If I left now, they'd see me. They already knew I was inside. What were they waiting for? I had to get out of there, but I couldn't let them know I was nervous.

Taking a deep breath, I squared my shoulders, trying to calm the frantic beating of my heart. I moved as quietly as I could, back toward the front, peeking through the window once more. The cigarette was still glowing faintly in the darkness, a small, ominous beacon. Whoever was out there, they weren't leaving soon.

Clutching the duffle bag close to my side, I slipped out the side door, keeping to the shadows as I made my way back to the car. My every nerve was on high alert, expecting a figure to appear from behind a building, or worse, from that car down the street. But nothing. The cigarette was still glowing. They were letting me leave—for now.

I started the car and pulled away, forcing myself to breathe deeply and relax.

I glanced into the rear-view mirror and watched as the black sedan pulled out, its headlights glaring, staying a careful distance behind me. Far enough to seem inconspicuous, but close enough to send a chill down my spine.

My grip tightened on the steering wheel. Turning onto a quieter street, I made a sudden left, then a quick right, trying to throw them off without being obvious.

Still, the car followed. Panic gnawed at the edges of my composure. Going straight home wasn't an option—not if they were tracking me.

I drove aimlessly for a few blocks, weaving through familiar streets in a clumsy attempt to lose them. At one point I thought about pulling over, demanding to know what they wanted but my better judgement kept me moving. At a red light I glanced back. The car was gone, swallowed by the darkness as if it had never been there.

The air felt heavier as I drove toward a well-lit café instead of home, needing time to think.

I wasn't sure what I'd do with the safes contents just yet—but one thing was clear—it was probably time to swallow my pride and talk to Gideon.

He would not be happy when I did.

Chapter 26

The sun had been up for a few hours when a knock came at the door. The steady thud jarred me from the file I'd been reading, and I hesitated before getting up. A sense of dread crept up my spine as I reached for my phone, checking the security camera.

Gideon.

I stared at the screen, my pulse quickening. Of all the people who could have shown up today, he was the last person I expected to see standing on my doorstep. He hadn't called. He hadn't texted. Just him, standing there with that same brooding look he wore far too often these days. His hand rose, poised to knock again, but he paused, as if reconsidering.

For a split second, I considered not answering, letting him stand there until he got the message and walked away. But that wasn't me. Even if it felt like we were galaxies apart right now, I couldn't avoid him forever.

I unlocked the door and pulled it open, the sunlight spilling in behind him. His eyes met mine, unreadable, but I could sense something just below the surface—tension, regret, something unspoken.

"Chili," he said, his voice rougher than usual.

I crossed my arms, leaning against the doorframe, my heart pounding in my chest. "What are you doing here, Gideon?"

He shifted his weight, his gaze momentarily dropping to the ground before meeting mine again. "Your dad told me I needed to see you. He's worried about you."

I bristled at the mention of my father. "So, what, you're here on his orders? I don't need anyone checking up on me, least of all you."

Gideon stepped closer, and I instinctively backed up a fraction, trying to maintain the wall between us that had been building for weeks. "It's not just about your dad. I'm worried too. You've been shutting everyone out, burying yourself in this investigation like you don't care what happens to you."

"What I do is none of your concern, Gideon. You're the one who wanted space, remember?"

His eyes flashed. "This isn't about space. This is about you diving headfirst into something that could get you killed. You're being irresponsible."

"Irresponsible?" I laughed, though it held no humour. "You don't get to stand there and lecture me about how I handle things. You're the one who's kept me at arm's length, Gideon. Every time I get close to the truth, you pull me back."

"I'm trying to protect you, Chili. Whether you believe that or not is up to you," Gideon said, his tone firm but not unkind.

"I don't need protection," I snapped. "I need answers. About Coco, about the Van Horne's, and about whatever it is you're not telling me."

Gideon took a deep breath, his expression softening as he stepped closer, closing the space between us. "I'm not the enemy here," he said quietly.

"Then stop acting like one," I whispered, the words catching in my throat, barely audible past the lump that had formed.

Every instinct screamed at me to keep my distance, to lock him out like I had so many others. But the truth gnawed at me, raw and insistent. I couldn't do this alone anymore—not if I wanted to uncover what was really going on. With a sigh, I stepped aside and motioned for him to come in. "There's something you need to know," I said, my voice softer now. "I found something."

Gideon's brow furrowed as he stepped past me into the house, the tension between us still palpable. He didn't say anything—just waited.

I closed the door behind us, unsure how to continue. Maisie could wait for now. What mattered more was the safe and its contents—it felt like the key to everything we'd been chasing.

I led Gideon into the living room, where the coffee table was cluttered with files, photos, and documents. It was a mess—papers scattered everywhere, none of it organised. I noticed his gaze linger on the pile before returning to me, his silence pressing me to explain further. He took a seat on the couch, but his body was tense, coiled like he was ready to spring into action. "Okay, what is all this?"

I sat down across from him, rubbing my hands together as I tried to figure out where to begin. "I found everything here in the Van Hornes' safe."

His eyes widened slightly, but he didn't interrupt. He just waited, his patience unsettling.

"Delia knew there was a safe in the store, but she didn't know where it was." I shrugged. "She gave me the key to the shop and asked me to find it, hoping whatever was inside could clear her husband's name."

"Go on."

I gestured to the stack of documents on the table. "I found these. Some of it's blackmail material—photos, emails, private correspondences. It's all here. People being pressured to do favours for land developers. Politicians, business owners ... they're all involved."

Gideon leaned forward, his expression sharpening. "Blackmail?"

I nodded. "That's just the start." I picked up a sheet and handed it to him. "Fake diamond certifications. Dozens of them. They've been passing off synthetic diamonds as the real thing, inflating prices and laundering the money through shell companies."

He stared at the document, the gravity of my words sinking in. "Money laundering and fraud. This is huge."

"And there's more." I slid a series of bank statements across the table. "Offshore accounts. They've been funnelling money through these for years. It's systematic, almost too well-organised."

Gideon exhaled sharply, tapping his fingers against the couch. "Chili ... how did you even get your hands on this?"

"I told you, Delia gave me the key to the store," I replied, frustration creeping into my voice.

He raised an eyebrow. "And you broke into the safe?"

That wasn't a topic I wanted him lingering on—especially since carrying lock-picking tools, and using them, could land me in serious trouble.

Gideon's eyes widened as he flipped through the bank statements, his brow furrowing deeper with each page. "This is ... extensive," he muttered, more to himself than to me. "Van Horne must have been running this scheme for years, right under our noses."

I leaned forward, my earlier frustration fading as I focused on the evidence. "It's not just him. Look at the transaction dates. Some of these go back years—long before William Van Horne even moved here."

Gideon's expression darkened. "You think there are more people involved?"

"I'd bet my last cup of coffee on it." I tapped one of the documents, pointing out a pattern. "See these transfers? They're too regular, too precise. This isn't just one person's dirty laundry. It's a full-blown operation."

I couldn't help but feel a small sense of satisfaction. "Still think I'm being reckless?"

He shot me a pointed look, though his tone was calmer. "That doesn't change the fact that going back to that store was incredibly dangerous, Chili. You could've been caught—or worse."

"But I wasn't," I countered, leaning in. He didn't need to know about the car following me, not yet. "And now we've got proof. This isn't just about a random murder anymore. Whoever's behind this is deep in illegal activity, Gideon. This could be the key to unravelling everything."

"You're right. This could be enough to blow the whole thing wide open."

"Exactly." I leaned back, crossing my arms. "But now we need to figure out what happens next. The developers don't seem like the kind of people who'll just let this slide."

Gideon leaned forward, his brow furrowed as he sifted through the documents, his fingers tracing the edges of the pages. He was quiet, focused, his eyes scanning each line like he was piecing together a puzzle only he could see. I watched him, the familiar tension in his jaw, the way his eyes darkened when he was deep in thought. Even now, after everything, there was a steadiness to him I couldn't deny.

He wasn't just a cop to me—not anymore.

As we sat, Almond, my cat, padded softly across the floor, her tail flicking from side to side as she approached the couch. She brushed against Gideon's leg, but when he didn't notice, she turned her attention to me. I reached down, pulling her onto my lap, grateful for the minor distraction. Stroking her fur helped calm the storm inside me, if only for a moment.

"There's more," I said my voice barely above a whisper. And there was.

So much more that I hadn't told him yet.

Chapter 27

Gideon's head snapped up, his eyes locking onto mine. "More? What do you mean 'more'?"

"Morgan's involved," I said, bracing myself for his reaction.

He sighed. "Why doesn't that surprise me?"

I shifted on the seat and thought about everything Morgan had shared with me. "He didn't know what he was getting involved in, at least not at first."

Gideon frowned, crossing his arms. "Do you believe him?"

"I do," I said. "Morgan may be a lot of things, an idiot being one of them, but he's not a felon. He didn't realise what was happening until it was too late."

Gideon shook his head, clearly unconvinced. "He's mixed up with a smuggling operation. That puts him in very dangerous territory."

"I know," I admitted. "But he's not the mastermind behind the operation. He's just ... caught in the middle."

Gideon pinched the bridge of his nose. "Caught in the middle or not, he's still involved in a criminal enterprise. I can't just ignore that, Chili."

I leaned forward, my voice urgent. "I'm not asking you to ignore it; I'm asking you to help me figure out who's really behind all of this. Morgan's just a pawn in their game."

"A pawn who made a choice," Gideon countered, but I could see the conflict in his eyes.

"Maybe," I conceded. "But he's also our best lead. He knows things, Gideon. Things that could help arrest everyone involved."

Gideon was quiet for a long moment, his gaze fixed on the documents spread out before us. When he finally spoke, his voice was low, almost resigned. "What else did Morgan tell you?"

I took a deep breath, steeling myself. "He overheard conversations. Names. Dates. Locations. I think the Van Horne's are just the tip of the iceberg."

Gideon's eyebrows shot up. "What names are we talking about?"

"Big ones," I said. "Including someone in the police department."

Gideon cursed under his breath. "This is getting more complicated by the minute. We need to tread carefully, Chili."

"I know. But we can't just sit on this information. People could be in danger."

"Including you," Gideon said, his eyes meeting mine with an intensity that made my breath catch. "If what Morgan's saying is true, and someone in the department is involved, we're dealing with people who have a lot of power and influence. They won't hesitate to silence anyone who threatens their operation."

For a moment, we just looked at each other, the air between us thick with unspoken words and the undeniable pull of the history that connected us. Something in his eyes softened, like he wanted to say more, but then he cleared his throat, breaking the spell.

"Alright," Gideon said, his tone shifting into something more professional. "We need a plan. We can't go to the department with this yet, not until we know who we can trust. But we also can't handle this alone." He ran his hand across his jaw. "I have a friend in a task force who can help. I'll give them a ring once we've gone sorted through the paperwork."

I nodded, feeling the seriousness of the situation settle in. Gideon was right—we were in over our heads, and one wrong move could unravel everything we had uncovered.

"In the meantime, I want you to write everything Morgan told you," Gideon continued, his voice steady and firm. "Every detail, no matter how small it might seem. We need to know exactly what we're dealing with."

"Already done." I picked up my notepad detailing my conversation with Morgan and handed it to him. He removed the papers from the pad, took an evidence bag from his pocket and placed them in it.

Gideon's jaw tightened as if he were wrestling with something. "Chili, promise me something."

"What?" I asked, wary of the intensity in his gaze.

"No more solo investigations. No more breaking into places or confronting suspects on your own. We do this together, or not at all." He paused, his voice softening. "What if they were to break in here? I can't risk losing you as well."

I felt ill. Someone *had* been in my house. They'd used a key. I admitted as much to Gideon.

"Why didn't you tell me?" Shock filled his voice. "Do you really think that little of me that you wouldn't say something?"

"I'm sorry," I said, guilt twisting in my chest. "It wasn't that—I just didn't want to worry you." I hesitated, then added, "I've got security footage. You should see it." I pulled up the footage, my stomach tightening as I fast-forwarded through the timestamps. Then, there it was—a hooded figure moving through the grainy image.

My chest tightened.

Gideon leaned closer, studying the screen. "Looks more like a young man than someone tied to a vast criminal enterprise," he said after a moment. "In my experience they don't tend to wear hoodies or pet cats."

He straightened and squeezed my hand. "Still it must've been scary for you."

"It was," I admitted, my voice barely above a whisper. The memory of knowing someone had been inside still made my skin crawl.

"I really don't think they'd have access to a key," he said, his voice steady. Then he frowned. "Could it be one of the original set of keys that came with the house?

I hadn't thought of that. Checking the time, I grabbed my phone and sent a quick message to Mary the owner. Her reply came back almost immediately: her nephew had a key when he was staying with them but lost it. I sent her a photo still from the security footage and she confirmed it looked him.

When I told Gideon he nodded, satisfied. "I think I might get someone at the station to have a friendly chat with him. Just to be on the safe side."

We spent the next hour combing through the papers, piecing together timelines, names, and transactions. The more we uncovered, the clearer the scope of the operation became. I highlighted names and noted potential links between the Van Hornes and various shady businesses.

As I worked, I caught Gideon glancing at me from time to time, his expression a mixture of admiration and concern. It was both reassuring and unnerving. The warmth in his gaze that made me feel seen, but it also reminded me of the risks we were taking.

"What are you thinking?" he finally asked, breaking the silence.

"Just gathering my thoughts." I forced a smile, but my mind was racing. Was Morgan truly innocent, or was he playing us all? And then there was Maisie. I hadn't forgotten her. She was another thread in this tangled mess, but asking Gideon about her now wouldn't help. Not yet.

When I finally leaned back in my chair, fatigue washed over me. "I think we've made some genuine progress."

Gideon glanced at the mess of papers spread across the table, a hint of satisfaction in his eyes. "Yeah, we have. Great work." He smiled, a brief flash of warmth cutting through the heaviness of our task. "And Chili?"

"Yeah?"

"Just remember, no more solo runs, alright?"

"Alright," I promised, though I knew the temptation to act on my own would be hard to ignore.

Gideon's hand brushed mine, so softly I almost missed it. I glanced up, surprised by the look in his eyes—something different, something I'd almost given up hoping for. My heart stuttered, and before I could process what was happening, he leaned in. His lips met mine, gentle and hesitant, like he was giving me the chance to stop him. But I didn't move. I couldn't. The kiss was soft, careful, and for a moment, the noise of everything else faded. Just his warmth, his breath against mine, and the quiet space between us.

I didn't want it to end.

When Gideon finally pulled away, I felt dizzy, my mind struggling to process what had just happened. His eyes searched mine, a mix of vulnerability and determination in their depths.

"I'm sorry," he whispered. "I shouldn't have—"

"Don't," I interrupted, my voice matched his. "Don't apologise."

He nodded, a small smile tugging at the corner of his mouth. "Okay."

We sat there for a moment, the air between us charged with possibility and uncertainty. Part of me wanted to throw caution to the wind, to lose myself in the warmth of his embrace and forget about the danger lurking just beyond these walls. But the rational part of my brain—the part that had gotten me this far as a PI—knew we couldn't afford such a luxury.

I still had one more thing to tell him. I hesitated, knowing that once I told him what I'd discovered, our worlds would change forever. A part of me wanted to be selfish, to build on this moment and explore the possibilities of a future with this man. To dream and plan like normal couples.

I just hoped he wouldn't hate me when I was done.

As he stood to leave, I took a deep breath and swallowed hard, my fingernails driving into my palms. "There's one more thing."

He squeezed my shoulder, giving me his full attention. "Go on."

I stood up and walked over to a cupboard and retrieved a box from it. I could feel my heart pounding in my chest as I stared at it. My palms were sweaty, my breath shaky. I didn't want to say it, didn't want to drop this on him, but I had no choice.

"Gideon," I said, my voice barely above a whisper, "I found something else. In the safe, hidden." My hands trembled as I dumped the contents on the table—jewellery, passports, small things that shouldn't have meant anything. But I knew they did.

As his fingers made contact with the items a mix of emotions flitted across his face like fleeting shadows. The confusion etched on his brow gave way to a growing horror that twisted his features. When his hand closed around a watch, he froze. He sat down hard and the colour drained from his face. He turned it over in his hand, staring at it like it might disappear.

"This ... this was hers," he said, voice strangled. His eyes met mine, wide with shock and something darker, rawer. "It's Sarah's. It has her name engraved on the back. How is this possible? She went missing five years ago."

My stomach twisted, guilt and fear crashing over me in waves. I opened my mouth, but nothing came out. I didn't know how to fix this, how to make any of this okay.

The silence that followed was deafening. I watched as Gideon's fingers trembled around the watch, his knuckles turning white. The pain etched across his face was almost unbearable to witness.

"Gideon," I whispered, reaching out to touch his arm. He flinched away, his eyes never leaving the watch.

"How?" he repeated, his voice hoarse. "How is this possible?"

I swallowed hard, trying to find the right words. "I don't know. But I think ... I think it means that Sarah's disappearance is a part of all of this. The Van Hornes', the diamond smuggling, everything."

Gideon's head snapped up, his eyes blazing with a mixture of grief and fury. "You're telling me that the people responsible for my pregnant wife's disappearance have been right under my nose this entire time?"

Chapter 28

I nodded, the ache in my chest spreading as I searched for the right words. "I think so. Gideon, I ... I'm so sorry. I didn't know this would lead here when I started digging."

He shot up from his chair so fast it scraped against the floor; the sound making me wince.

Back and forth he paced, like a caged animal desperate to break free, his movements sharp and agitated. His hands flexed open and closed at his sides, the veins in his forearms standing out as he clenched his fists. Rage poured off him in waves, the heat of his anger an almost palpable force.

"Five years," he muttered, his voice low and trembling with rage. "Five years I've been chasing shadows—every lead, every dead end. And they've been here all along. Here. Living their lives like nothing happened, like they didn't ruin mine."

I stood too, my legs shaky under me, but I couldn't stay still. The energy in the room was electric, dangerous. I took a small step toward him, keeping my voice soft, careful. "Gideon ... we don't know everything yet." I reached out and touched his arm, just lightly. This time, he didn't flinch or pull away. "We need to slow down, be smart about this. If we don't ..." I hesitated, choosing my words. "We could lose everything."

He turned so fast I felt my breath catch. His eyes burned—wild, red-rimmed, and desperate. "Smart? You want me to be smart?" His voice cracked on the last word. "Chili, they took my wife. They took my unborn baby. Do you know what it's like? Five years of wondering—if they were alive, if I'd ever find them, if—" His voice broke completely, and he bent over a groan escaping from his lips.

A lump rose in my throat. "I know," I whispered, my hand tightening on his arm. "I know. And we're going to figure this out. Every piece. But if we rush in without thinking, without being sure ... they might never get the justice they deserve."

He stood there for a long, agonising moment, his chest heaving as he stared past me at something I couldn't see. Then he exhaled a shaky breath. "You're right," he said, his voice raw and broken. For a long moment, he stood frozen, his chest rising and falling as he fought to rein in the storm inside him. Then, finally, he drew a deep, shuddering breath and ran a hand through his already dishevelled hair. "You're right," he repeated, his voice stripped bare. "Of course, you're right. But it doesn't make this any easier."

The walls seemed to close in on us. The air in the room was thick—dense with emotions neither of us knew how to name, let alone confront. Outside, the wind howled, shaking the house to its bones. Tree branches scraped against the roof, and the windows rattled in their frames as if trying to break free. A low growl of thunder rolled in the distance, a warning of the storm to come. Inside, though, the veritable storm raged in Gideon.

I stayed quiet, giving him room to pace. His boots thudded dully against the worn floorboards as he moved from one side of the room to the other. One hand trailed along the edge of my desk, brushing against the small, scattered details of my life—family photos in mismatched frames, a cold cup of coffee with a faint lipstick smear on the rim, the pile of case files I hadn't yet filed away. His fingers paused briefly on one frame, the photo of me and my mum at the beach. He didn't look at it long, though. He saw an old murder book I'd dug out, where I'd pinned the pieces of my private investigation into his wife's disappearance were—newspaper clippings curling at the edges, surveillance photos so grainy they were almost useless, and notes scrawled in my barely legible shorthand.

I could see the tension in his shoulders from where I stood, with his whole body coiled tight, ready to spring. The anger was still there, simmering beneath the surface, but it had given way to something heavier. Grief, maybe. Or the exhaustion that only comes when you've carried too much for too long.

"Gideon ..." I started, but my voice faltered. What could I say? What could make this right?

He stood still, his back to me, one hand braced against the wall as if he needed it to stay upright. When he finally turned to face me, his eyes were shining with a grief so deep it made my chest ache.

"I can't do this," he said, his voice hoarse. "Not right now. I just ..." He shook his head. "I need air."

Before I could respond, he strode to the door, yanking it open with more force than necessary. The door slammed against the wall, making me jump, and for a moment, I thought he was gone. But then I heard it—the sharp intake of breath, the awkward shuffle of feet.

Morgan stood in the doorway, one hand raised as if he'd been about to knock. His expression shifted from surprise to confusion as Gideon shouldered past him, nearly knocking him off balance. Morgan spun on his heel to watch him go, his mouth opening as if to call out, but I shook my head.

"Leave him," I said.

Morgan turned back to me, his brow furrowed. "What's going on?"

I stepped aside and gestured for him to come in, my stomach churning as I tried to find the right words. He hesitated for a moment, rain dripping off his hair before stepping inside, closing the door behind him.

"It's a long story," I said, my voice heavy. I grabbed a towel from the cupboard and gave it to him. He shook off his jacket, hung it on the coat rack, and dried his hair. I sank into the chair Gideon had vacated moments ago, closing my eyes. "We found something that none of us were ready for."

Morgan's gaze shifted to the table, taking in the chaos of evidence there. His eyes narrowed as he tried to piece it together.

"What did you find?" he asked his voice low.

I leaned back; the chair creaking under my weight, and gestured to the table. "For five years, Gideon has been searching—digging through every lead, chasing down every shadow, trying to find them. His wife and unborn child." My voice wavered as I spoke, the weight of it hitting me all over again. "All we know is ... her watch was in the Van Horne's safe."

Morgan blinked, confusion flickering across his face. "Her watch?"

I nodded, feeling the knot in my chest tighten. "The one she was wearing the day they disappeared. Gideon gave it to her as a wedding gift—he had their initials engraved on the back. There's no mistaking it."

Morgan's eyes darted to the table, then back to me. "But that doesn't mean ..." He trailed off, as though afraid to say the words aloud.

"No, it doesn't mean they're dead," I said, my voice flat. "But it doesn't mean they're live, either. It means someone knows what happened. Someone had that watch all this time and hid it away."

"What do the Van Horne's have to do with this?"

I shrugged. "All I know is the watch was in a bag containing other items. That bag was in the safe."

"How did you get it?" he asked, then held up his hands to ward off my answer. "Forget I asked."

He stared at me for a few seconds as his expression darkened, his jaw tightening. "And Gideon? How's he taking it?"

I let out a shaky breath. "He's barely holding it together. That watch was hope for him, Morgan. Proof that he hasn't been chasing shadows all these years. But it's also a slap in the face—a reminder that whoever did this has been living their life, free and untouched, while he' been drowning in grief."

Morgan rubbed the back of his neck, his eyes fixed on the table again. The storm outside rattled the windowpanes, as if echoing the tension in the room.

"So, what now?" he asked finally, his voice low but steady.

I exhaled, the sound shaky, and met his gaze. "Now ... we have to find out the truth. All of it. Because if we're wrong about this—or if we act too soon—it could destroy Gideon. For good this time."

The room fell silent, save for the storm's relentless howl.

Morgan nodded slowly. "Then we'd better get it right," he said.

Chapter 29

Two days had gone passed before I heard from Gideon. He'd ignored my messages and calls and while initially I was concerned, now I was just plain ticked off.

His message this morning was short and straight to the point. *Meet me at the morgue. You bring coffee, I'll bring lunch.*

As far as dates went, it wasn't the worst invitation I'd ever had.

The morgue was colder than I'd expected. I'd been in plenty of morgues before—came with the territory—but this one felt like a freezer someone forgot to defrost. It was the kind of cold that burrowed under your skin if you stood still too long. The autopsy room was in the hospital basement. Stark and clinical, the walls tiled in white to ensure easy cleaning. Overhead lights cast a harsh, sterile glow, reflecting off steel countertops and a gleaming metal examination table at the centre. Cabinets lined one wall, neatly labelled, while the faint scent of disinfectant and chemicals I couldn't name lingered in the cold air. Against one wall, a rolling cabinet held a variety of surgical tools and photographic equipment, while on the wall above was an x-ray box.

I approached the autopsy table where Gideon was waiting. I took a steadying breath and steeled myself as I looked down at the body, the mottled skin a harsh reminder of a life snuffed out too soon. The bruises and pale discoloration told a story of pain and struggle, each mark cruelly testifying to a life stolen. Her name had been Harper Foley. Last week she'd been alive.

Gideon stood beside me, arms crossed, face tight. Both of us were wearing the required PPE; boots, gloves, gowns, face shield and hair nets, to avoid cross-contamination. He said little, but then, he never did when it mattered most. I glanced at him out of the corner of my eye, wondering if he was seeing the same thing I was: the bruises on Harper's wrists, the faint marks around her neck that screamed restraint, not accident.

"This wasn't random," I said, my voice barely above a whisper.

"No," he agreed, and the weight of that single word felt like it could crush us both.

The silence that followed stretched like elastic, tight and ready to snap. I turned away from Harper's body, swallowing hard against the bile rising in my throat. I wasn't squeamish—I couldn't afford to be—but something about this case was digging its claws into me. Maybe it was the way Harper's face still looked surprised, like she couldn't believe how it had all ended. Or maybe it was the thought that this was how Gideon's wife may have ended up; we just hadn't found her body.

I curled my hands into fists, rocked back on my heels, and concentrated.

"Do you think the boyfriend was behind this?"

He shook his head. "No. His alibi checks out. In fact, the alibies of everyone who knew Harper check out."

"So what do you think happened?"

"I can't confirm it until after the autopsy, but it seems like someone kidnapped her, tortured her, and somehow she either escaped or died while in her kidnapper's hands and got dumped."

My stomach sank. Even though the evidence hadn't caught up yet, Van Horne had scrawled his name all over this. The problem was, from what we'd seen, it wasn't a syndicate you could pin down. They slid through loopholes, bought off the right people, and made anyone who got too close vanish without a trace. "You think Barrett'll listen?" I asked.

Gideon sighed, the sound heavy with frustration. "Barrett's tricky. I'm not sure he can be trusted, but I've been in touch with someone on the task force. They're making inquiries."

That was the thing about small towns: everyone knew everyone, but loyalty always came at a cost. Barrett's price? Van Horne's allies could pay it easily.

I glanced back at Harper, swallowing the lump in my throat. Someone had to care about her, even if it was just me. I resisted the urge to remove my clammy hands from the gloves. She'd been a student once. Someone's daughter. Someone's friend. Now she was a case in a file.

Gideon stood next to me, quiet as a shadow. His expression was unreadable, the way it always got when the world tipped a little too far out of balance. I wanted to say something, but what do you say in a morgue, standing over a young woman who deserved better?

Gideon's phone buzzed and we left the room, moving into an antechamber where we removed the PPE and disposed of it in the hazardous waste bin. I scrubbed my hands until they were raw and joined Gideon in the waiting room.

We were only there a few minutes when the door opened, and a tall man with salt-and-pepper hair walked in, his brightly coloured scrubs at odds with his job. He nodded at us briskly, setting a clipboard down on the counter. "Sorry to keep you waiting. I'm Dr. Patel."

"Chili Beane," I said, offering my hand, though it felt strange, almost too polite, given the circumstances.

Patel glanced at his notes and then gestured toward Harper. "We haven't completed the full autopsy yet, but I can share some preliminary findings. It appears the cause of death was an undiagnosed heart condition. The heightened stress she experienced likely triggered a fatal episode. The bruising on her wrists suggests she was restrained for an extended period, and suffered extensive abuse."

I glanced at Gideon, whose jaw was tight, a muscle twitching near his temple. He was looking at Harper like he could will her back to life, just to give her a fighting chance.

"Anything else?" I asked, my voice steadier than I felt.

Patel hesitated, flipping a page on his clipboard. "We found traces of adhesive residue consistent with duct tape. Those findings, combined with the ligature marks, point to her being held against her will. It's consistent with similar cases we've seen."

The room suddenly felt smaller, like the walls were pressing in. I needed air. "Thank you, Doctor," Gideon said. "We'll let you get back to it."

The staff room was a little better, mostly because it opened out onto a courtyard with a few overgrown shrubs and a crooked wooden bench. Contrary to his promise, he'd forgotten to bring lunch. Gideon handed me a ham sandwich from the vending machine. "Eat," he said, sitting down heavily.

I un-wrapped the plastic, but my appetite was non-existent. "She didn't deserve this," I said.

"No one does," he replied, staring at the ground.

We sat in silence for a while; the breeze carrying the faintest hint of eucalyptus. Just as I thought I could breathe again, my phone buzzed on the table. Maisie McClintock's name flashed on the screen.

I hesitated, glancing at Gideon, but answered. "Maisie?"

"You need to know this," she said, her voice sharp and urgent. "The property deals? They're tied to the mayor's cousin. He's targeting struggling homeowners, forcing them out. Chili, I think the mayor's in on it."

My stomach twisted. I didn't know what angered me more—that the town's highest office might be corrupt, or that Maisie, of all people, was the one bringing me the news.

"What is it?" Gideon asked, his voice sharp with concern.

I looked at my phone, absorbing Maisie's words before repeating them. "She said those property deals are tied to the mayor," I repeated.

Gideon's brows furrowed but, he said nothing. I felt like a knot twisted in my stomach.

"Is that Gideon with you?"

I looked at him, hesitating for a moment. "Yep, he's right here."

"Can you tell him thanks again for the other night?" Maisie continued her tone light but still edged with something else. "My ex got the message. I don't think he's going to be bothering me any longer."

My heart skipped a beat. "What message?"

"Tony's been pestering me," she said, the words coming out in a rush. "He wants to get back together."

I felt the air leave my lungs, a mix of anger and disbelief filling the space between us. "What? That's horrible. Are you alright?"

"I am now," she said, and I could almost hear her smile through the phone. "After Gideon's charade, I'm fine. He pretending to be the new love of my life did the trick. Tony has left town to head back east."

I exhaled in relief. "Wow. That's great news."

"It sure is," she said, her voice warmer now. "I have to go; I just wanted to let you know what I found out."

"Thanks, I'll look into it," I replied, ending the call with a soft sigh. Gideon hadn't moved on after all. There was still hope for us.

Gideon raised an eyebrow as I put the phone down. "What was that about?"

I stood up, my mind already shifting back to the case. "Corruption," I said, my voice tight with resolve. "It looks like the mayor's going down."

Chapter 30

I splashed cold water on my face, hoping it would cool the heat crawling up my neck. It didn't help. The hospital bathroom was stuffy, the fluorescent lights buzzing overhead, and my reflection looked about as frazzled as I felt. I was supposed to meet Gideon in the lobby, but I needed a minute to pull myself together.

Drying my hands, I smoothed my hair back and headed for the door. That's when I heard him.

Gideon's voice.

It came from just outside, low and urgent, but I could make out the words. I froze, my fingers still gripping the bathroom door.

"I told you, Barrett, it's all connected." His tone was sharp, like he was holding back anger. Or fear.

Barrett's response was muffled, but it didn't matter. My focus was locked on Gideon's next words.

"Chili has the evidence. From Van Horne's safe." A pause, then, quieter, "If they figure that out, she's dead. Hell, we both might be."

I leaned closer, my stomach flipping. Evidence? Dead? My pulse quickened, and I held my breath, afraid to miss anything.

"Plus," Gideon continued, his voice thick. "I think ... I think it's tied to Sarah."

The air left my lungs in a rush. Sarah. His wife.

Another pause and this time Barrett's voice came through clearer. "You think this is the same trafficking ring?"

Gideon didn't answer right away. When he finally spoke, his voice was tight with worry. "I don't know. But if high-profile figures are involved ..."

The door creaked as I pushed it open. Gideon spun around, pressing the 'end' button on his phone.

"Chili—"

"Don't." My voice trembled, a mix of anger and hurt. "I thought you didn't trust Barrett."

"He's my boss," he said, stepping toward me.

"So? Two days ago you didn't trust him—or anyone at the station. And now, suddenly, you do? What's going on?"

"It's not what you think—"

"Then explain!" I snapped, cutting him off. "What's going on?"

Resignation flickered across his face. He cupped my elbow gently and guided me into an empty office, shutting the door behind us. "Sit," he said, motioning to a chair.

Reluctantly, I obeyed, watching him pace for a moment before he spoke. "My friend on the task force, Travis, looped Barrett and myself into a major investigation. You were right about someone in the office being dirty, but wrong about who it is."

Shock rippled through me. "You're saying it isn't Barrett? Then who is it?" My stomach churned at the thought that it could be someone I knew, someone I trusted.

"At this stage we don't know." He held up a hand as I started to protest. "The task force has taken the lead on the case. That's why only Barrett and I have been given information: the fewer people who know about it, the better."

"So we trust them?" I asked, scepticism colouring my voice.

"We don't have much choice," Gideon replied. "But they're our best shot at cracking this wide open without tipping off whoever's involved locally."

I chewed my lip, considering. "You're right, none of us want that." I said quietly. "What do you want me to do?"

For a moment, he didn't say anything, just stared at me with a surprised expression. Guilt flooded me. Was I really that opinionated and hard to put up with? Did everyone around me feel this way?

Gideon leaned against the desk. "For starters, we need to be more careful about what information we share and with whom. No more discussing details over the phone or in public places. We'll need to set up secure communication channels. Perhaps a VPN. In the meantime, you can use this phone." He handed me a sleek device, its screen glinting under the dim light. "It's pre-configured with the necessary apps to keep things private. I've also installed tracking software on it, so I can make sure you're safe and that no one else can trace you."

"And what about the evidence I found?" I asked. "The stuff from the Van Horne's safe?"

Gideon's eyes met mine. "We need to secure it. Somewhere safe, where no one else can access it. And Chili," he paused, his voice softening, "you can't tell anyone else about what you found. Not even Bonnie or your father. The fewer people who know, the safer we all are."

I chewed my lip, considering. "Alright. So what's our next move?"

"You go home. I'll call you as soon as I know more."

I wanted to argue, to insist that I could handle whatever came next. But something in his expression stopped me. The worry lines etched around his eyes, the tension in his shoulders—it all spoke of a man with the weight of the world on his shoulders.

"Fine," I said my voice barely above a whisper. "But you better call me the second you know anything. And I mean anything, Gideon."

He nodded. "I promise."

I hesitated at the door, my hand on the knob. "Gideon?"

He looked up, his eyes questioning.

"Be careful," I said softly. "I can't lose you either."

A small smile tugged at the corner of his mouth. "I will."

With a deep breath, I stepped out into the hallway, my mind racing. Hospitals always felt like a strange mix of chaos and calm. The nurses bustled through the halls with practiced urgency, but the air was heavy with quiet tension. I scanned the ward, searching for someone—anyone—who could tell me where Morgan was. I had to find out if he was okay.

It was a young nurse, barely out of school, who finally stopped long enough to answer. "Dr. Morgan? I ... I don't know where he is. He hasn't been in for days."

Her voice was hesitant, her eyes darting nervously around the room like she was afraid someone might overhear. My stomach clenched.

"Days?" I pressed. "Did he say anything before he left?"

She shook her head, and her lips parted as if to say more, but she stopped herself.

That was all I needed. Something was wrong.

Chapter 31

I couldn't stop pacing the length of my kitchen, my phone clutched tightly in one hand, the other pressed to my temple. The talk with Gideon was still fresh, leaving me on a heightened sense of alert. But I wasn't going to sit on my hands while corruption and lies spread like poison through our town. I just needed to be cautious.

I took a deep breath and scrolled through my contacts until I landed on the number I needed: Tunbridge. The mayor's cousin. My thumb hovered for only a second before pressing the call button. Langford wouldn't suspect a thing. To him, I was just another player in the game, one he thought he could outsmart.

The phone rang twice before he picked up, his voice smooth and too confident. "Tunbridge speaking."

"Hi, Mr. Tunbridge," I said, pitching my voice with the right mix of entitlement and sweetness. "This is Tania Dorsey, Mr. Dorsey's granddaughter. I understand you've been working closely with my grandfather."

There was a brief pause, just long enough to tell me he hadn't seen this coming. "Ah, Tania. Of course! Your grandfather speaks highly of you. What can I do for you?"

I forced a polite laugh, even though it made my skin crawl. "Well, you see, Grandpa's been talking about some ... plans. He mentioned selling the property. Naturally, I want to make sure he's making the best choice for our family."

Tunbridge's tone brightened immediately. "Oh, absolutely. Your grandfather's property is a real gem. I have a buyer who's very eager to get their hands on it."

I leaned into the role, letting a hint of concern colour my voice. "A buyer, already? Wow, that's quick. Why are they so interested?"

He chuckled, the sound smug enough to make my teeth clench. "Let's just say the area's undergoing some exciting changes. Zoning adjustments are turning it into prime real estate."

"Zoning adjustments?" I feigned confusion. "I don't know much about that sort of thing. Could you explain?"

"It's all above board," he said, his confidence unshaken. "When you have the right connections, you can move things along quickly. The area is going to be rezoned residential and the lots subdivided. As I told your grandfather, if you don't get in now the price won't be as good in a few months time."

A gold mine. Sure, for people like him. I hesitated, pretending to weigh my options. "That's fascinating. Maybe we should meet to discuss this further? I'd hate for Grandpa to make a decision without considering all the angles."

"Of course," Tunbridge said smoothly. "I'd be happy to meet. The sooner, the better. Once the deals start closing, the market could shift."

When the call ended, I sat back, stomach churning. Tunbridge was as dirty as I'd expected, but now I had confirmation. He wasn't just taking advantage of Mr. Dorsey; he was part of something much bigger—and he wasn't working alone. And only one name rose to the surface: the mayor.

I didn't wait to second-guess myself. Grabbing my keys, I headed out the door, determined to confront the man who'd been lurking in the shadows of this whole mess.

Back in town, I marched straight into City Hall, determination coursing through me like wildfire. My boots echoed sharply against the marble floor as I stormed toward the mayor's office, the heavy oak doors standing like a challenge. Each step was fuelled by anger and certainty—I wasn't here for games or politics. I had evidence, and someone was going to answer for it.

Inside, Mayor Sealey sat behind his oversized desk, all smug authority. His surprise at my unceremonious entrance lasted a fraction of a second before his expression shifted into that practiced politician's calm. He tilted his head slightly, smirking like he had the upper hand. "Ms. Beane," he drawled, "what brings you here today?"

I slammed the file onto his desk with more force than necessary, the sound slicing through the tension in the room. "Drop the act. I know everything."

He barely glanced at the folder before meeting my gaze, his smirk deepening. "Everything? That's a bold claim, even for you."

I leaned in, meeting him eye-to-eye, my palms pressed flat against the polished wood. "Shady rezoning deals. Your cousin's cut from the property development scam. And Sarah St. James. Don't play dumb—you're tied to all of it."

The confidence in his grin faltered, just for a second. But then, like a curtain being drawn, it was back. He chuckled softly, shaking his head. He reached forward and hit a button on the phone. "You've got a vivid imagination, Ms. Beane. I'll give you that."

"I've got evidence," I shot back, my voice steady despite the anger boiling under the surface. "Dates, signatures, wire transfers. And I'm not leaving until I hear the truth."

Sealey leaned forward, his voice dropping to a near-whisper. "And if there is such a truth, what exactly do you think you'll accomplish? If you're as smart as I've heard, you'll walk away. Now."

It wasn't a suggestion. It was a threat. But instead of scaring me, it only steeled my resolve. I folded my arms and said, "Funny. That's what I"ve heard about you, too. From Sarah. Before she disappeared."

His face drained of colour. Finally, a crack in the armour. For a second, I almost felt pity for him. Almost. "I don't know anything about that," he stammered, his bravado slipping. "You're barking up the wrong tree."

"You're lying," I snapped, stepping closer. "Sarah's dead, Morgan's missing, and Van Horne's name keeps coming up. Start talking, or I'll take what I know straight to the press."

His eyes darted around the room like a trapped animal. "Look, I don't know where he is, alright? I'm just the middleman."

"Middleman for what?"

Before he could say more, the sound of the door opening made me whip around. Two men stepped in, both broad-shouldered and unflinching, their faces carved from stone. They didn't need to say a word; the menace rolled off them in waves. My heart sank. I knew trouble when I saw it.

"Sealey," the taller one said his voice low and razor-sharp. "What's this?"

Sealey stumbled back like a guilty child caught with his hand in the cookie jar. "I ... I didn't know what else to do," he stammered, gesturing vaguely toward me. "She's asking too many questions."

Neither of them spared him a glance. One man closed the distance between us in two strides, his hand latching onto my arm with an iron grip.

"Let go of me!" I shouted, thrashing against him, but it was like trying to fight a statue. A meaty hand clamped over my mouth, muffling my cries. Sealey stayed rooted to the spot, his expression flickering between guilt and cowardice. His betrayal felt like a knife twisting in my gut.

They hauled me out of the office through a side door. My heels scraped uselessly against the polished floor as I kicked and writhed, but their grip was vice-like, unrelenting.

Outside, the cold air hit me like a slap, but there was no time to think—I was shoved roughly into the back of a waiting van, my shoulder colliding painfully with the metal floor. Someone picked me up and threw me against a pile of dirty rags. The door slammed shut behind me, the sound echoing in the confined space. My breaths came fast and shallow, panic clawing at my chest as the engine roared to life, its growl vibrating through the van. Darkness closed in around me, thick and suffocating. I tried to push myself up, my mind racing for an escape plan, when something cold pressed against my neck.

I froze, a sharp prick biting into my skin. My pulse thundered as I realized what was happening. A needle. Warmth spread from the puncture point, cold at first, then unnaturally heavy, pulling me down into a haze. My limbs felt leaden, my head spinning as the edges of the world blurred and folded in on it-self. I fought against it, clawing at the van floor, but it was no use. Everything dissolved into black.

When I came to, it was the smell that hit me first—rotting wood, mildew, and the unmistakable tang of blood. The room was damp and cold, shadows pooling in the corners. Faint moonlight filtered through a broken window, just enough to make out the shape of someone slumped against the wall.

"Morgan?" My voice cracked as I crawled toward him, dread tightening around me like a vise. His face was pale, his shirt soaked with blood. Too much blood.

"Chili ..." His voice was barely audible, but hearing it was like a jolt of electricity. I reached out, my trembling hands hovering over his wound.

"Stay with me," I said, trying to steady my voice. "Morgan, just—stay with me."

He gave me a faint, crooked smile, his lips tinged with dry humour despite the pain. "Wasn't planning ... on going anywhere. Not yet."

Tears burned behind my eyes, but I blinked them back. "What do I do?" I whispered, desperate.

"Pressure," he murmured, his eyelids fluttering. "Stop the bleeding ..."

I pressed my hands to his wound. The sticky wetness of his blood coated my fingers as I pressed my palms against his wound. His skin was clammy with sweat, and his body trembled with pain. His breathing hitched, shallow and uneven, but I wasn't letting him slip away. "Don't you dare close your eyes," I snapped, my voice breaking. "You don't get to leave me here, Morgan. Not like this."

Desperation clawed at me. I grabbed his shirt, tearing a strip from the fabric with a savage rip. The sound barely registered over the pounding of my heart. I pressed the makeshift bandage to his wound, feeling it grow warm and heavy with blood almost immediately.

He fought to stay conscious, his words a faint but determined promise that we would get out of this together. And I prayed, with all my being that we would.

Chapter 32

The warmth of Morgan's blood soaked through my fingers as I continued to press the wadded-up piece of his torn shirt against the wound on his chest. The sticky sensation made my stomach churn. The sweat trickling down his temple only heightened my sense of urgency.

I tried to focus on breathing steadily, but my pulse pounded in my ears, threatening to drown out the whispers of my own thoughts. "Talk to me, Doc," I said, my voice shaking despite my best efforts to keep it calm. "How bad is it?"

"Not ... as bad as it looks," he rasped, his voice barely audible. "Knife hit the clavicle. Tore more than it cut. Hurts like anything, though."

His words didn't reassure me. My eyes flicked to the jagged wound starting from above his collarbone and finishing a couple of inches below. Blood seeped steadily, vivid against his pale skin, but I could tell he was right—it wasn't deep enough to kill him. Still, the sight of it made my stomach twist. I shifted the makeshift bandage slightly, hoping to slow the bleeding.

"I need to hold this in place. What can I use?" I muttered, my eyes darting around the dimly lit room.

"Something tight," Morgan croaked. "Belt ... cord ..."

My gaze landed on a thin, frayed rope tied to a rusted hook on the wall. It wasn't ideal, but it was all I had. I grabbed it and worked quickly, wrapping it around his chest to secure the bandage. My fingers fumbled, slick with his blood, but I forced myself to concentrate. Morgan winced, sucking in a sharp breath, but didn't make a sound beyond that. His jaw tightened, and his eyes met mine with a steadiness that belied his obvious pain.

"Who did this to you?" I demanded, my voice sharper than I intended.

"Jessica," he whispered, his words like a knife slicing through the air. "Delia's daughter. She said … I knew too much."

The room tilted for a moment as rage flared in my chest, white-hot and searing. Jessica. The polite smiling nurse, the model of professional care who had played her role so convincingly at the hospital while behind closed doors destroyed lives. I could picture her now, standing over Morgan with a knife, her mask slipping to reveal the monster beneath. The image sent bile rising in my throat

"She won't get away with this," I muttered, more to myself than to him. The anger pulsed through me, begging for release, but I swallowed it and focused on Morgan.

His breathing hitched, and his skin remained pale despite my efforts. He was alive, but he wasn't out of the woods yet.

I sat back on my heels and surveyed my work. The rope would hold for now, but it wasn't a long-term solution. Wiping my hands on my jeans, I felt a bulge in my boot. They hadn't searched me thoroughly which both a blessing. They'd found my main phone, the one I'd used to reach out for help, and tossed it aside without a second thought. They assumed I only had the one. The other phone, the one Gideon had given me, slipped by unnoticed in my pocket.

I held it up. The screen was cracked and the phone showed no bars—no signal, no way to reach out for help.

"I need to look around," I said, keeping my voice steady. "There might be something here to help us. I'll be quick."

Morgan gave a weak nod, his eyelids fluttering as he slumped against the cold stone wall.

The air hung heavy with the stench of mould and decay, every breath tainted by the damp, rotting scent that clung to every crevice. Chains dangled from the stone walls like forgotten remnants of a twisted past, their rusted surfaces rough against the flickering light. Stained mattresses lay scattered across the floor, each a testament to the horrors that had occurred there. Every inch of the place whispered of suffering, of lives left in ruin. My stomach churned as I surveyed the space, the weight of it pressing down on me, like the walls themselves were suffocating under the secrets they held.

In one corner, a pile of papers caught my eye. I picked my way through the clutter, careful not to disturb anything that could be evidence. I rifled through them, my hands trembling as I used a stick to turn over the pages. The edges were yellowed and curling with age, but the contents made my blood run cold. Names, dates, horrifying details—all meticulously recorded, like someone cataloguing lives destroyed. The words blurred as my hands trembled.

A flash of something shiny caught my eye in the dim light. I crouched and gently pulled a gold locket from the pile. The broken chain's delicate links were twisted beyond repair. My thumb brushed over the small latch, and it popped open to reveal a photo of a young girl with sparkling eyes and a carefree smile. My chest tightened painfully. This locket belonged to someone, someone who had likely suffered in this place.

On the far wall, faint carvings marred the surface of the stone. Names. They were uneven, some barely legible, others gouged deep into the rock with a desperation I could feel in my bones. Sarah. Harper. I ran my fingers over the letters, the rough grooves cutting into my fingertips like an echo of the pain that had carved them. The names stuck in my throat like shards of glass.

Had these people hoped someone would find their names, remember them? Or had they etched them here in defiance, a last mark to say, I was here. I mattered. Each name was a story, a life, now reduced to a few rough letters on cold stone. I imagined trembling hands, raw and bleeding, forcing those names into permanence. The effort it must have taken to scratch them there—to leave a mark in this place of darkness—felt overwhelming.

Using the phone Gideon gave me I snapped photos of everything—the documents, the chains, the scrawled names. Each image felt like a lifeline, proof of what had been hidden here. I couldn't afford to miss a single detail.

I stepped back, and my foot slipped on chains, the metallic clatter loud in the oppressive silence. The sound reverberated like an accusation, cutting through the stagnant air. It made me flinch as though I'd disturbed something sacred, something left behind to bear witness.

"What ... did you find?" Morgan's voice pulled me back, weak but insistent.

"Evidence," I said, my throat dry. "Personal belongings. Documents. And ..." I trailed off, glancing around the room. "And things people left behind. It's horrible."

I knelt beside Morgan, brushing the hair from his sweat-soaked forehead. "Morgan," I whispered, my voice trembling. "I found something on the wall. Names. Carved into the stone." His eyelids fluttered, and I swallowed the lump in my throat. "Sarah and Harper," I said. "They fought to leave them there. It felt ... desperate, like they wanted to be remembered. Like they knew they might not make it out."

His gaze locked onto mine, weary but firm. "It's their story," he murmured, voice barely audible.

"It's ours now," I said, gripping his hand. "We'll make sure no one forgets."

Morgan's eyes opened a fraction, his gaze steady despite the pain etched across his face. "Get out of here," he said his words heavy with urgency. "Before anyone comes back."

"I'm not leaving you," I said. My voice cracked, but I didn't care.

"You have to. You need to get help," he insisted.

I knelt beside him, checking the rope and the makeshift dressing. The bleeding had slowed, but his skin was still too pale, his breaths shallow and laboured. I cupped his face, my thumb brushing against the grit on his cheek. "You're not giving up on me, got it? We'll get out of here. You just need to hold on a little longer."

A faint smile ghosted across his lips. "Stubborn as ever."

"Darn right I am," I shot back, though my voice shook. My eyes flicked to the door. Every second felt like borrowed time.

Silence hung between us broken only by his laboured breathing. Then, from somewhere beyond the heavy door, I heard it—the unmistakable sound of footsteps.

My heart leapt into my throat. Our captor hadn't finished with us yet. We weren't safe yet.

I pressed the record button on the phone, the cool metal of the device almost a relief in my palm. The sound of my pulse still hammered in my ears, but I focused. This was it. The one chance I had to document the truth. My fingers trembled, but I steadied myself and took a breath.

The recording icon blinked on the screen, and I could almost hear the weight of the evidence starting to build.

Whatever lay beyond that door, I was ready to face it. For Morgan. For the names carved in the wall. And for every life this place had tried to bury.

Chapter 33

The metallic scrape of a key turning in the lock snapped my head up. Fear crept up my spine. The door creaked open, revealing Jessica, her once-perfect nurse's demeanour replaced by something feral. The gun in her hand glinted under the dim light, and the smile curling her lips made my stomach churn.

"Well, well," she purred, stepping into the room and kicking the door shut behind her. Her voice dripped with malice, every syllable sharp enough to cut. "How cosy. Here you both are, the good doctor and the nosy investigator, playing house in my little hideaway."

Her boots caught my attention, the scuffed brown leather worn in the exact same places as the pair I'd seen when I hit the ground in the jewellery store. My stomach twisted as the memory resurfaced—the last thing I saw before everything went black. It was her.

"It was you. You killed William Van Horne," I blurted.

She bowed. "He'd outlived his usefulness. The moment he decided to try and save your sister by having the fake argument with her, his time was limited. He knew that."

I shook my head. "I don't understand."

"The whole idea was to draw your sister in, much like I did Morgan. Threaten her children and she would have done anything to save them. William, however, was genuinely fond of her. A staged argument was the easiest way for him to keep her out of my reach." She shrugged. "It worked."

"And then I showed up."

"It was quite the surprise when you walked in. I was even more surprised when that heavy glass jar hadn't shattered; quite the testament to craftsmanship."

"What do you want, Jessica?" My voice came out steadier than I expected, but the tension in my jaw betrayed me.

"What do I want?" She tilted her head, as if the question amused her. "That's a loaded question, isn't it? What I want is for you two to stop meddling. You've made this far more complicated than it needed to be." Her gaze shifted to Morgan, her smile widening. "Especially you, my dear cousin."

Morgan let out a weak, disbelieving laugh. "Cousin?"

I stared at her, the pieces clicking into place. Jessica had been the one to attack me. And now, she was here, ready to finish what she started.

"Yes, dear cousin," Jessica said with a mock pout. "You didn't know, did you? Mommy dearest doesn't like to share her secrets. Allow me to enlighten you." She stepped closer, her voice taking on a sing-song quality. "Delia, my darling mother, is the daughter of *your* grandfather and his little side piece, Anna. That makes me your blood. Family."

"That's not possible," Morgan muttered his voice weak but laced with anger.

"Oh, it's very possible." Jessica's expression darkened her tone dropping into something cold and menacing. "Your precious grandfather had his fun on the side, and Delia was the result." She shrugged. "My mother grew up bitter and hungry for the power she was denied. She married Van Horne because he offered something she couldn't resist—a way to make her empire untouchable."

I swallowed hard, my mind racing to piece everything together. "And what empire is that, Jessica? Diamonds? Human lives? What's the endgame here?"

Jessica's eyes gleamed with twisted delight. "Ah, clever Chili. Yes, diamonds and people, a perfect cycle of human greed. Van Horne's business connections gave us the picture-perfect front. The diamonds keep our accounts clean, and the trafficking ... well, it's lucrative. Everyone wants to turn a blind eye when there's profit involved."

"You're sick," I spat, my voice trembling with fury. "Both of you."

"Sick?" She chuckled and then conceded. "Perhaps. But it's funny, isn't it? How easily the world lets it happen. We're just the middle men; all we do is supply people what they're willing to pay for."

It was the second time I'd heard the phrase 'middle men.' It was a convenient excuse, a way for cowards to distance themselves from the damage they caused. Calling themselves that let them pretend they weren't responsible, that they were just cogs in the machine, instead of active participants in ruining lives. It was infuriating. Sealey had called himself the same.

She laughed when I told her so.

"You can't get away with it forever. Sooner or later someone will stop you," said Morgan.

"Oh, Morgan," Jessica said with a mock sigh, the gun in her hand twitching toward him. "Still clinging to those silly humanitarian ideals, I see. You really are my favourite cousin. Too bad I'll have to tie up this little loose end."

I stepped forward before I could think better of it, my body tensing. "He's right. Eventually someone will get caught and when they do your name will be mentioned and your whole world will be destroyed."

Jessica's smile faltered a flicker of something unhinged flashing in her eyes. "Those are big words from someone in your position. But maybe I'll let you live long enough to see how wrong you are."

Her grip on the gun tightened, and I felt the weight of her madness press down like a suffocating fog. I didn't dare move, my mind spinning for a way out. One thing was clear—Jessica wasn't just a player in this game. She was a true believer, intoxicated by the chaos her family had created.

Before she killed us I needed to know the truth.

"Jessica," I said, forcing my voice to stay steady. "What happened to Sarah and the baby?"

Her face twisted into a mockery of regret, a sneer creeping into her expression. "Sarah? Oh, she had the baby, don't worry. A beautiful little girl. There's always a market for infants, especially for couples desperate to start a family." She tilted her head, eyes glinting with something cold and cruel. "We sold her to the highest bidder. Perfect little life for a perfect little baby. Isn't that what everyone dreams of?"

My stomach churned, but I kept my face blank, refusing to let her see how her words cut me. "And Sarah? Where is she?"

Jessica's expression darkened, her lips curving into a cruel smile that didn't reach her eyes. "Sarah didn't make it. She bled out after the birth—complications, they said. These things happen, you know? A real shame." Her tone was cold and dismissive. "Not that it mattered. She was always so fragile, always whining about wanting to tell someone. As if anyone would have believed her. Honestly, it's better this way. No loose ends." She shrugged as if she were describing a minor inconvenience, not a human life snuffed out. "She would've been miserable knowing her daughter was gone."

Each word hit like a punch to the gut, but I forced myself to stay calm, to keep her talking. Slowly, deliberately, I shifted my weight, inching toward the door. The movement was small enough not to draw her attention, but my heart thundered in my chest, each step calculated and measured. I kept my gaze on her, feigning a grim fascination with her story.

Jessica's voice grew sharper, more unhinged. "You know, it's funny. People think they're so moral, so above it all. But when it comes to getting what they want, they'll pay any price. A baby, a diamond, a life—it's all just currency in the end."

Behind me, Morgan stirred, a low groan escaping his lips.

Jessica's head whipped toward him, her eyes narrowing. "Oh, for goodness sake, can't you just—"

She didn't finish. I didn't give her the chance.

I lunged for the gun and knocked it out of her grip. It skittered across the floor, just out of reach. Before I could react, her arm shot up nails tearing across my face as she clawed at me, wild and feral. Blood poured down my forehead, stinging my eyes and clouding my vision.

The next moments were chaos. I swung blindly, my fist connecting with her jaw in a solid, satisfying crack. We hit the ground hard, the concrete unforgiving beneath us. Her head struck the concrete and for a moment her body went still.

Then her eyes fluttered open. Fury replaced dazed confusion and she let out a savage growl. With surprising strength she bucked beneath me, her knee driving into my stomach and knocking the air from my lungs as she tried to twist free.

I gasped, my lungs burning as I struggled to keep her pinned. Her claws tore into my arms, the pain sharp and relentless but I refused to let go. Jessica reared up, her forehead slamming into my face with brutal force. Pain exploded through my skull as my teeth smashed against my gums. The metallic tang of blood flooded my mouth, warm and nauseating. She writhed beneath me and I grabbed her wrist, twisting it hard. She screamed and with one last burst of strength, I slammed her back down the force sending a shudder through both of us.

Her head hit the concrete again with a sickening crack.

This time she went limp. Silence fell, heavy and suffocating as I collapsed beside her, trembling and gasping for air.

I forced myself to move, my fingers shaking as I reached out to check her pulse.

Relief washed over me—she was still alive.

Panting, I scrambled to my feet and picked up the gun thrusting it into my back pocket. "Morgan," I gasped, rushing to his side. "Come on, we've got to move."

He nodded weakly, leaning heavily on me as I hauled him upright. We staggered to the door.

The sunlight outside was blinding, a harsh contrast to the dim, suffocating gloom we'd just escaped. I raised a hand to shield my eyes, blinking against the glare as it washed over us. For a moment, I stood still, breathing deeply, letting the fresh air fill my lungs and the warmth settle on my skin. "Let's go," I whispered, tightening my grip on Morgan. We weren't safe yet, but we were free. And that was enough for now.

Chapter 34

The bush swallowed us whole, a labyrinth of shadows and whispers. The undergrowth grabbed at our legs like it was alive, desperate to drag us down into the earth. My boots slipped on the slick leaves, and I stumbled, my palms slamming against the rough tree trunk. Bark scraped my skin leaving it raw.

"We need to keep moving." Morgan's voice cut through the roar of blood in my ears.

"I'm trying," I shot back. I couldn't hide the tremor in my voice. Fear leaked through and I hated he could hear it.

I pushed off the tree, forcing myself upright and scanned the area ahead. "This way," I muttered though I wasn't sure. The trail we'd been following had vanished under a tangle of ferns and roots, the bush conspiring to swallow any trace of direction.

I seized Morgan's arm, yanking him upright again as my knees nearly buckled beneath his weight. His staggering steps were slow and heavy, but they kept us moving forward. The branches clawed at my skin, leaving stinging scratches, and the uneven ground made each step feel like a gamble. My focus zeroed in on one thing—escape.

The cool air burned with every breath, slicing through my throat like a blade. My pulse thundered in my ears, drowning out everything except the relentless echo of our steps and the faint shouts closing in behind us. A snap of a twig somewhere nearby jolted my senses, and

I whipped my head toward the sound, half-expecting to see shadows moving between the trees.

Morgan faltered again, his legs trembling beneath him. "No," I hissed, gripping his arm tighter, my voice raw with desperation. "Not now. We have to keep going!"

He stumbled, and before I could steady him, we both went down in a chaotic heap. I hit the earth hard, the jarring impact rippling through me as damp soil clung to my skin. My fingers scrambled for the revolver, but it was gone—lost somewhere in the undergrowth.

The sound of footsteps grew closer. My heart seized. We were out of time. "I can't," he gasped, his face ashen and slick with sweat. His breath came in ragged bursts, shallow and uneven, his body trembling like a wire stretched too tight.

"Yes, you can," I hissed. My fingers scrabbled through the dirt until I found the revolver and shoved it back into my waistband.

Chili ..." His voice was barely audible now, a whisper carried on the wind.

"Lean on me," I said, looping my arm around his waist. He was heavier than he looked, his body sagging against mine like dead weight. Every step forward was agony, his weight threatening to topple us both.

Morgan swore under his breath, but his steps faltered, and I tightened my grip. "Keep moving," I whispered, unsure if I was telling him or myself.

The gully ahead was a sunken shadow in the dense undergrowth, surrounded by a tangle of lantana that clawed at us as I dragged Morgan off the trail. The air was thick and heavy, carrying the sickly-sweet smell of damp earth and rot. My boots slipped on the loose dirt as we stumbled downward, and I barely managed to keep us upright.

"We need to hide," Morgan muttered, his voice strained and hoarse.

"No, we need to get out of here," I snapped back, though deep down, I knew he was right. He couldn't go much farther, and I couldn't carry him much longer.

At the bottom of the gully, a fallen tree stretched across the space, its bark rough with moss and decay. "Here," I whispered, easing him down behind it. His breath hitched as he clutched at his chest, his face pale and slick with sweat.

"Stay low," I added, crouching beside him. The lantana closed in around us, a cocoon of prickly branches and leaves, its pungent scent lingering in the air like an unwelcome, bittersweet memory. It wasn't perfect, but it would have to do.

Morgan's lips parted as if to speak, but his gaze shot upward. My stomach twisted. I strained to listen, my heartbeat pounding painfully in my ears.

Then I heard it—boots crunching on rocks and branches above us, slow and deliberate. A man's voice growled, "They went this way."

My stomach plunged. The voices were too close, far too close. I pressed myself against the fallen tree, my breath caught in my throat.

Morgan met my eyes, and the raw fear there was like a punch to the gut. He'd always been calm, always steady, but now his face was drawn tight with the realisation that we might not get out of this.

My hand tightened around the revolver, the cool metal biting into my skin. I hated the way it felt, the weight of what it meant. I hated more that I might have to use it.

Morgan's hand brushed mine, a small, almost imperceptible gesture. When I looked at him, his face was grim. "If they find us—"

"They won't," I said, cutting him off. My voice was sharper than I intended, but I couldn't let him finish. Couldn't let him voice that possibility.

He didn't argue, just leaned back against the log, his shoulders sagging under the weight of exhaustion and pain.

I swallowed hard and scanned the gully, searching for anything, any glimmer of a plan. "Stay here," I whispered, my voice low and urgent. "I'll draw them off and come back for you."

"Chili, no," he said, his hand weakly grabbing at my arm, but I shook my head.

"I'll be back. Just stay hidden," I insisted.

Before he could protest again, I slipped into the shadows, leaving Morgan hidden behind the log. The sound of my own breath drowned out the whispers of the bush, but I didn't dare look back.

I grabbed a rock and hurled it into the bushes furthest away. It crashed through the undergrowth, loud and deliberate rolling even further down the hill.

"Over there!" someone shouted, and I heard the crash of heavy footsteps as they veered toward the sound I'd created moments earlier.

This was my chance.

I hauled myself up the gully, every movement a battle against the loose soil and tangled roots. My palms slipped, raw and stinging as I clawed at the earth. A sharp sting ripped through my hand, and I yanked it back, blood welling up from a jagged cut where a buried shard of glass had sliced me.

I bit the inside of my mouth, clutching my hand to my chest for a heartbeat before forcing myself to keep moving. The burning in my arms screamed for me to stop, but I didn't dare. Above me, the rim of the gully seemed impossibly far, like a goal that shifted with every desperate pull.

The shouts behind me faded but didn't vanish. Each echoed word sent a new jolt of panic coursing through me. They were searching, closing in. My heartbeat thundered in my ears, blending with the rustle of leaves and the scrape of my boots against the shifting earth.

Finally, my fingers grasped at solid ground. I heaved myself up, rolling onto my back for a brief second. The sky peeked through the canopy above, mocking me with its stillness. My breath came in gasps, my cut hand throbbing with every beat of my heart.

No time to stop. I scrambled to my feet, ignoring the sticky warmth dripping down my palm. The bush stretched out before me like a maze, every shadow a potential threat. The faint shouts below grew sharper, a reminder of how little distance I'd gained.

I stumbled forward, wiping my hand on my shirt, leaving a smear of blood behind. The air felt heavy, the silence between their calls thicker than the noise itself. Each step felt like a dare—escape or collapse. Every breath I took sounded deafening in the stillness, and I bit down on the metallic tang of fear that flooded my mouth. My clothes clung to my skin, damp with sweat, and the cool damp air chilled me.

Then, a gunshot cracked through the night, splitting the air like lightning.

I froze, the sound reverberating in my chest. My fingers automatically tightened around the revolver in my waistband.

The voices were louder again, nearer. They were closing in.

Another gunshot rang out, sharp and deliberate, much closer this time. I ducked instinctively, my body pressing into the coarse bark of a towering gum tree. Every muscle in me screamed to move, to run, but the sound of approaching footsteps rooted me to the spot.

Leaves rustled, branches snapped, and the unmistakable crunch of boots on dry earth pierced the quiet. My breath hitched, my throat tightening until even the air refused to move.

I raised the revolver, my arm trembling. The gloom stretched in front of me, shadows shifting but giving no clear target. My hands were slick with sweat, the gun slipping slightly in my grip. I bit my lip to stop from crying.

Then, through the maze of branches and undergrowth, a flicker of light caught my eye—red, then blue, then red again.

I blinked, convinced I was imagining it. But there it was, steady and real, piercing the suffocating dark.

"Police," I whispered, the word barely audible over the thundering of my pulse.

Hope surged through me, sharp and painful. But it wasn't over yet. The lights were distant, the safety they promised still too far away.

I had to lead the others from Morgan, buy him time. I stepped away from the tree, my every instinct screaming against the move. The lights ahead seemed to blink in approval, urging me on.

I took a deep breath and started to sprint towards safety.

A sharp crack came from my left—someone stepping on a branch. I skidded to a stop, my finger hovered over the trigger, my heart hammering so hard it hurt.

"Chili!"

The voice was sharp, desperate, and familiar.

I froze. My brain struggled to process what I'd just heard.

"Chili! Morgan!"

I blinked, my heart skipping a beat. The voice called again, closer this time. "It's me—Gideon!"

Gideon?

Relief flooded through me, so sudden and overwhelming that it left me light-headed.

"It's him," I whispered, my voice breaking. "It's really him."

Tears flooded my eyes.

"I'm over here!" I shouted.

The bushes rustled violently, and dark shapes emerged from the shadows—figures with guns glinting in the dim light, their eyes cold, calculating. Jessica's men, drawn in by the shout, were closing in fast, relentless and unforgiving. My pulse raced as their boots crunched against the undergrowth, the sound of pursuit growing louder with every passing second.

Then, a force exploded through the trees. Gideon, moving like a predator, came into view—an avenging angel with no time for hesitation. The underbrush splintered beneath him, branches snapping like twigs as he navigated through the thicket. His gun was raised before I even registered his presence. The blast that followed was deafening, echoing through the trees, a violent punctuation to the silence. One of Van Horne's men crumpled to the ground, lifeless, a puppet whose strings had been severed in an instant.

The other turned on his heel and bolted, disappearing into the darkened wilderness, no match for Gideon's precision.

"Chili!" His voice was raw with urgency, frantic, and when his eyes locked on mine, they softened in relief, only to harden in horror at the sight of me. In an instant, he pulled me into his arms, a buffer against the terror swirling in my chest. He hugged me tightly, as if willing the fear out of me. But just as quickly, he pulled back, searching my face.

"Morgan?" His voice dropped an octave, laden with worry.

I pointed toward the gully. "Back there. Near a fallen tree, hidden under lantana."

His eyes creased with concern. "Is he okay?"

I swallowed hard. "He's still alive. Badly hurt but alive." Gideon didn't hesitate, turning to bark orders at the officers emerging from the bush. "Send a team now! Search the gully, near a fallen tree. Move!"

One of the officers grabbed a radio, relaying the instructions as Gideon turned back to me. His hands hovered near my shoulders like he wasn't sure if I'd collapse or run.

"Are *you* okay?" he asked.

"Yeah," I said, the word barely a whisper. My legs wobbled, but I stayed standing, my resolve the only thing keeping me upright.

Gideon drew me into another hug. "You did good," he said, his tone softer now, the tension in his voice easing.

I wasn't sure I believed him. But at least Morgan had a chance now.

Chapter 35

The ambulance doors slammed shut with a finality that sent a pang through my chest. I sat on the bumper of another one, the blanket someone had draped around my shoulders doing little to stop the tremors running through me. Morgan was on his way to the hospital now, pale and battered but alive. That word carried a weight I wasn't sure I could unpack yet.

Barrett stood a few yards away, huddled with a group of men who looked like they meant business. Some wore suits; others looked more tactical, the kind you'd see in undercover movies. They moved with quiet precision, their voices low, but every so often, I caught fragments of words: 'trafficking,' 'network,' 'intelligence.' These weren't your everyday cops. This was something bigger, something darker than I'd dared imagine when this nightmare began.

I couldn't focus on the group for long. My gaze kept drifting back to the gravel driveway where Morgan's ambulance had disappeared, its sirens silenced, leaving only the eerie echo of their absence. The flashing lights left a strange stillness in their wake, the world feeling too quiet, too heavy. My hands curled into fists beneath the blanket, the fabric tight against my palms. I tried to push the thought of him out of my mind, but it kept creeping back. He'd be fine. He had to be. I couldn't afford to think otherwise. Not now. Not when so much had been lost.

Movement caught my eye. Gideon broke away from Barrett's group, his steps purposeful as he crossed the space between us. His face was grim, tension in his shoulders, but as he reached me, it softened. Without a word, he crouched in front of me, his hand gentle on my arm.

"Chili," he said, his voice low and thick with emotion. "I'm so glad you're okay."

I let out a laugh that sounded more like a sob, shaking my head. "I barely kept it together."

"You kept yourself and Morgan alive. That's more than most could've done."

I nodded then a thought came to me. "How did you know we were here?"

He hesitated, his hand squeezing my leg. "We found you because of the phone I gave you."

I blinked at him, the words taking a moment to register. "The phone?"

He nodded. "The tracking didn't work until you were out of those stone walls. Must've blocked the signal. The second you got outside ... we were on you."

His hand tightened on mine, his grip warm and steady. "I'm sorry we didn't get there sooner. I should've—"

"Don't," I cut him off, the lump in my throat making it hard to speak. "You got here when you could. That's what matters."

Gideon didn't answer right away. Instead, he leaned forward, wrapping his arms around me and pulling me to his chest, the warmth of his body engulfing me in an unexpected wave of comfort. I froze for half a second, taken aback, before I allowed myself to sink into him. His heartbeat was steady against my ear, a grounding rhythm in the chaos of the day. The frantic pace of everything that had just happened—the rush, the fear and uncertainty—seemed to slow down as I focused on the sound of his heart. For the first time in hours, I could breathe, my shoulders easing, the tension finally starting to ebb.

"On second thoughts, you *were* late," I said into his shirt, my voice muffled but teasing, "but I'll let it slide this time."

He laughed softly, the sound vibrating through me. "You're unbelievable."

I stayed there for a moment longer, letting his presence soothe me. The world felt heavy, like I was seeing it through water, but for the first time in what felt like forever, it didn't feel completely hopeless. We'd made it out.

And I wasn't alone.

Gideon pulled back from our embrace, his hand lingering on my arm as he stood. His gaze flickered back to the group of men gathered near Barrett. With a small squeeze of reassurance, he said, "Stay put. I'll be right back."

I nodded, watching him walk away. His shoulders were squared, his strides confident, but there was something in his posture—a heaviness, maybe. This wasn't over, not for him, not for any of them.

Barrett noticed him coming and gestured toward the others. They leaned in closer, their conversation taking on a new intensity. Every so often, one of the men glanced my way, their faces a mixture of respect and something more complicated—sympathy, maybe. Barrett nodded in my direction, and the others followed suit, their acknowledgment making my stomach twist. I wasn't sure if it was pride or something closer to dread.

I waved for Barrett to come over and moved a few feet away from the back of the ambulance.

He approached, his gaze flicking between me and the phone in my hand. Without saying a word, I handed it to him.

"There's something on there you and your team need to hear," I said, my voice tight. "It's about Gideon's wife."

Barrett took the phone, his expression unreadable, but I saw the flicker of concern in his eyes. He was already bracing himself for what I was about to tell him.

I quickly outlined what the recording revealed—Gideon's wife had been kidnapped, tortured, and held captive, and in the process, her baby was stolen. The horror she'd endured was far worse than any of them had imagined.

Barrett swallowed hard, his face softening with the knowledge. "I'll take care of it," he said, his voice rough. "We'll make sure the team knows, and we'll get answers. Don't worry about it now."

I nodded relieved that someone was going to take action. A paramedic approached me, clipboard in hand, her expression kind but businesslike. "Let's check you out." She crouched down, shining a small light in my eyes and inspecting the multitude of scrapes, cuts and bruises.

"I'm fine," I said, my voice raspier than I intended.

She raised an eyebrow, clearly unimpressed with my self-assessment. "You've been through a lot. Adrenaline can mask things. But from what I can see, you're in decent shape. That said, you'll need a proper check-up at the hospital."

I nodded, knowing she was right, even if the thought of sitting under fluorescent lights surrounded by the sterile smell of antiseptic wasn't exactly appealing.

Gideon headed back toward me, his expression lighter than before but still shadowed by the weight of everything that had happened.

"You're all good?" he asked the paramedic, his tone tinged with concern.

"She'll be fine," the woman replied, standing and snapping her clipboard shut. "But I'd feel better if she got checked out at the hospital."

Gideon nodded. "She will."

The paramedic gave me one last smile before walking away, leaving us alone again.

Gideon crouched beside me, his hand brushing against mine. "I'll catch up with you at the hospital in a little while," he said gently. "I want to make sure Barrett has everything he needs to wrap this up. After you visit Morgan, I'll drive you home, okay?"

"Okay," I whispered, my voice barely audible.

He stood, helping me to my feet with an ease that belied how shaky I felt. The blanket slipped from my shoulders as he guided me toward the open ambulance. Before I could climb in, he stopped me, his fingers brushing against my cheek as he tucked a stray lock of hair behind my ear.

His touch was light, almost hesitant, but the intensity in his eyes rooted me in place. "You scared the hell out of me, you know," he murmured.

"Didn't mean to," I replied, a small, tired smile tugging at my lips.

I swallowed hard, my throat dry and aching. "Jessica," I asked. "Did they get her?"

His expression darkened, a mix of frustration and regret clouding his face. He shook his head. "She's gone. Must have slipped out in all the mêlée. Don't worry, we'll find her."

The words rang hollow, but I nodded, my chest tightening. Jessica had done this—left Morgan bleeding, left me in the dirt—and now she was free to do it again. The thought chilled me, but I forced myself to focus on the steady strength in his gaze.

"You'll find her," I echoed, though the promise felt like a fragile thread in the face of everything she'd already done.

He leaned in, pressing a soft kiss to my forehead, then to my lips. It was brief but full of unspoken promises, a basic reminder that I wasn't alone in this.

"Go," he said, his voice low but firm. "I'll see you soon."

With his hand steadying me, I climbed into the ambulance. As the doors closed, the last thing I saw was him standing there, watching as I was driven away.

Chapter 36

I sat on the edge of the hospital bed, the fluorescent lights above me buzzed and flickered, while the hospital hubbub could be heard outside my curtained cubical. A nurse had dabbed antiseptic onto the gash across my hand, the sting sharp enough to draw a hiss through my teeth. Then she added an injection or three of an anaesthetic to numb the area. She offered a tight, apologetic smile before starting to stitch the wound. My body ached in places I didn't know existed, and the dried blood on my skin felt like an accusation. Every prick of the needle was a reminder of how close we'd come to losing everything.

When it was over, I gently flexed my fingers. The pain knifed through me, but the hand still worked. After washing up in the tiny sink and signing a myriad of forms, I left the room to find Morgan.

He lay in a private room, an IV drip taped to his arm and bandages stark against his pale skin. The sight made my chest tighten. He was awake, though, and his lips quirked in a weak attempt at a smile when I entered.

"You look like you've been through hell," he rasped.

"Funny, I was about to say the same to you," I replied, pulling a chair close to his bed.

He leaned back against the hospital bed, his face a mask of exhaustion and grief. His voice wavered as he began to speak. "When I first went to Africa, I thought I was leaving behind every messy thing in my life." He looked at me. "Our breakup, hospital politics ... I just wanted a fresh start. Jessica was different back then. She was confident and intelligent, passionate about people, and could ignite a room with that passion. She said she wanted to help. Said I could help too. But now ..." His voice cracked, and he reached for a glass of water. "Now I can't stop thinking about all the people I didn't see. The ones I didn't save."

"She monitored inpatients for potential victims," I said softly, my stomach twisting. "The ones she thought no one would miss. The vulnerable, the forgotten. Then funnelled them into their operation."

Morgan's fingers tightened around my good hand. "You have to believe me, Chili, I didn't know. Not at first. And by the time I started to suspect ... "He trailed off, his eyes dropping to the IV taped to his arm. "I didn't know how to stop her."

"I know you didn't," I said, squeezing his hand in reassurance. "But the police will want your statement. They'll need everything you know."

Morgan nodded, his jaw tightening. "I'll tell them everything. Every meeting, every shipment. Even the things I didn't fully understand at the time. It's the least I can do."

A heavy silence settled over the room as we sat together, the memory of what had happened hung over us like a storm cloud.

I broke it first, unable to let his earlier words go. "You said you saw the signs too late. What did you mean?"

He let out a long, weary sigh. "It started with the diamonds. Jessica claimed they were ethically sourced and that the profits would fund healthcare initiatives and education in rural villages. It sounded ... noble. But then shipments would go missing. New faces would show up with no explanation, people who didn't belong. She brushed it off and said it was just business."

"And you believed her?"

"For a while." His gaze was distant, haunted. "But then I started seeing things that didn't add up. A shipment marked as medicine arrived, but when I checked the crates, they were filled with diamonds.

Then there were the people—young women, mostly. They'd come through the hospital, terrified and injured. Jessica said they were refugees, but they'd disappear as quickly as they came."

"Jessica and Delia were trafficking them," I said, the words bitter on my tongue.

Morgan's face crumpled, the realisation hitting him anew. "I'm related to them," he whispered. "To Delia, to Jessica. It makes me sick."

"Family doesn't define who you are," I said firmly. "You're not like them."

He nodded, though the anguish in his eyes didn't fade. "I tried to fix it, Chili. I thought if I stayed close, I could find a way to shut it all down. Instead, I just got tangled deeper."

"You're out now," I said, meeting his gaze. "That's what matters."

Morgan sighed. "I hope it's enough." His hand fell away from mine, and he stared at the stark white hospital sheet draped over his legs. His jaw worked like he was chewing over words he wasn't sure he wanted to say. Finally, he looked up, his expression raw. "What do you think the police will do to me?"

The question caught me off guard. I opened my mouth, then shut it, unsure how to respond. "I don't know," I admitted, my voice quiet but steady. "It depends on what you tell them and how much they believe you didn't know."

Morgan let out a low, bitter laugh. "So it depends on whether they think I'm a fool or a liar."

"Maybe," I conceded. But you're cooperating. That has to count for something. And they'll see you weren't in this for money or power. You were just ... in over your head."

"That's putting it mildly," he muttered, his fingers twisting in the blanket. "I was blind, Chili. Stupid. Jessica—she knew exactly how to play me. I thought I was doing something good, that I was helping people. And all the while ..."

His voice broke, and I reached out, resting my hand on his arm. "You made mistakes, Morgan. Big ones. But you're not the villain here. Jessica and Delia are. That's where the focus will be."

His eyes searched mine, desperate for reassurance. "And if it's not? What if they decide I'm just another cog in the machine?"

I shrugged. "Then we'll fight that. You're not alone in this."

Morgan leaned back against the pillows, his face etched with exhaustion. "I guess we'll see."

"We will," I said firmly. But for now, just focus on getting better. The rest will come when it comes."

He closed his eyes while I sat by his bed, my hands clasped tightly in my lap. His face was pale, the deep shadows under his eyes a stark contrast against his skin. He shifted restlessly, his breath uneven and I reached out stopping short of touching his arm. I wasn't sure if he would welcome the comfort or push it away.

Morgan's eyes fluttered open for a moment, his gaze cloudy with exhaustion and something deeper. Guilt, maybe. Or fear. "I'm fine," he muttered, though his voice was thin barely convincing even to himself.

I swallowed my voice tight. "Just sleep. We'll figure it out tomorrow."

Tomorrow. The word felt like a heavy mass pressing against my chest. What if there wasn't a way out? Worst-case scenarios played on repeat in my mind. If the truth came out—the whole truth—Morgan could lose everything. His license. His career. His freedom.

My pulse quickened as I thought about him in jail, his sharp mind caged, his hands useless. It wasn't right.

When his breathing finally settled into a fragile rhythm, I stood my chair scraping against the floor. I hesitated, heart heavy and slipped silently from the room.

Chapter 37

As I stepped out of Morgan's room, the dim corridor seemed heavier, every shadow stretching longer than it should. My mind churned with worst-case scenarios, each one worse than the last, until a flicker of movement pulled me from my thoughts. A shadow shifted just beyond the edge of my vision. My breath hitched, and I froze, instinctively pressing myself against the wall.

A figure darted ahead, her stride purposeful, her silhouette all too familiar. Jessica. That sharp tilt of her head, the unyielding set of her shoulders—it couldn't be anyone else.

My pulse quickened as I pushed off the wall and began moving. My steps were slow, deliberate, my boots barely brushing the floor. She didn't look back. Her pace quickened as she neared the stairwell at the far end of the hallway.

The heavy door creaked faintly as she slipped through it, and I hurried to follow, slipping inside before it closed fully. The narrow stairwell felt suffocating, the echoes of her steps bouncing off the concrete walls. I stayed one step behind her, my breath shallow, my heart pounding in my ears. Each sound beneath my feet felt deafening, but she didn't seem to notice. Her movements were frantic now, as though she knew time was running out.

The closed-off basement reeked of mildew and something sharper, like scorched wires. Exposed pipes crisscrossed the ceiling, dripping occasionally onto the cracked tiles below. Yellow tape marked off sections of the room, half-hearted warnings of the hospital's ongoing renovations. Shelves sagged under the weight of forgotten records, and the hum of ancient fluorescent lights buzzed against my ears like an angry wasp.

"What's in those files, Jessica?" I asked again, my voice steady despite the anger clawing at the edges. "Names? Dates? Something worth throwing your whole life away for?"

She started at the sound of my voice, twisting toward me like a cornered animal. Her shoulders tensed, a visible ripple of fight or flight running through her. Her gaze flicked to the door, calculating, before settling on me with narrowed eyes. Recognition flared, quickly masked by a wall of disdain.

Her lips curled, caught between a smirk and something more brittle. "Really, Chili?" she said, her tone oozing scorn. "Sneaking around like some wannabe hero? Haven't you got anything better to do?"

"Not when you're down here trying to erase the truth," I shot back. My hands itched to grab the crumpled papers she held so tightly, the sharp edges bending under her grip.

Jessica scoffed, the sound sharp and hollow. "The truth?" she said, her voice rising. "You wouldn't know the truth if it hit you in the face. You're so wrapped up in your little crusade; you can't even see the bigger picture."

"Then enlighten me," I said, taking a slow step forward. "What's so big about this picture that it's worth breaking the law?"

Her jaw tightened, a flicker of something—fear, maybe—crossing her face before she buried it under a mask of defiance. "You wouldn't understand," she said, her voice lower now. "You never could." I stepped closer, the faint hum of the industrial shredder filling the silence like a threat. "Try me."

Her laugh was sharp, almost cruel. "You think this is about me? About money or power? It's about survival. These people—these names—are insurance. Without them, I'm just another loose end."

I shook my head, disbelief tightening my chest. "So, you'd ruin lives to save your own? Who's coming after you, Jessica? Who's pulling the strings?"

Her eyes flashed, something raw and unguarded slipping through—regret, fear, or both. For a moment, I thought she might answer. Instead, her lips twisted into a bitter snarl. "You don't get to judge me," she snapped, her voice cracking under the strain. "Not when you've never had to choose between your life and theirs."

The air between us felt charged, every nerve in my body braced for her next move. "Then stop running," I said, my voice firm, the words hitting the charged space between us like a dare. "Face it, Jessica. Whatever this is, running won't fix it."

Her knuckles whitened around the papers, the tension in her shoulders pulling her taut like a bowstring. "And trusting you will?" Her words cut sharp, her tone daring me to respond, as if I were a fool for even suggesting it.

I opened my mouth to speak, but before I could find the words, she moved. Quick as a viper, she darted toward the door, her body colliding with mine as she passed. The papers crumpled between us before scattering to the floor, but she didn't stop.

I stumbled, caught off guard, as the door swung open and Jessica disappeared into the shadows beyond. She didn't head for the exit but toward the industrial shredder humming ominously in the corner. Her heels scuffed against the polished tiles, her movements frantic, unrestrained.

Without thinking, I surged forward, adrenaline overriding the sharp sting radiating from my stitched hand. My shoulder slammed into hers with enough force to send us both careening to the ground.

The folder burst open as it hit, its contents exploding into a storm of papers that fluttered around us like oversized confetti.

Jessica scrambled, her nails clawing at the floor in a desperate attempt to gather the papers. Her breath came in harsh gasps, her movements erratic. I grabbed at the nearest handful, clutching them to my chest as I blocked her path.

"You can't destroy this," I said, my voice hoarse, the desperation in my words a stark contrast to the chaos around us. "These aren't just files—they're people, Jessica. Their lives, their families. What are you so afraid of?"

Jessica fought like a wild animal, every move brimming with raw, unfiltered panic. I gripped her wrist as her nails raked across my arm, leaving searing trails of pain, and I struggled to maintain my grip. Her knee drove into my ribs, forcing the air from my lungs in a sharp gasp.

"You have no idea what you're doing!" she snarled, her voice breaking, equal parts rage and desperation.

"I know enough," I ground out, the edges of my vision blurring as my strength began to waver.

She wrenched her wrist free, her movements sharp and erratic, like a cornered animal with nothing left to lose. Before I could react, she shoved me with every ounce of strength she had.

The force sent me stumbling backward into a row of filing cabinets. My shoulder struck the edge first, and the impact jarred my entire body. One of the cabinets tipped, its metal frame groaning as it toppled over. I landed hard on top of it, the rusted corners biting into my back.

A sharp jolt coursed through me, stealing my breath. The world tilted as I tried to make sense of the chaos. Metal screeched against the floor as the cabinet shifted beneath me, and I grabbed at its edge to steady myself.

Above the ringing in my ears, I caught Jessica's ragged breaths and the frantic scuff of her boots against the floor. Pain rippled through my back and shoulders as I forced myself upright, adrenaline screaming louder than the ache. My gaze locked onto her as she bolted for the shredder, her focus sharp, her movements desperate.

The room swayed, the edges of my vision threatening to close in, but the faint crunch of scattered papers beneath her feet snapped me back. My fingers clawed at the overturned filing cabinet for leverage, the cold metal biting into my palm.

Jessica was already halfway to the door, her silhouette sharp against the dim hallway light. The sight of her retreating figure reignited my urgency.

"Jessica!" I shouted, my voice cracking as I stumbled forward. She didn't look back, her movements quick. Then, with a sudden, calculated movement, she reached for the fire alarm, her fingers gripping the lever with a finality that sent a chill down my spine.

The fire alarm blared to life, its shrill, piercing scream shattering the fragile silence of the hospital. It tore through the air with brutal force, raw and relentless, a physical shockwave that reverberated through my chest, sending panic spiraling through my veins. The sound was deafening, a thousand voices screaming all at once, but louder, far louder than any sound I'd ever heard. Through the chaos, I saw her figure dart into the hallway, her shadow flickering like a ghost in the strobing light. And then she was gone.

I forced myself upright, my head pounding and my stomach churning. Ignoring the vertigo, I fumbled for my phone, my fingers trembling as I dialled Gideon's number. He picked up on the second ring.

"Chili?" His voice cracked through the static, sharp and filled with worry. "What's going on?"

"She was here," I gasped, urgency in every syllable. "Jessica. I found her in the basement in the old records room, going through files on missing people."

A heavy silence followed, thick with tension. I could almost hear his thoughts racing before he exhaled sharply. "Are you alright? Did she hurt you?"

"I'm fine," I lied, feeling the lingering ache in my skull, the tremor in my hands betraying me. "She got away, but she might still be in the building. I managed to save the files, though."

"Listen carefully," Gideon's voice turned commanding, strong with authority. "Stay where you are. Barrett and I are on our way. If you see her again, don't engage. Stay out of sight. She's dangerous, Chili."

I gripped the phone tighter and nodded even though I knew he couldn't see me. "Please hurry, Gideon. I don't know what she's planning, but it's bad. Really bad."

"We're coming. Stay sharp, don't take any risks." The call ended, and I jammed my phone back into my pocket. The stack of papers felt like it was burning through my fingers, the pressure of everything suddenly too much to bear.

Chapter 38

By the time Gideon and Barrett arrived, Jessica had slipped away through the throng of people heeding the alarms blare and exiting the hospital. The frustration on Barrett's face mirrored my own, but we couldn't waste time dwelling on her escape. Barrett opened his mouth to say something, but Gideon cut him off, holding up a file.

"The mayor's cousin cracked," Gideon said his voice tight. "Spilled everything in exchange for leniency."

I stared at him, letting the words sink in. "Everything? Names, connections, the whole operation?

Gideon nodded grimly. "Enough to take down more than just Delia."

I leaned in, scanning the file over Gideon's shoulder. "Does this mean we have confirmation on the offshore accounts?"

"Not just that," Gideon replied. "We've got records of payments, coded messages, and a list of known accomplices. It's a gold mine."

I couldn't hide the flicker of hope rising in me. "So, we've got them cornered?"

"Cornered, but not caged," Gideon said, his voice steady but cautious. "Delia won't go down without a fight. Neither will the others." We left the hospital and headed outside.

Barrett sighed, the kind of sound that carried the weight of annoyance he didn't bother to hide. His boots scraped against the gravel as he turned to face me, arms crossed tight over his chest.

"You might as well come with us, Chili," he said, his voice sharp. "That way we can keep an eye on you. Just remember, Delia's estate isn't some sightseeing tour. It's messy, and it's going to get worse before it gets better."

"I'm not here for fun," I said, squaring my shoulders, my voice steady. "We all know Delia's tied to this case. You might not want me involved, but without me you'd have nothing."

Barrett's jaw clenched, his gaze hardening as he weighed his options. For a long moment, it seemed like he might push back. Then, with a sharp, reluctant nod, he gave in.

"Fine," he muttered. "But you follow my lead. You stay out of the way unless I tell you otherwise."

I understood exactly what he was saying, and I wasn't about to argue. This wasn't about stepping on toes; it was about getting the job done. I nodded, not trusting myself to speak. For now, it was enough. We piled into Barrett's car and drove straight to Delia's estate. The mansion sprawled over the hill like a monument to greed, all gleaming stone and immaculate lawns. Even from a distance, it screamed excess.

Delia met us at the door, her expression unreadable but her eyes cold and calculating. "Chili. Detectives." she said, her tone laced with false warmth. "To what do I owe this ... unexpected visit?"

Barrett stepped forward, his badge gleaming under the harsh light. His voice was firm and authoritative as he addressed Delia. "Delia Van Horne," he stated coldly, "a warrant has been issued for your arrest. You are not obliged to say or do anything unless you wish to do so. But it may harm your defence if you do not mention when questioned something which you later rely upon in court. Anything you do say and do may be given in evidence. Do you understand?"

Her only response was a slight nod of her head. He continued, "I am arresting you on suspicion of human trafficking and on suspicion of collusion in order to commit murder."

His words echoed in the tense silence, each one deliberate, underscoring the gravity of the charges against her. The police began to fan out, their movements synchronized and efficient as they moved into the hallway, clearing the area. One officer, a burly man with a grim expression, guided the mayor from a back room. He looked smaller now, his usual swagger gone, replaced by a pallor that drained his face of any remaining colour. His bluster filled the room as he stepped forward, trying to command attention, but the desperate tone in his voice betrayed his fear.

"You can't do this," the mayor said, his voice rising with panic. "Do you have any idea who we are?"

Barrett didn't flinch, his posture unshaken. His eyes locked on the mayor's, and his reply was cool, almost dismissive. "That's exactly why we're here."

The unmistakable snap of handcuffs echoed through the hallway as they clicked into place. First, they secured Delia's wrists, her icy poise returning—her head held high. Yet, even in her composed manner, her eyes were darting around, searching for an escape, as if she could still slip away from the inevitable.

Then, the handcuffs were placed on the mayor. His bravado faltered, his voice growing desperate. "You don't understand. I didn't—"

Barrett cut him off with a sharp, commanding tone. "Save it. Your cousin's already given you up. Every deal, every payment, every threat—you're tied to all of it. There's no way out."

The mayor's mouth opened, but no words came. The defiance drained from him, his face crumbling with realization. His bravado, once a shield, now lay shattered on the floor. "This is a mistake, it's all her doing," he sputtered.

Delia hissed, her voice cold and venomous. "I'll have your badges for this."

Her words landed like hollow threats, but I could see the cracks in her armour. She didn't believe them anymore. The evidence was overwhelming, airtight. Everyone in the room could feel it. Yet something lingered, an unsettled feeling gnawing at the edges of my mind. Jessica's disappearance, the way she'd vanished into the night, hung over us like a dark cloud. Her absence wasn't just a missing person—it was a silent question, casting a long shadow over the moment, making everything feel incomplete.

Then, the mayor spoke, his voice shaky but loud enough to fill the heavy silence between us. "You don't understand," he said, his eyes wild, frantic. "You think you've won? No. It's over for me, I know that. But not for her. Delia ... " He faltered, his breath ragged, struggling to find the words. His eyes darted from Delia to the floor and back again, his mind scrambling for a way out. "You've got it all wrong. Van Horne was innocent. A pawn in her game. She set everything up. All of it. From the very beginning."

For a brief moment, something almost like regret flashed across his face. "I should have known. I should have stopped her." The words hung in the air, pregnant with meaning, as though he was finally seeing the pieces of the puzzle come together—but it was too late for redemption. Delia's lips curled into a sneer. "You're pathetic," she spat. "You think they'll believe you?"

But the mayor wasn't finished. His voice grew louder, more frantic, each word tumbling out in a rush. "Morgan ... he's innocent. She used him too—manipulated him. Now she's going to throw him under the bus just like she did with Van Horne. She's the one pulling all the strings. The whole rotten operation—everything. I just played my part, like anyone would." He repeated a variant of the same words over and over, his frantic tone edging on hysteria.

For a moment, doubt gnawed at me. Was there some truth in his words? The pieces didn't fit perfectly, but I wasn't sure they ever would.

Deep down, I knew the mayor was just scrambling, trying to shift the blame onto someone else. It was too late for that. He had already played his part, and now he was desperate to save himself, no matter the cost to anyone else. Delia didn't flinch. She merely gave him a cold, almost pitying look. "You're weak," she said softly, and there was something so final in her voice that it left no room for doubt. "You've always been weak. Always."

We moved toward the door, Delia's wrists still secured, her posture unyielding, head held high despite the venom in her words. She cast one final, sweeping glance around the room, as if searching for a way out, but the moment of escape had long passed.

Once Delia and the mayor were escorted out, Barrett turned to me, his usually calm demeanour now frayed, frustration evident in his voice. "This should feel like a win," he said, his jaw tight with suppressed tension. "But with Jessica still out there, it doesn't."

I nodded, clutching the stack of papers I'd taken from the hospital. "Something tells me this is just the tip of the iceberg."

Gideon stepped closer, his hand resting on my shoulder. The warmth of his touch steadied me. "We'll find her and the people she's working with," he said, his tone firm, unwavering. "This isn't over."

It wasn't a promise he could guarantee, but I needed to hear it, needed that spark of hope. It was the only thing that kept me moving forward, the only thing that made this fight feel worth it.

The drive back to the station felt longer, the silence between us heavier than the chaos we were leaving behind. The image of Delia and the mayor in cuffs should have offered some sense of justice, but it didn't. Not with Jessica gone. Not with the knowledge that she had planned her escape, that every step of tonight had been part of her scheme.

I stared out the window, my thoughts racing as the scenery blurred past. Jessica wasn't just out there; she was waiting. Watching. Plotting her next move. I could feel it, a pulse in the back of my mind, a presence

I couldn't shake. She was always one step ahead, and I hated that we were playing catch-up in her game.

The stack of papers sat on my lap like a lead weight. Every mile we covered back to town made them feel heavier. They weren't just documents; they were fragments of her plans, pieces of a larger puzzle I couldn't quite put together. We had made progress tonight—arrests, evidence, steps toward justice—but it felt hollow. Jessica wasn't just a loose end; she was the knot holding everything together.

At the station, as we crossed the car park, I turned to Barrett. The exhaustion in his eyes mirrored my own. "Have you told Gideon?" I asked my voice quieter now, as if the weight of the question might tip the balance.

Barrett glanced at Gideon, who was still standing by the car talking to another officer. "Not yet," he admitted. "I'll do it when we debrief. It's not the kind of news you drop in the middle of this mess."

I nodded, understanding his hesitation. Gideon didn't know about Sarah and the baby, not yet. It wasn't my place to tell him, but the thought of it made my chest tighten. He deserved to know, but how do you deliver something like that?

As we walked toward the station, the tension in the air followed us. Inside, everything was waiting—the paperwork, the processing, the hours of unravelling the night's chaos. But above it all, Jessica loomed, her shadow falling over every step we took. We had struck a blow tonight, but the war wasn't over.

Chapter 39

Three weeks later, Morgan stood in the same parking lot, but his posture was different—lighter, perhaps. The decision not to charge him had come down the week before, a direct result of his full cooperation. He had given up everything—names, dates, places—to ensure Delia and the others would face justice for their crimes. In the end, the board had acknowledged the good he'd done and spared his medical license, though he'd be on probation for a while to come.

"I'm grateful," he said, staring out across the lot, his voice softer than usual. "But it doesn't feel like I deserve it. Not after everything."

Morgan's decision to leave hit me harder than I had expected. We stood soaking in the quiet morning, both of us deep in thought. He leaned against the driver's door, his shoulders slumped, his clothes loose on his frame. Gone was the man constantly looking for reassurance and in his place stood someone who'd walked through fire; a lot of his own making.

"I need distance," he said finally, breaking the silence. "From this place, from the memories. I can't stay here and pretend it didn't happen. I can't move forward if I'm still looking back."

I leaned against the car beside him, the morning breeze tugging at my hair. "You've paid your dues, Morgan. Giving evidence, facing the board, losing what you've lost ... You're still here because someone up there thinks you've got more to do."

He nodded slowly, his hands flexing at his sides as though testing their strength. "Maybe. I just hope I can live up to that."

I nodded, my throat tight. I couldn't speak right away, but when I did, my voice was firm. "You will," I said. "You have a second chance. Not everyone gets that." I nudged his arm with my own. "Besides, Africa will be good for you. You've got work to finish there, people who need you. It's a fresh start."

He smiled faintly, the kind of smile that carried more sadness than joy. "I owe you my life, Chili. You and Gideon. Don't ever think I don't know that." His voice was filled with a sincerity that made my chest ache. "You saw the good in me when I couldn't. You gave me a chance to be something better."

"Just make it count, Morgan. Do the work. Be better. For them—and for yourself."

He nodded and pulled me into a hug. I gripped him tight. Who knew when we'd see each other again? "I will," he said. He climbed in but hesitated before pulling the door shut. "You'll keep an eye on things here? On Gideon? My folks?"

"Always," I promised.

For a moment, he just sat there, looking at me with an expression I couldn't quite place—gratitude, hope, maybe even relief. Then he shut the door and started the engine. As the car rolled away the dust from the lot swirled in the air marking his departure.

Morgan had a long road ahead, but for the first time, it felt like he was heading in the right direction. It felt like the end of something important, but also the beginning of whatever redemption he was chasing. He had a lot to make up for, and I hoped he'd find it out there, among the people he had left behind.

Barrett arrived as the sound of Morgan's car faded into the distance. He didn't say much, but the grudging nod he gave me spoke volumes. "You did good," he said after a moment. His voice carried that familiar gruffness, but there was no mistaking the respect beneath it. "Even if you did make my job harder."

Barrett had been nothing if not stubborn since the moment we met, most of that due to his history with my parents, but now there was something different in his expression—a flicker of camaraderie I hadn't expected.

"I couldn't have done this without you," he said, his voice softer than usual. He hesitated for a moment, then added, "Call me Gordon."

I blinked, caught off guard. The surprise must've been written all over my face because he gave a small shrug, almost sheepish, as if he wasn't sure how I'd react.

A smirk tugged at my lips. "Admit it, I've grown on you ... Gordon," I teased, my tone playful.

He shook his head, a rare smile threatening to break through. "Yeah, maybe," he admitted, his voice tinged with reluctant humour. "But don't push it," he added, though the warning lacked any real bite.

I chuckled, appreciating the moment for what it was—an unspoken truce between two people who'd somehow managed to find common ground amid bedlam. Maybe we weren't friends—not yet—but we weren't enemies anymore, either. That was progress.

Gideon lingered behind, his broad frame shrouded in shadow despite the golden spill of morning light. He stood a few steps away, close enough to reach, yet lost in a world of his own thoughts.

The news had shattered him. His wife—gone. His baby—sold like a possession. And the discovery of bodies buried on the grounds where I'd been held? It was a horror that no one could easily process, least of all him. He'd carried so much for so long.

When he finally turned to me, his gaze was heavy, his eyes haunted by unspeakable grief. The lines on his face told a story of sleepless nights and relentless searching. When he spoke, his voice was raw, a crack in the otherwise unyielding armour he wore. "I think I always knew Sarah was gone," he said quietly. "But the baby? For years, I told myself I'd find her. I held onto that hope like a lifeline. I never stopped looking."

I stepped closer, placing a hand on his arm. It wasn't enough, but it was all I had to give in the face of so much loss.

"The trafficking team said they'll do everything they can to find her," he continued, his voice rough, barely holding together. "My daughter. She'd be five years old now. I keep wondering ... does she have Sarah's eyes? My chin? What's her favourite colour? What's her laugh like?"

The ache in his voice was palpable, and I swallowed hard, forcing my own emotions down. "We'll find her," I said meeting his eyes. "No matter what it takes, Gideon. We'll get answers. For Sarah. For your daughter. For you."

He nodded but the pain in his expression remained. The road ahead would be long, but for the first time, there was a sliver of light at the end of it. Forensics would take a long time to determine the identities of the bodies found. More were being uncovered every day. One of those bodies, we both thought but didn't say. One of them was Sarah.

The wind whipped through the car park, tugging at my jacket and stinging my face with cold. Overhead dark clouds swirled as if the sky itself was mourning. It wasn't raining yet, but the air was thick with the promise of a downpour, heavy and oppressive.

The silence grew again, stretching out as we stood there, anchored by a hope neither of us wanted to name. It felt breakable, but it was all we had.

Chapter 40

The backyard hummed with life, strung with fairy lights that swayed in the light evening breeze. Their warm glow cast the space in a golden hue, making the gathering feel magical. Laughter rippled through the air, rising from small groups scattered across the yard. The tension of the last few weeks lifted, replaced by joy and the simple comfort of being surrounded by family and friends.

Bonnie stood near the grill, talking animatedly with my dad, their easy connection undeniable. I caught the way her hand rested on his arm as she spoke, a subtle gesture that said everything. They'd been through so much together. Seeing him happy again made my chest ache in the best way.

Dudley, Mr. Dorsey's yellow Labrador, decided to steal the show. He darted through the crowd, barking at shadows and chasing his tail, earning peals of laughter from the kids—and more than a few adults. I found myself laughing, the sound unfamiliar but welcome, like an old friend I hadn't seen in years.

The scent of burgers and sizzling sausages filled the air, mingling with the sweet tang of grilled vegetables. Bonnie had brought her homemade potato salad and Dad's famous coleslaw was in a large bowl at the centre of the picnic table. Drinks clinked in glasses as people raised them in a toast to another year, another chapter.

"Why don't skeletons fight each other?" my dad shouted from across the yard.

Coco shouted the punch line arm in arm with Sommer, both laughing so hard they could barely stand. "They don't have the guts!"

The sound of their laughter echoed across the yard, infectious and bright. My dad, standing by the grill with a spatula in one hand, grinned and threw up his arms in mock exasperation. "Hey! I was telling that one!" he called out, his voice carrying easily over the chatter and music.

Coco pointed at him, still giggling. "You've got to be faster than that, old man!"

Sommer nudged her playfully. "Pretty sure you just stole his big moment."

"Worth it!" Coco declared before they both doubled over in fresh peals of laughter.

Even I couldn't help but chuckle as the moment spread like wildfire, pulling smiles from everyone in its path. My dad shook his head, a mock scowl on his face, but the twinkle in his eye betrayed him. "Fine. Next time, I'm going for the long joke."

Coco threw him a thumbs-up, still catching her breath. "Can't wait. Bring your A-game!"

The laughter that followed was easy, flowing like the love and friendship that seemed endless tonight. Even the kids got in on the fun, their faces smeared with sauce as they chased each other around the yard, a blur of energy and joy.

I grabbed a plate, piled high with food, and sat on the edge of the verandah, feeling the cool evening air brush against my skin. For a moment, it was as though everything had come full circle. Then Gideon arrived, slipping through the gate at the back of the yard. His tie hung loose, and his shirt sleeves were rolled to his elbows, giving him a look that was both weary and endearing. His gaze swept the crowd until it found me, and when he smiled, something inside me steadied.

"You made it," I said as he reached me. I patted the seat next to me and gestured to the esky. "Pick your poison."

"Wouldn't miss it," he replied, lowering himself beside me. He grabbed a can, opened it and took a long, slow sip.

For a moment, we sat there under the soft glow of the fairy lights, the noise of the party fading into the background. His hand enveloped mine, his thumb tracing the scar on my palm with a tenderness that made my chest ache. "I love you," he said, his tone steady but quiet, like a truth he'd carried for a while, waiting for this very moment to release.

The world seemed to hold its breath as his confession settled over me, filling me in a way I didn't know I needed. I smiled feeling a calm certainty I rarely experienced, as though every jagged piece of my life had fallen into place. "I love you too," I said, my voice soft.

Around us, the party continued—voices rising, laughter spilling out— but we stayed in that quiet bubble for just a moment longer, savouring the stillness between us. Then someone called Gideon's name, pulling him away from the calm we'd found. He gave my hand a gentle squeeze before standing. As he walked toward the others, I watched him go, a sense of peace settling over me.

The night peaked when Bonnie and Dad stood together on the makeshift stage near the garden. Dad cleared his throat, his cheeks redder than I'd ever seen. He looked nervous, which was rare for him.

"Bonnie and I have an announcement," he said, his voice carrying across the yard. "We're engaged."

A collective gasp of surprise rang out, followed by loud cheers. Bonnie beamed her smile wide enough to light up the whole yard as Dad held up her hand. The ring caught the light, shining like a promise. My throat tightened, a mix of emotion and something I couldn't name. But I didn't hesitate—I clapped, hollered, and cheered along with everyone else.

In that moment, I felt something shift. The past few years had been hard, full of loss and uncertainty. But this? This felt like the beginning of something new. Something to hold onto. My family, despite everything, was healing. And for the first time in a long time, I believed in the possibility of a fresh start.

The hours passed, and as the night wound down, I found myself standing alone, watching the familiar faces of the people who made this town home. So much had changed—fractured, mended, shifted—but tonight, none of that mattered. This moment, the soft chatter, the clinking of glasses, the bursts of laughter carried by the cool evening breeze felt like a memory worth holding onto.

Gideon caught my eye from across the yard, a quiet smile spreading across his face, softening the edges of his usually serious expression, and then he winked. For a moment, the noise and crowd faded into the background leaving just the two of us in this fleeting, unspoken connection. My heart gave a small flutter, and I smiled back, feeling an unexpected lightness.

I thought of Jessica, still out there, and the fight that wasn't over. But for the first time, I didn't feel concerned by it. The uncertainty of the future no longer consumed me like it once did. The warmth of the evening, the steady presence of the people I cared about, and the certainty of Gideon's love made everything else seem distant.

Whatever came next, I was ready.

I wasn't facing it alone anymore.

Recipes

courtesy of Rebecca McLeod
from www.Becs-Table.com.au

Rock Cakes

Ingredients

I 30 g sultanas (I used a total of 90g of dried fruit, you can use anything you like)

30 g currants

30 g dried cherries

300 g plain flour

2 1/2 tsp baking powder

½ tsp flaked salt or ¼ tsp fine salt

1/2 tsp mixed spice or 1 tsp if you like the flavour

90 g caster sugar

20 g raw sugar or a courser sugar than caster for sprinkling on top

100 g unsalted butter cold cubes

1 egg beaten

125 g milk

Instructions

Set oven to 200°c or 180°c fan

Boil the jug, weigh the dried fruit into a bowl, when the water has boiled pour the water over the dried fruit and set aside for 5 minutes. Once the fruit has plumped up a bit drain in a sieve or colander.

Line a couple of cookies sheets with baking paper. No need if you're using good non-stick pans.

Weigh the flour, baking powder and mixed spice into a bowl and mix with a whisk or fork to combine.

Rub the butter into the flour with your fingertips

Add sugar and drained dried fruit along with the egg and milk, mix to form a stiff dough

Place spoonfuls of the dough mixture onto your prepared oven trays (I got 11 portions)

Sprinkle with a little raw sugar then Bake until golden brown (around 20 mins)

Cool on cake rack,

Notes

These will keep for 3 – 4 days in an airtight container

Don't over mix.

Don't over bake.

Take them out when they start to appear golden brown. Too dark and they'll dry out.

Zucchini Slice

INGREDIENTS

300 g Zucchini

120 g Onion

120 g Cheddar Cheese

150 g Plain flour

2 tsp Baking Powder

4 eggs

50 g Olive Oil

200 g Bacon Sliced (lardons)

Instructions

Preheat your oven to 170°C fan and line a baking tin with parchment paper to make this recipe.

Weigh your flour and bicarb into a large mixing bowl and mix well with a whisk to ensure your baking powder is evenly distributed.

Add the four eggs and the olive oil to the flour mix and whisk to combine.

Using a hand grater, grate the zucchini, onion and cheese into the same large bowl.

Chop the bacon into lardons (long strips) and stir through the batter.

Next, pour the mixture from the bowl into your prepared baking tin and bake in the oven for around 30 minutes.

Finally, serve the zucchini slice warm or cold with a side salad. Enjoy your delicious and easy-to-make zucchini slice!

Bec's White Chocolate Mud Cake

INGREDIENTS

For the cake:

300 g plain flour all-purpose

1 tsp baking powder

250 g butter

180 g White chocolate I used Cadbury 180g baking blocks for this recipe

330 g castor sugar

180 g milk

1 tsp vanilla

110 g eggs lightly whisked to break up that's 2

You will need a 20cm deep-sided cake pan

White chocolate Ganache:

360 g white chocolate chopped into cubes for TM or chopped fine for stovetop

125 g cream

Decorative crumb:

30 g pistachios

30 g walnuts

30 g coconut shredded

30 g green sugar crystals *See tips

1 tsp of culinary matcha powder optional (if you can't find it – usually available from Health Food Stores)

Edible rose petals

1 pack of speckled easter eggs

Instructions
Start by reading the whole recipe first.

Add the butter, sugar and milk to a saucepan and set the heat to medium. Bring it up until it's just under a boil, remove from the heat and add the cubed white chocolate. Stir the chocolate in until it's melted and transfer into a large bowl for mixing later. Allow this mix to cool for around 15 minutes before proceeding to add the dry ingredients.

While you're waiting, prepare your pan—grease with butter or pan release. Line the base and sides with baking paper. (Using butter or pan release helps the paper to stick.) If you have baking strips, apply them now.

Now set your oven to 160°C (320°F) fan.

Start by sifting or whisking the flour and baking powder and set aside.

In a separate small bowl, crack the eggs, add the vanilla and whisk to break up the eggs a little, set aside.

Add the eggs to the white chocolate mixture and stir to combine.

Then add the flour mix and stir to combine.

Pour the mixture into the prepared pan and bake. My cake in my oven takes 1 hour and 30 minutes. I bake for 30 minutes, then add a hood (baking paper-lined foil cap) and continue to bake for another hour. Remove the hood and check if it's done. Cool the cake in the pan overnight with the hood back on.

Ganache:
Place the finely chopped white chocolate into a heatproof bowl and set aside.

Add the cream to a saucepan and bring to the boil.

Pour the boiling cream over the white chocolate, cover it, rest for 2 minutes, then stir until smooth.

Cover and place in the fridge. Allow the ganache to chill until it's spreadable. Bring it out and stir every so often. This should take 30 minutes to an hour.

Crumb:

Using a food processor, chop the pistachios and walnuts to the desired size. *see tips

Add the coconut and matcha if using and stir to combine.

Add the sugar crystals. Stir to combine.

Bec's Tips:

Do not mix the flour into your melted white choc/sugar mix until it has cooled, or you will end up with a gluey cake.

Making a baking paper-lined cap. Cut a sheet of baking paper slightly larger than the top of your cake tin. Cut off a sheet of tin foil around 4 cm larger than the baking paper. Sit the baking paper on top of the foil, then crimp the edges to make a round shape, just the right size to fit over the top of your cake tin.

Chopping nuts for the crumb topping without a food processor or TM: You can place the nuts in a zip lock bag and use a rolling pin to crush them or place them on a cutting board and chop with a chef's knife.

Allow your cake to chill in the fridge before working with it. It will really firm up.

For the best texture, allow your cake to come to room temp before serving.

A crumb coat is a thin layer of the icing or ganache you're using on the cake. You then allow that coat to chill until it's firm, preventing the next coat from picking up crumbs in the topcoat.

You can buy coloured sugar crystals from cake decorating shops. They come in all sorts of colours. You can sometimes find them in a small range of colours at larger supermarkets too.

Acknowledgements

Writing this novel has been an incredible journey filled with creativity, late-night brainstorming, and more than a few cups of coffee. The process of bringing these characters to life has been both challenging and rewarding. Any mistakes within these pages are mine alone.

A HUGE THANK YOU TO my incredible support group—Pierce, Rosemarie, Mike and Angie, Graham and Moyra, Fiona, Bek and Sue. Your constant encouragement, insightful advice, and ability to listen (even when I ramble!) have made all the difference. I'm lucky to be surrounded by such a wonderful, slightly dysfunctional, and always supportive crew!

I'D LIKE TO SEND A heartfelt thank you to the multi-talented pastry chef, Rebecca McLeod, whose incredible recipes grace these pages, adding sweetness and creativity throughout. You can find her cooking up a storm at www.Becs-Table.com.au[1]

---

1. http://www.Becs-Table.com.au

AND FINALLY: DUDLEY and Bella, my loyal Labradors, who fill my life with unconditional love, endless joy, and the purest companionship imaginable. You're truly Labradorable!

Don't miss out!

Visit the website below and you can sign up to receive emails whenever Dixie Leigh publishes a new book. There's no charge and no obligation.

https://books2read.com/r/B-A-RUNBD-UYDMF

BOOKS 2 READ

Connecting independent readers to independent writers.

About the Author

Dixie Leigh lives with her husband and two constant companions, Labradors, Dudley and Bella, in a charming port town.

When not in the kitchen, she enjoys capturing moments through photography or spending time with friends.

A true admirer of winter and rainy days, she finds comfort and creativity in the cosy atmosphere they bring.

Whether exploring her coastal surroundings or enjoying quiet moments, she cherishes life's simple pleasures and the connections that make them special.